VIOLET

S. J. I. HOLLIDAY

First published in Great Britain 2019
by
Orenda Books

First Isis Edition
published 2020
by arrangement with
Orenda Books

The moral right of the author has been asserted

This is a work of fiction. Names, characters, places and incidents are either products of the author's imagination or are used fictitiously. Any resemblance to actual events, locales or persons, living or dead, is entirely coincidental.

A catalogue record for this book is available from the British Library.

ISBN 978–1–78541–904–1

PUBLISHED BY
ULVERSCROFT LIMITED
ANSTEY, LEICESTERSHIRE

Set by Words & Graphics Ltd.
Anstey, Leicestershire
Printed and bound in Great Britain by
T. J. International Ltd., Padstow, Cornwall

This book is printed on acid-free paper

To JLOH — my favourite travelling companion.

"If you tell the truth, you don't have to remember anything"

— Mark Twain

Prologue

The body lies broken on the dusty, potholed track. The sky is a fading bruise of purple and grey, the alleyway illuminated by the faint lemony glow from one of the low-level windows at the back of the hotel. Parched, weedy-looking shrubs; gritty, dirty soil, and the ever-present hum of a generator somewhere close by mingles with the tinny sound of a radio from one of the rooms higher up. A mangy dog appears, its unclipped toenails scraping the cracked concrete. It sniffs. Whimpers. Before starting to lick at something dark and wet that's pooling on the ground near the dead man's head.

The hooded man pushes the body slowly with his boot and the dog starts circling, saliva dripping from its hungry mouth. The man makes a clicking noise with his tongue, stamps his foot once, hard.

Shttt shttt.

The dog whimpers once more, then slinks away into the thick night.

"Tell me what happened," the hooded man says. He spits out a chewed matchstick and takes a pack of crumpled cigarettes from his back pocket.

"I told you on the phone." The young woman's voice shakes as she tries to compose herself. "He fell . . . He was climbing up the balconies. He was nearly at ours. I . . . we . . . we shouted at him. We threw things. Tried to get him to stop. We told him we would call the police."

"What did he say?" He lights a cigarette. Puts the used match back into the box.

"Nothing. He just . . . He laughed. Then he said, 'Let me in, little pig . . . Or I'll huff and I'll puff, and blow your house down.' It was creepy."

The hooded man snorts. "What does this mean? 'Little pig . . .' "

Leetle peeg.

She shivers. "It's from a nursery rhyme. It's the Big Bad Wolf —"

"Wasn't he with Red Riding Hood?"

"Another one." She shakes her head. "I guess there are lots of wolves in fairy tales."

He blows a series of perfect smoke rings into the air above him. "Not just in fairy tales." He coughs up a ball of phlegm and spits it on the ground, and she feels a light spray misting across her sandalled feet.

She swallows hard, trying not to retch. Whimpers, just like the dog. "Please," she says. "Please help me."

The hooded man shrugs. "Why don't you go to police? If it was accident? Like you say?"

"But . . . but what if they don't believe it? I've heard things. Bad things."

"Bad things about wolves?"

Bad things about Russians, she thinks.

Finally, she looks him in the eye. Holds his gaze. He's not that bad-looking. This is not the worst thing she's ever done.

"Please," she says. "Can you make this go away?"

He comes closer to her, stepping over the body. She can smell him now. His hot, stale sweat. She wonders when he last washed. She shudders, imagining the smell inside his clothes to be much, much worse. Hot acid roils up her throat and she swallows it back. She has no choice about this. She needs his help.

"And the other girl?" he says, blowing smoke slowly into her face. "Where is she now?"

"She's . . . I . . ." Her eyes flit up and left, towards the balcony. His eyes follow, and then back to her again. His stare is hard, his expression unreadable.

She says it again, more pleading. More desperate. "*Please*. Can you make this go away?"

He grins, revealing sharp, wolfish teeth, and she hears the chink of metal on metal as he unclips his belt. There's a brief pause, while he removes the cigarette and drops it on the ground, grinding it into the dirt, then without breaking eye contact, he slowly pulls down his zip. His huge, dark pupils gleam in the moonlight, full of want. She can't look at him anymore.

She closes her eyes and tries to imagine herself somewhere else. With someone else. Somewhere far from here. Somewhere long ago.

He shuffles closer towards her and his trousers slide down to his ankles. The sour milk smell of him hits the back of her throat, but she won't cry. She refuses to cry. She can do this. She has to.

He lays a rough, warm hand on top of her head, exerting just enough pressure to force her to her knees. Gravel cuts into her bare flesh, but she barely feels it. She is numb.

"Oh yes, *leetle peeg*," he says, "I can make this go away."

CHAPTER
ONE

Beijing

I'm sitting alone on a concrete bench. Around me, people are swarming, shouting quickly in a language that I can't understand. Above me, the sky is a thick powder blue, like dirty paintbrushes swirled in water. The smog is so dense I can taste it. Waves of panic wash over me as I try to inhale some fresh air, and I wonder how anyone can breathe in this city. What started out as an exciting, fun morning has rapidly declined into panic and frustration; and not for the first time, I regret leaving Sam behind in Bangkok.

There is something *easy* about that place, with the swarms of British backpackers and grinning Aussies, men on stag parties, cold beers and menus written in English. Even though Thailand is as far away from the English countryside as can be, there is a certain warmth. Familiarity. Despite all the stories you hear, I felt completely safe there. But then me and Sam had that stupid falling-out in the hotel lobby. I can't even remember how it started.

And so here I am, sitting outside the Beijing international train station, no boyfriend, only half my luggage — since my rucksack went AWOL somewhere

5

on the way to China — and still no ticket for the train I want, which leaves tomorrow morning. I could call Sam, beg for his forgiveness, ask him to follow me out here. But firstly, I know he doesn't want to, and secondly, I'd only be doing it out of desperation. He got sucked in, in Thailand, didn't want to follow the plan — *my* plan — loop back via China and the Trans-Siberian Express to Moscow, before flying home from there. He'd gone into an Internet café and resigned from his job; he was getting more excited than I liked by the cheap beer and the hordes of stunning young women that seemed to flock to him on a daily basis. "I'd just like to hang about here a bit longer," he'd said. "Lighten up, sweetheart. You need to smoke some more weed."

Idiot.

He'd changed since the group of German students arrived. There'd been a wild night. I'd felt uneasy, but he'd felt the opposite. "This is the kind of fun I came for," he said. To them, not me. I knew then that my Sam was gone. Was I angry? Not really. I just hope he stayed sober enough to do the appropriate *checks* on some of those beautiful "women" that he and the German lads were spending so much time with.

Now I'm alone, in Beijing, a bustling metropolis of nearly twentytwo million people, feeling properly homesick for the first time in months. I did have fun yesterday, going for a proper Chinese tea ceremony with a young couple I'd met in the gardens near the Forbidden City. The tea had been ridiculously expensive, and I'd realised early on that it was a scam

6

of some sort, but as scams go, it was pretty friendly. And I know more now than I ever thought I needed to about the many different kinds of Chinese tea.

This morning I was buzzing, ready for another full-on day, making sure I could fit in as many crispy duck pancakes as I could manage. All I had to do was pop down to the train station and buy my ticket. The station is huge, the guidebook said, but buying a ticket should be simple. Just make sure you go to the international section. When they said huge, I hadn't quite realised what that meant. But while I sat outside, waiting for the sun to push its way through the everpresent smog — it didn't, by the way — it dawned on me that small towns in China have five million inhabitants, and that huge really means the station is the size of Manchester, and after walking around the whole place for two hours, being jostled and stared at, pointed at, pointed out and misdirected for hours on end, what I realised was that foreigners can't buy international tickets in the station after all; they have to go to a travel centre in some business hotel, streets away . . . and that I am so over this now. This so-called "adventure".

And so I sat myself down on this concrete bench, and all I want to do now is cry. But that's not going to get me anywhere. Certainly not to Moscow, which is where I really want to be. I need to move on. Find another companion for my trip. So I take a swig of water, then I pick up my backpack and head back into the throng.

CHAPTER
TWO

The Beijing International Hotel is seriously plush. Marble pillars, velvet sofas. There's a long black bar made of smooth, sparkling granite. A good-looking Chinese man with neatly gelled hair is standing behind it, polishing glasses. I could sit there, ask him to mix me a cocktail. Something classic, old fashioned — like a Brandy Alexander. Then sip it seductively and see who might come in and offer to buy me the next.

But that's for another time.

I don't want to stay here alone in this city full of noise and smog. It's too big. Too impersonal. There's a reason why most backpackers follow a trail, go to the same places. I'd always thought that wasn't for me, and yet here I am alone, and I'm not happy about it at all. I'm kidding myself if I think I prefer my own company.

What I need now is a new friend. A replacement for Sam. I pause. Thinking again about the barman. No. What I need more than anything else is a ticket out of this place, and I just have to hope that my bag turns up before I move on. I look down at my skirt, wondering why I'd chosen this particular look for the flight. I bought a load of things in Bangkok, thinking I might head to the beach before moving on, but that never happened, and now I look like a goddamn hippy. I don't fit in here, in this hotel. But without the rest of my clothes and my hair stuff and everything else I need, I'm just going to have to style it out. I suppose I will just have to be who this outfit suggests.

The hotel travel centre is a small room filled with too many rubber plants. There's a small leather sofa, and one desk where someone is being served by a beautiful Chinese woman with her hair pinned up with chopsticks. I've seen this before, but not on someone wearing a navy business suit. I like the contrast.

The air conditioning is on full, and I'm relieved to be out of the thick, sticky heat, but after a few moments I'm already feeling a chill on my legs. I watch the woman with the chopsticks, smiling and nodding at the customer. Blonde, hair in a messy ponytail. Shorts. Backpack on the floor. Another traveller. Another me?

I hope so.

"So you're saying I can't get any sort of refund on this, even though I booked it six months in advance?"

Chopsticks nods again. "So sorry. We cannot do it."

The blonde sighs in frustration. "It's an expensive ticket. I did call before I left the UK and was told you could deal with it here . . ."

Chopsticks shakes her head gently. She's still smiling.

The blonde stands up. "Fine," she says. "I assume the ticket is transferable? If I can find someone else to take it . . ."

"You can do that, yes." Chopsticks is beaming now. All sorted, and she didn't have to do a thing.

The blonde hitches her backpack onto her shoulders, giving me a wry smile and a massive eye-roll as she leaves the room.

Chopsticks is heading towards a door at the back. I glance up at the clock. The minute-hand ticks and the hour-hand clicks into place at the top. Five o'clock.

I jump up off the sofa. "Wait . . . I need to buy a ticket."

"Sorry, we closed now," Chopsticks says, her smile dipping just a little. "We open nine am."

"No . . . I need to get the ticket now. The train is at seven-thirty tomorrow."

She frowns. "You want Trans-Siberian?"

"Yes. Yes, please."

"No ticket left. Come back tomorrow, and you can get ticket for another day, OK?"

It's not OK, but she's disappeared through the back. *Shit*. I grab my bag and slink out of the room, beaten. For another brief moment, I want to cry. But I bite it back. Looks like I'm going to be getting to know the barman after all.

There are a few others in the bar area now. A couple of businessmen in suits on the high stools at the bar. A tanned couple with umbrella'd drinks and their faces stuck in the *Lonely Planet*. The blonde is sitting on her own, a tall glass of beer in front of her. She's gazing out of the huge windows, watching the hordes of ant-like humans going about their business.

I hesitate, not sure whether to approach her, but before I can make up my mind, she turns around and sees me.

10

She looks confused, just for a second, then she smiles. "Hey. You were in the travel centre, weren't you? Did you get sorted?"

I shake my head. "Sold out. I need to rethink my plans." She just stares at me, saying nothing, and I stand there feeling a bit awkward. "That beer looks good." I smile at her, nod towards her glass. The condensation is trickling slowly down the sides, and suddenly I am so thirsty, I have to fight the urge to pick it up and sink it in one. When did I last have a cold drink? The water in the bottle I've been lugging around with me all day is so hot now I could probably use it to make tea.

"Tsing Tao," she says. "Sounds all exotic back home, but it's cheap and nasty here. Even in this place."

"Mind if I join you?"

She moves her laptop over to the far side of the table and gestures towards the empty seat opposite. "Be my guest."

I've barely sat down when a smiling woman appears at my side, asking me what I want to order. I return the smile and point at the beer.

"One of these. Unless you want another?"

The blonde shakes her head. "Not yet. Thanks, though."

"I'm Violet," I tell her. "I —"

"Carrie," she says, offering me a small, lightly tanned hand. "So where were you trying to buy a ticket for?"

The woman returns with a tray. We wait patiently while she lays down a white paper coaster with a frill around the edge and places the glass carefully on top.

Then she lifts a bowl of unshelled peanuts off the tray and places it down in the middle of the table. She smiles and gives me a small half-bow, and I thank her and take a long drink. It tastes like heaven, and I already feel more relaxed.

"I wanted to get the Trans-Siberian. I wasn't fussed about which branch, as long as it gets me to Moscow. I'm supposed to be meeting friends there." The last part is a lie. I have no particular reason to want to go to Moscow other than I haven't been yet, and I'm getting a bit bored with Asia. It's all a bit predictable after a while — same sorts of people on the trail, doing the same things. I think Russia might spice things up a bit. Take my mind off Sam, and everything else. It's not like I've got anything to rush back to the UK for.

"Oh cool. Me too," Carrie says. Then, "Oh shit, sorry — you just said you couldn't get a ticket." She slaps herself on the head, then laughs. "Let's have a few drinks and you can forget abour it for now. The train tracks will still be there the day after tomorrow."

CHAPTER
THREE

Her accent is more pronounced after four beers. In the travel centre, I'd only caught a subtle lilt, but now, as we sit here de-shelling peanuts and complaining about the smog, it is undeniably Scottish.

"Where are you from?" I ask. "I have relatives in Glasgow. You don't sound quite like them, but maybe somewhere nearby?"

She snorts. "Wrong coast. Totally. I'm from Edinburgh. I get mistaken for Northern Irish a lot though. You southerners never get it quite right."

"I'm from Nottingham," I say, laughing. I throw a peanut in the air and catch it in my mouth. I've no idea where that came from. The city, or the peanut trick.

She raises her eyebrows. "Impressive." She lifts her beer and takes a long drink. Her eyes are sparkling. "You don't sound like you come from Nottingham. That's the Midlands, isn't it?"

"Hmm. I've moved a lot. Lived all over. I don't think I have any accent now. Not like you."

She leans forwards and smirks. "Do you need me to speak slow . . . er?"

I pretend to look confused. "I've *no* idea what you're saying."

"Funny. Would you believe, I spend a *lot* of time pronouncing my words carefully for non-natives. I'm quite good at accents, actually." She throws a peanut and tries to catch it, but it goes way wide of the mark. She swears under her breath, but she's grinning. "Oh damn it," she says in a good approximation of my accent. She's right. She's a decent mimic.

I toss another peanut and catch it. I'm clearly on a roll. Maybe this boho look I've adopted comes with extra skills. "Don't worry. I've spent years perfecting this as my party trick," I lie. "I'd always hoped I could try that holding-lipstick-in-your-cleavage thing that Molly Ringwald does in *The Breakfast Club*, but I don't wear lipstick and my tits aren't big enough." The last part is true, at least. Something that caused many sleepless nights when I was a teenager, but is actually quite a relief now, when my peers are complaining about sagging and I barely need to bother with a bra. Besides, I've never had any complaints.

She laughs. "Oh . . . well, if we're talking party tricks, I've got something much more impressive . . ."

Before I can ask what it is, she's got two fingers in her mouth and she's whistling — high pitched, loud — like a builder hanging out of a white van. Everyone in the bar looks at us, and the waitress scurries over, smiling.

"More beers?" She does another semi-bow and scuttles back off. We collapse into fits of laughter.

"Oh man, I didn't expect her to come over like that . . . she must think I'm so rude!"

14

I drain the rest of my pint. "Oh, you *are* rude. They're probably spitting into your glass as we speak."

"Don't. I used to work in a pub. I never actually saw him do it, but the chef was always threatening to do disgusting things to people's dinners. Especially if they were the 'oh can I have salad not chips and the sauce on the side, and is it possible to have the fish grilled instead of fried?' type."

"I thought everyone in Scotland ate everything fried."

"Racist." She throws a peanut shell at me and it gets trapped in my hair. We start giggling again, and as we shake with laughter the poor waitress has to dodge in between us to lay our pints on the table, and we ignore her. I'll make sure we leave a good tip. Assuming Carrie has cash, that is.

"We have to cater for the tourists," she says. "Some of them eat vegetables."

"Except the Americans."

"Well, unless they're Californians. But not many of those make it all the way to Scotland. It's a long way to travel to wander about in the rain looking for haggis." She snorts.

I can't stop laughing. My face aches from it. My throat dry, so dry that I almost choke, and while I'm choking, Carrie throws another peanut shell at me, and she's off again. I can't remember the last time I've laughed like this. Not with Sam. Not with anyone. Not for a very long time.

Carrie wipes her face with a cocktail napkin. "Besides . . . spitting is actually OK in this country. As is squatting on toilet seats."

I pull a face. "Only the squat-hole ones."

"I went into the public toilets near Tiananmen Square and it was full of squat-holes and no doors, and all these girls were just there, squatting and texting madly on their phones."

She starts laughing again. A wave of dizziness hits me, and I sway slightly in my seat.

"Bloody hell," Carrie says. "I think we need to eat. We're getting hysterical."

I fan a hand in front of my face. "It's the heat."

"It's Baltic in here! It's the shady beer . . . Come on, let's neck these then go and grab some food. You know what, since it's our last night here, I really fancy going to the Hard Rock Cafe. I know it's cheesy as fuck and lacking any sort of cultural awareness, but . . ." She pauses, leans in closer to me. "I am *so* sick of rice." She laughs and de-shells another peanut. "Plus, Laura collects the badges so I want to get her one —"

The laughter drains out of me, like water down a plughole.

"Who's Laura?"

She waves a hand in front of her face. Her face crumples slightly. "I told you, didn't I? I was meant to be travelling with her. She's my best friend from school. We went out on a big night before we were due to leave and she fell down the stairs wearing stupid heels . . ." She pauses, takes a long drink. I watch her throat moving as the liquid moves downwards. A long, slender

16

neck. Perfect pale skin. "OK, we were actually a bit pissed." She puts the glass down and raises an eyebrow. "A lot pissed. A lot more pissed than this. Anyhow, the travel insurance wouldn't cover it. She was gutted. I was gutted . . . I nearly didn't come. But then I thought, you know what? Why should I not come? Why give up the chance of a trip of a lifetime? Neither of us would be able to save for it again . . . So I came —"

"Good for you," I cut in, relaxed again now that it's clear that Laura won't be joining us. "So how long have you been here?"

"Oh, here, not long. A few days. I was in Vietnam . . . Thailand . . ."

I feel sober all of a sudden. "Were you in Bangkok? I've just come from there . . ." I wonder now if I have seen her before. That maybe this is why I feel connected to her.

"Nah, just the airport. I was meant to spend a night in the city, but the taxi driver recommended this trip to Ko Samui and told me the beaches were better than the stinking city streets — his words, not mine. I kind of regret it now. But hey, I've been in the night market here. I've eaten locusts. I've done the things. Anyway, what are you doing here on your own? Been dumped?"

I don't want to get into this right now. "Something like that," I say.

She sits back in her chair and I realise then that she's quite drunk — her eyes glazed, swimming in and out of focus. It's good that she's relaxed, because the more relaxed she is, the better chance I have of convincing

17

her to let me have her spare ticket for the train. I like what I've seen so far. I want to get to know her better.

CHAPTER
FOUR

We're giggling as we fall into a taxi outside the hotel, and the beginnings of drunkenness start to fade, turning instead into a state of blissed-out happiness that I haven't felt since I arrived here.

The driver is infected with our laughter and blurts out random names of rock stars as he drives us through the endless streets, horns honking around us. Bicycles weave by us, as our driver calls out "Jon Bon Jovi" and "Bruce Springsteen guitar", and starts to sing the chorus of "Born to Run" in heavily accented English, and Carrie waving a hand in front of her face, mouthing, "I can't breathe," which only makes us laugh more.

Carrie's laughter has turned into hiccups by the time we reach the entrance. A huge, concrete block of a place, with the usual Hard Rock Cafe logo and various memorabilia adorning the walls as we head up the steps.

A grinning waitress leads us to a table, and before I can even look at the menu, Carrie says, "Two Long Island Iced Teas."

The waitress does a little bow then scurries off, still grinning.

"Oh, God," I say, fanning myself with the menu. "I think I might need a Coke or something —"

"Shut. Up. You're not going soft on me already are you, V?" She laughs again. "See what I did there? Soft?"

I roll my eyes, but she doesn't see because she's picked up the menu and is studying it intently as if she's reading the instructions for the most difficult exam she's ever taken, and is determined not to fail. Her face is scrunched in a cute approximation of drunken concentration, and it makes me happy. And she called me "V", which makes me happier still. We've only known each other for a few hours and she already has a pet name for me. After my earlier despair, it seems like the planets may have collided at just the right time after all.

The waitress returns with the drinks and places them on the table on top of two small black napkins. "Are you ready to order? Do you need help with menu? The Local Legendary burger is really good —"

"Yep, two of them please," Carrie says, snapping the menu shut. I haven't even had a chance to look yet, but I don't really care what I eat. I'm just glad to be here with this vibrant, buzzing ball of energy that I've stumbled upon.

She lifts her drink. "Cheers," she says. "To new friends and new adventures."

We chink glasses, and I take a sip. Carrie downs half of hers in one. The waitress is still gathering up the menus, tidying up the table, and I grab her arm, gently. "Could we have a jug of water too, please?"

"Of course!" She grins at me and scurries off.

20

Carrie rolls her eyes. "You trying to stop me getting drunk?"

"No, of course not . . ." I pause, worrying now that I've upset her. "I just need a drink of water or I'm not sure I'm going to get through this cocktail. I'm a bit of a lightweight. What's in it?"

She laughs. "Oh my God, you mean you didn't go out underage drinking in places like this and order the cocktail with the most alcohol you could find, cos you could only afford one?"

I shake my head. "I didn't really do anything like that. There was nothing like this near where I grew up."

"Me and Laura used to go up to this American diner place on the High Street . . . you know, The Royal Mile? That road that all the tourists love because it links Edinburgh Castle to Holyrood Palace, and it's full of tacky tartan, fudge and bagpipers?" She laughs again, and takes a sip of her drink. "It was called the Filling Station. When I first heard of it I thought it was a garage. Anyway, it was a great place for underagers. I think they thought we wouldn't stay too long, so they could get away with it. Saying that, most of the bars around The Grassmarket and The Cowgate let us in too. Starting the night with one of these was our wee tradition."

I take a sip, and it's actually quite nice. Sweet and sour, but with a definite kick. I feel the warmth hit my stomach, and I let myself relax again. I'm not that much of a lightweight. Far from it. I'm just trying to keep my wits about me so I don't blow it with my new potential friend.

The water arrives, and then the burgers, and we don't talk for a while as we eat. Carrie picks up the burger and squashes it together as much as she can, opening her mouth and taking a huge bite. Sauce dribbles down her chin, and she wipes it away quickly with a napkin before taking another bite. She is devouring it, as if she hasn't eaten for days — whereas I have removed the salad and the bacon, and have cut the burger in half, nibbling on it. I feel self-conscious as I eat, but Carrie is one of those people who just gets stuck in — and I think this says a lot about her.

"Tell me about this ex then," she says, still chewing. "Did he dump you on the trip or before you left home? Come on, V, what's your story?"

I lay the burger back on the plate and nibble on a couple of fries. "It was in Bangkok. He just dumped me. Just like that. No explanation. I didn't bother to hang around."

"Fucksake, what a prick." She takes a long drink of water. She seems less pissed now that the food has started to soak up the alcohol. "Were you together long?"

I make a non-committal face and hope that she takes the hint.

"I've been plagued by bad luck on this trip," I say, finishing the last of my cocktail. The waitress must be watching us, as she comes scurrying over to collect the glasses.

"Two more?" she says. "You enjoy the food?"

Carrie nods, and the waitress grins at us again, before disappearing off towards the kitchen.

"Go on," she says. "I was feeling sorry for myself not being with Laura. Hearing about other folk's travelling disasters is making me feel better."

"Well I've been away for a long time now. Nearly a year. Before Sam —"

"That's your Bangkok bastard?"

I laugh. "Yes. Well before him, there was Michael . . ."

"Oh, don't tell me, he was a bastard too? I'm starting to think they really are all the same. My ex was called Greg. I dumped him just before we left . . ." She pauses, and takes an angry bite of her burger. "Someone sent me a message telling me he was cheating on me."

"Shit," I say. "Did you confront him?"

She laughs, but it's humourless. "You could say that. Anyway. Old. Fucking. News."

The waitress places two more drinks in front of us, and Carrie holds hers aloft.

"Cheers," she says.

I tap my glass against hers and take a long, slow drink.

She didn't give me a chance to tell her what happened to Michael, and the moment is gone — and that's fine. It's probably better she doesn't know. For now, at least.

"You know," she continues, "I think I might be off men altogether. Pointless, useless and far too much hassle." She puts her glass on the table. "Give me a Rampant Rabbit and a few semi-naked pics of Gerard Butler in *300* and I'll be fucking sorted." She laughs, then she leans across the table and puts both of her hands on top of mine. Her expression turns serious. "Listen. Don't suppose *you* want my spare ticket? It's for the Mongolian branch and I've got a couple of planned stop-offs. I kind of thought it might be interesting." She takes her hands away and leans back in her chair, picks up her napkin and wipes her mouth, then folds it into a neat square and lays it on top of her empty plate. "Like I said, Laura had to cancel, so I came on my own, but to be honest, after having a laugh with you tonight, I'm not sure I'm really up for being on my own anymore. Plus, it's a total waste of a ticket —"

To: lauralee@gmail.com
From: carrie82@hotmail.com
Subject: Got a new pal, you're dumped

Haha — only kidding! Right, so I tried to get a refund on your portion of the train ticket but the woman was, like, computer-says-no. Ragin'! Anyway, met this woman at the travel centre — she'd been dumped by her useless boyfriend (sounds familiar, eh?) and they said there were no tickets left . . . Anyway, I saw this girl and I thought she might be an interesting travelling companion (mainly because she headed straight to the bar when they told her there were no tickets left) so I just blurted it out and asked if she wanted to take the ticket and she said yes. Yay! Maybe because I didn't say she had to pay for it, but we can work that out. Anyhoo, we went out for dinner and she's a total riot.

I'll email you again ASAP. Reply when you can and tell me your news? I am so out of the loop over here.

Love you!

Cx

P.S. Hope you're recovering and not too jealous about me jet-setting around the globe while you're in your jammies

25

with that big stookie! You know what? I think we (but mainly you) need to start wearing more sensible drinking shoes . . .

P.P.S. I know you keep banging on about me using Messenger but I am trying to avoid being on there because . . . YOU KNOW WHY . . . and anyway, you can look forward to my emails like I'm sending you a postcard — in fact, maybe I will send you a postcard #oldskool

P.P.P.S. I got you a badge ☺

CHAPTER
FIVE

Beijing–Ulaanbaatar

We made it onto the train without any issues. Smartly suited but unsmiling hostesses showed us to our cabin, and we immediately went off to find the dining car, to have a drink and to see who else was around, and now that the buzz has worn off a little, and the hangovers are kicking in, we're back in the cabin, sitting on the edges of our beds. I've dealt us both our cards and placed them on the small table under the window between us, but they remain untouched next to two plastic cups filled with warm Coke. It was Carrie's idea to play poker, but apart from her telling me the rules, we haven't got very far. Carrie gazes out of the window and I watch her, watching the landscape.

Flat fields of cracked ochre mud. Pylons and rundown shacks. I have no idea where we are. Other than that we are still in China, because we haven't stopped yet to let the border guards come on. I heard someone earlier — one of the old ones from the organised tour group — say that we would hit the border late at night. Or early in the morning. They'd slow down the journey on purpose, so that the guards could join the train when most people were sleeping.

Then we'd sit for a while as they changed over the wheels on each carriage, because of the wider tracks outside of China.

We saw the sellers clambering on at the last stop, laden with chequered laundry bags filled with cheap jeans, fake branded T-shirts, bags and caps. The guards might let some of them through without paying import tax, or they might not. It was a risky business, but it was better than drugs, and people had to make a living somehow. Those sellers won't be sleeping tonight. They'll be waiting in their cabins, drinking black coffee to stay alert. Their gifts for the border guards stashed under the bunks, hoping for a sympathetic ear.

I wanted to take a sleeping pill and avoid the whole thing. I'd experienced it all before at other border crossings, and I knew the guards would be loud and rude and unreasonable. They could search the whole of our cabin, *toss* everything on the floor if they wanted. I didn't know if Carrie knew any of this.

"Have you crossed a border on a train before?" I ask her.

She snorts. "Of course. In Europe, though, not in Asia. I once smuggled a lump of hash from Amsterdam to Paris in a sock. I was terrified the whole time. When the guards came on. I nearly peed my pants. But they didn't even look at me. I guess I don't look like an international drugs mule." She laughs, takes a sip of Coke. "In fact, that means I might make a good one . . . Maybe I'll look into it." She winks.

Perhaps I've made a big mistake. I don't even know her. She found me at my most vulnerable, and she helped me. I appreciate it. We had fun. We can have more fun, if she lets me stick around.

"I was just thinking about dinner last night," she says, as if she has just read my mind. "As predicted, it was totally cheesy and we could have been anywhere, but I kind of liked how excited that group of students were to see us. So random that they wanted to take so many photos of us."

"They think we're exotic," I say. "With our pale skin and wide eyes. Our height too. We're like goddesses to them. They've no idea that they're the beautiful, exotic ones."

"Speak for yourself," she says. She licks her top lip with the tip of her tongue.

I feel something stir inside me. She *is* exotic, more so than me. Her skin is smooth and lightly tanned. Her blonde highlighted hair is naturally straight and shiny. She wears neatly fitting shorts and vest tops. She smells of lemons. I, on the other hand, seem to be clad in rags beside her. My long gypsy skirt and faded Nirvana T-shirt don't really show me off like her clothes do, my henna'd hair is in need of some TLC; it's been so long since I brushed it, it's turning into dreadlocks. I'm always pale, avoiding the sun. I smell of rose and jasmine, a blend of oils that I've been wearing since I was thirteen years old when I first mixed them together in an atomiser that my grandmother left me when she died. We are very different, and yet here we are.

She offered me the second bed in her cabin. She let this happen.

She let me borrow whatever I needed until my bag turned up. Of course it didn't turn up and probably never will. I will buy what I need when we get there. I'll change my sryle again. I don't know what people dress like in Ulaanbaatar, but it won't be long before I find out. I glance at Carrie. She's lying on her bed now, still and quiet. One hand resting on her chest. Her rib cage gently rises and falls. I can see the perfect mounds of her breasts above her thin vest. Her clavicle stands high and sharp, and I have to try very hard not to lean over and run my finger across it.

"I'll pay for the ticket. When we get to the next stop," I say quietly. I hope she'll let me stay with her in Mongolia. I feel like we're only just getting started.

"Whatever," she says. In a way that says she's chilled, not indifferent. She doesn't open her eyes.

I stare out of the window. Those same bleak fields. The rhythmic *badum badum* of the train on the tracks. I lean back against the wall, letting the sounds hypnotise me.

Badum badum.

A screech, now and then. The train lurches from side to side. I close my eyes and wonder what would have happened if I hadn't walked into the travel centre and found her there, and me so desperate to take this trip.

She's my beautiful, perfect saviour.

I've barely thought about Sam since I met her. She's going to be good for me, I think. I just hope I can control myself this time.

To: carrie82@hotmail.com
From: lauralee@gmail.com
Subject: RE: Got a new pal, you're dumped

OMG, you've replaced me already? Seriously, Caz, that is GREAT. I didn't tell you how much it was stressing me out about that bloody ticket. To be honest, I'm not even bothered about the money that much. I'm glad it's gone to a good home. You need to tell me everything about your new friend though -come on! Are you on the train yet? What's it like? And can we please use Messenger? I hate waiting for your emails . . . I miss you! Nothing much is happening here, as I am sure you can imagine. Edinburgh is cold and wet and full of tourists. Sheila from work has taken your place in the quiz team. She lacks your musical knowledge, but she knows everything else . . . She's actually quite a laugh after a couple of shandies.

Tell me everything!

Miss you,

L xxx

P.S. I saw Greg. I know that's what you were hinting at but are refusing to acknowledge. Why won't you tell me what happened with you two? He looks forlorn . . .

★ ★ ★

To: lauralee@gmail.com
From: carrie82@hotmail.com
Subject: RE: RE: Got a new pal, you're dumped

Her name is Violet and she reckons she's from Nottingham, but she sounds more like a home-counties rich kid and she dresses like a proper nineties grunge-hippy (is that a thing?). She has terrible hair — all matted henna dreads. She really needs a makeover! She looks like she's been travelling for twenty years. I'm pretty sure she's our age though. But apart from that, we seem to be totally on the same wavelength and I'm loving hanging out with her. We'll see how it goes . . .

Yes, we are on the train! I am writing this from the toilet. I went for a walk along the carriages and there's a massive tour group full of pensioners and they are bloody loving it. Me and you need to do massive trips when we're pension-ers. None of that bingo-fish-and-chips Friday shite.

I TOLD you I'm not using Messenger . . . Anyway, the time difference means we'll hardly ever be online at the same time so email makes more sense, plus I can write loads without you butting in.

I'm not talking about Greg.

Will email more when we get to the next stop. The train is great. It's like the Orient Express, except not as fancy. You would love it.

Cx

P.S. There's a *very* sexy guy working in the restaurant. I think he's Russian, but that is based entirely on his brooding, Slavic cheekbones (can cheekbones brood? Are Russians Slavic? Ask Sheila if she knows so much!) — he's never actually spoken to us. He's given us free vodka at every meal. Maybe he gives it to all the guests, but I think he fancies me. Trying to decide whether to proceed . . .

P.P.S. I am not going to proceed. I am so off men right now.

CHAPTER
SIX

Ulaanbaatar

Carrie has been reading the guidebook enrry for Mongolia. The capital, Ulaanbaatar, is our first proper stop on this journey, where we will actually get off the train for longer than a five-minute cigarette break.

"'Genghis Khan was born around 1162 near the border between modern Mongolia and Siberia. Legend holds that he came into the world clutching a blood clot in his right hand'," Carrie reads aloud. "'Before he turned ten, his father was poisoned to death by an enemy clan. His own clan then deserted him, his mother *and his* six siblings in order to avoid having to feed them.'" She blows out a breath. "Harsh."

"That's all fascinating, obviously," I say, tipping a cigarette out of the packet from the fresh carton that we bought at the last stop — something else that the platform sellers are keen on hawking. I stick the cigarette behind my ear. "But have you booked accommodation here? Only ... well I don't have anything, obviously. And I can ask a taxi driver or —"

"Oh for God's sake," she says, jumping up off the bunk and dropping the book into her backpack. "You can stay with me. I've got everything booked for two, haven't I?" She hoists her backpack onto her shoulders. "Come on, let's go down to the door. We'll be stopping in a minute."

The train has slowed right down, and it's clear from the chatter outside in the corridor that the tour group are excited that we're approaching a major stop. I pick up my own backpack and follow Carrie out of the cabin. Our little home for the last twenty-four hours where we've started a new friendship, and a new adventure. I'd been scared to ask if she was happy for me to continue on the journey with her, wondering if maybe up to the first stop was all she was happy to share. I don't want to seem too needy.

I've made that mistake before.

"Have a wonderful time in Ulaanbaatar, girls," says a spritely looking lady in beige-pocketed jungle shorts. I can't remember her name.

"See you in Moscow, Marion. We'll get fired into the proper voddie there." Carrie pats her back pocket. "I've got your email."

"She's staying off the firewater from now on," the man next to her says. "Can't control her."

Carrie laughs. "Well, Steve, what kind of fun would it be if you could control her, eh?" She steps forwards and hugs them both. Then we climb down the steep metal stairs and onto the dusty platform.

"Right," she says, "let's go and find out what this place is all about."

I follow her down the platform, envying her warm, easy personality. She'd got to know the people in that tour group, while I'd been far more reserved —

spending most of my time watching her engage. She is fascinating.

I had planned to get off elsewhere, but Carrie's ticket had destinations pre-booked, and with her helping me out, I could hardly make a fuss. She hasn't said anything about paying her since she handed me the ticket, and she's paid for everything else too. I'm wondering if I don't bring it up, will she? It's not like I *can't* pay her. I assume I can withdraw what I need in Ulaanbaatar, and I have a roll of emergency dollars in a hidden pocket of my bag, but why pay for things if you don't need to?

We're outside the station now. I'm smoking, casting a surreptitious eye around the place but trying to look casual, while Carrie speaks to the station guard, showing him the map and the guidebook. He's shaking his head and pointing to the patch of land that seems to be the car park. Several men stand waiting. All of them are smoking. None of them look particularly threatening, but you never know. I would suggest that we walk, but my quick flick through the guidebook earlier makes me think it might be too far with our rucksacks to carry.

I take a moment to check Sam's Facebook, and see that he is "#hanging". What a surprise. All he seems to do there is party. There's a picture of him with one of the German lads, both of them grinning and holding massive beers. I enlarge the photo, trying to see if there are any girls in the background, but it's dark and grainy — probably in one of those awful clubs. I put my phone back in my bag.

36

Looking at the mainly elderly gents hovering around their tatty cars, I think it's unlikely that any will offer to carry our bags on their heads, like they did when I was in India. I told Carrie about this in the Hard Rock Cafe, and she snorted in an "I don't believe you" way, but the only places she'd been before Beijing were Vietnam and Thailand, and the culture there is not the same at all. The Indian bag-carriers are called "coolies", and they are waiting at every train station. Between them and the men lugging around the huge pots of steaming chai and tiny earthenware cups, it's a very different experience to this so far. Also, there are no monkeys scampering across the tracks here. So far, Mongolia is not particularly inspiring. A trickle of the younger passengers have set off on foot, while a few others have headed towards the taxis. There is a minor flurry of excitement and some rapid-fire conversation as the drivers decide between them who they will take, and probably, what inflated prices they can charge. Luckily Carrie has read the guidebook in more detail than I have and she won't let us be ripped off.

I drop my cigarette and crush it underfoot. Carrie comes back at last. The station guard has recommended a taxi driver who she assures me will not overcharge or kill us, so I hitch my rucksack onto my back and follow her to the car. She hands over the address, written neatly on a piece of paper.

"Let's drop our bags at the hostel, then get out and explore the place," Carrie says. We pass flats, low, ramshackle houses, a couple of fancy-looking glass buildings.

"I was looking at the guidebook earlier," I say. "Apparently there are two Irish pubs and a British pub here. Maybe we can head there for a bit." I really want her to say yes. As much as I love discovering new things, I'm feeling quite tired after the train journey, the effort of it all. I'd love to go somewhere that feels like home. Just for a bit. The culture will still be there tomorrow.

"Oh, definitely," she says. "I saw those too. I fancy a walkabout, then a proper night out." She leans over and takes a strand of my hair between her fingers. Twirls it around. "We can get dressed up."

"Have you looked outside," I say. "Not sure it's a very 'dress up' sort of place." The taxi driver looks into his rear-view mirror, and I catch his eye for a moment. He's smiling. Maybe he knows something we don't. Assuming he understands what we're saying.

"Good shop," he says, pointing out to the right.

We follow his line of sight to a monolithic building. It looks like a communist prison, but I try to be optimistic. A department store, maybe? From what I've seen so far, this place is such a mishmash.

"Brilliant," Carrie says. "Can you recommend a good restaurant?"

The taxi driver laughs. "No Mongolian barbecue here."

Carrie opens her mouth to question him further, but then the car swings around a bend and comes to a stop next to a cut-through to a small square lined with terraced houses. They've been painted various colours, but the paint is faded and peeling. One of them has a sign nailed on the wall next to the front door, but I can't make out what it says.

The driver points. "Sunrise Guesthouse," he says.

I turn to Carrie, trying to work out if there's been a mistake. It looks like we're in the middle of a housing estate, and not a particularly nice one at that. But she's already out of the car, handing over notes. Picking up her rucksack from where the driver has dropped both of them onto the rough, cracked concrete. Oh well. Beggars can't be choosers.

CHAPTER
SEVEN

The front door opens before we get all the way across the square.

"Welcome, welcome," says the woman standing on the doorstep. She is tall and slim, long dark hair in one braid over her shoulder. She has high cheekbones and shining almond eyes, and she is wearing faded blue jeans and a cream smock-top with multi-coloured tassels hanging from the neck. She looks fresh and welcoming, and I feel shabby in front of her. Even Carrie doesn't look so fresh after nearly thirty hours on a train without a shower.

As we get closer, I see that she has tried to make an effort with the garden. Despite the scorched patches of grass, there are planters lining the wall under the window, a mix of flowering and spiky cacti, and a few coloured rocks in the dry soil. She sees me looking.

"Best we can do in this climate. Nothing grows, you know. You might have noticed the fields — if that's even what we can call them. I'm Geriel," she says. "It means a bright light in Mongolian. We like to choose our names carefully in our culture. It's nice, to do this, is it not? And you must be Carrie —"

40

"Actually, I'm Carrie." She steps forwards and the woman at the door beams. "This is my friend, Violet."

"Hello," I say, feeling shy all of a sudden. I don't know why, but I hadn't expected this kind of welcome. This kind of accommodation. Meeting Carrie in the Beijing International Hotel, I had assumed that she would be staying in places like that all the time, but it looks like I misinterpreted that. It's unlike me to get it so wrong.

"Come inside, you must be desperate for some tea . . . and perhaps a shower?" Geriel says.

"In that order, definitely," says Carrie.

We follow Geriel into the house, and it's clear that she has put a lot of effort into the interior. I suppose I shouldn't have judged the place by its exterior, but it's a natural reaction. I saw something I liked in Carrie, and so far, she doesn't disappoint.

"This is the kitchen, and the lounge off it. Please come and go as you please. We like to gather here at the end of the day to chat, to drink tea. To talk about our day . . . and to give thanks."

There are various prints on the walls, Buddhas and sunsets. Beaches. Beautiful women in impossible yoga poses. Various words of wisdom printed in a pretty typeface on top of the images:

> "*It is better to conquer yourself than*
> *to win a thousand battles.*"
> "*The root of suffering is attachment.*"
> "*Speak or act with an impure mind and*
> *trouble will follow you.*"

I try to catch Carrie's eye, but she seems enthralled by them. Personally I think it's all a bit much, and the thought of sitting in the lounge with a group of strangers, giving thanks, makes me shudder. I might look like a hippy today but, like I said, it was meant to be beachwear. However, letting my hair go matted just makes it easier to handle, because I don't have to think about it. I know that one day soon, I'm going to have to let someone cut it all off, but for now, it's doing the job. Besides, if I dress like this, I blend in. And I've found that blending in is the best way to get what you want.

Finally, Geriel shows us to our room — two single beds with yellow crocheted bedspreads, a white painted dresser with another cactus sitting on a wooden coaster, and a small bathroom off to the side. Despite my initial reservations, it's perfect — and I am delighted to throw my bag on the floor and lie down on a bed that is at least double the width of my body. Don't get me wrong, I loved sleeping on the train — but this feels like luxury in comparison. There was barely room to swing a cat in the cabin.

"At last," I say, kicking off my boots. "I thought she was going to make us join a moon circle before lunch." I lift my head to look at Carrie, who is already unpacking, removing neatly rolled clothes from her bag and putting her toiletries on the dresser.

"She's all right. You need to play the game, Violet. Soak it all up then discard it. Smile in the right places. It gets you far in this world . . . especially if you want something."

42

I feel myself bristle at her words, at her insinuation that I am not doing things right. I've been travelling for long enough to know how it all works. I might not be a people-pleaser like Carrie, with the shiny hair and the fake smile, but I usually get what I want. She'll realise that soon enough. I say nothing — deciding that letting her believe she is educating me is the way to ingratiate myself further. I want something, all right. And I know I'll get it.

"Anyway . . ." she carries on, realising that I am not going to contradict her, "let's get freshened up and get out of here — I want to explore. It has to be more than cracked concrete and dull buildings. The guidebook said —"

"Do you want to have a shower first, or shall I?" I give her my best smile, and it knocks her off guard.

"Oh. Right, yeah. You go. Hang on . . ." She rustles about in her bag and pulls out a fat red tub. "Put this on your hair, leave it in while you get washed and whatever. It'll soften those tangles . . ." She cocks her head to one side, appraising me, like a little bird. "I might even be able to brush it for you." She stands beside me at the dresser and we look into the mirror together. She pulls my hair back off my face. "Smile," she says, and I have no choice but to oblige. She smiles too, both of us grinning like lunatics into the mirror. "See? We're quite alike, actually, when you get that mop out of the way. I'll give you a makeover and then we'll hit the town."

Any stab of annoyance I started to feel has disintegrated now, with the soft touch of her fingertips on the back of my neck.

To: carrie82@hotmail.com
From: lauralee@gmail.com
Subject: RE: RE: RE: Got a new pal, you're dumped

Bored to f**k here!

I phoned William Hill and put a bet on that you shagged the sexy Russian. Don't let me down . . . I must live my life vicariously right now.

Lx

★   ★   ★

To: lauralee@gmail.com
From: carrie82@hotmail.com
Subject: RE: RE: RE: RE: Got a new pal, you're dumped

Just a quick one to let you know that we're in Ulaanbaatar — that's in Mongolia, in case you didn't know. The locals call it "UB" which I suppose is much easier to pronounce, not to mention spell. Seriously, do you know anyone who's been to Mongolia? Mental! So far, no barbecues . . . I'm beginning to think we've been mis-sold the Mongolian experience. Haha! Staying in a wee guesthouse with *New Age Mama* type but she seems OK to be fair. Wants us to go all communal and do sun salutations before supper, but I cannae see it somehow. I gave her the smiley spiel and she likes us now — well, me anyway. Violet looked like I'd brought her into a cult — haha!

Anyhoo . . . getting changed and heading out on the town. I'll take pics! The guidebook is telling us to ditch the traditional restaurants and head to an Irish Bar — seems like slightly suspect advice, but we're gonna go for it I think. Maybe pop into one of the other places first, just to see.

Need to go shopping too — taxi driver pointed out this big hulk of a building that looks like it might sell ten-kilo bags of rice and shoes made from hessian sacks, but I'm trying to remain positive. I wonder what Mongolian chocolate is like? I'll bring you some.

Missing you, doll. Violet is nice but she's no' you. I'm giving her a makeover, if she ever gets out of the shower. Damn it, should've taken a "before" pic . . .

What's your news?

Cx

P.S. Hope you didn't bet your flat on the Russian. Told you, I'm off men. Too much stress!

★ ★ ★

46

To: carrie82@hotmail.com
From: lauralee@gmail.com
Subject: RE: RE: RE: RE: RE: Got a new pal, you're dumped

Glad to hear you're missing me! My leg has reached peak itchiness. Thankfully I had a knitting needle from that kit we both bought after the beginners' workshop, It's perfect for scratching down inside the cast, but I think I might actually start knitting something — might have a scarf for you by the time you get home!

Btw, I was expecting more from you on the Greg thing — mainly because you didn't even ask how I ended up seeing him, when I'm stuck here with this affliction? I'm actually quite good on the crutches. My mum came and took me down to Costa -I nearly cried! I hate being stuck inside, especially when you're over there, doing the most exciting things ever.

Buy me a handbag made from yak wool, or whatever weird animals they have over there.

Andy and Elaine are coming over later with Domino's and the new *Halloween* DVD. I'd say "what has my life become?", but it's better than sitting here on my own. At least I got out to the quiz the other night . . . I might replace you with Sheila long term (as if).

Keep having fun!

Love,

Lx

48

CHAPTER
EIGHT

She's done an excellent job with my hair. The tub of magical conditioner followed by her careful, methodical brushing with a Tangle Teezer has worked wonders. I need to dye it now, of course, to complete the effect. The henna is faded and it's about time I went back to my dark-blonde roots. Maybe a bit of bleach through the ends, to give it a sun-kissed look.

I used the time while she was in the shower to check Sam's Face-book again. Latest update: photo of him gurning disrespectfully outside a temple. What did I ever see in him? Then I had a quick root through Carrie's bag, being careful to put everything back where I found it. I tried to check her phone but she's got a password on there, so I had a squizz at her laptop instead.

"How are the shorts?" she says, glancing down at me as we walk. "The T-shirt really suits you, you know."

"Mmm," I mutter, catching my reflection in the dull glass of what looks like an electrics store. "Quite a transformation." She's done a great job with my impromptu makeover, but I don't want her thinking she's changed my life or anything. I've had many different looks. I've been fatter than this, I've been much slimmer. I've had black hair and piercings and leather-look leggings. I've had summer dresses and lightly curled blonde locks — with extensions, of course — there's no need to waste time growing your hair these days. But I feel like I am showing Carrie my vulnerable side by letting her take control of how I look, so I will give her the praise she craves. "I don't know how to thank you," I say. I stop walking, and lay a hand on her arm, exerting just the right amount of pressure so that she stops too.

She looks surprised, and then her face breaks into a huge grin. "You're *so* welcome, love. Now, let's get ourselves into this shop . . . see what magical wares are on display." She nudges me and I link arms with her. The building looms in front of us, and I'm glad to be going inside, away from the small army of feral children who have taken to following us along the streets. No doubt Carrie will want to buy things for them in the department store, but I'm sure that they're part of one of those begging gangs, and I'd rather not have any contact with them at all.

Inside, the shop is a little disappointing. I'd hoped that the harsh stone shell was protecting a precious gem, but actually it's all very functional, and is filled with the hollow echoes of an indoor market. I can't read the signs on the boards, but there are helpful graphics depicting food, women's clothes, men's clothes, shoes, and something a bit confusing that turns out to be local crafts.

50

"Right. We need some supplies," Carrie says. "I'll go and get snacks and drinks, and you can do a recce on the rest of the place — what do you think?"

I'm a bit confused as to why we need snacks and drinks when we're meant to be going out for dinner. "Sure . . . although I'm not really hungry . . ."

"Not for now, daftie." She rolls her eyes. "For the room. Here . . ." She rummages in her small bag and pulls out a roll of notes. "Take some cash. Buy us a surprise." She holds the money out towards me. The notes are unfamiliar, and I have no idea how much they're worth — she could be giving me fifty pence and waiting for me to make a fool of myself at the counter when I try to buy something for a fiver. You never know what these currencies are like.

"Where did you get that?" We've been together the whole time since we got on the train in Beijing. She definitely hasn't been to a cashpoint — because if she had, surely she'd have suggested I take some money out too? Somehow, up to now, I've managed to get away without spending any money. She seems oblivious to what she's paying out.

"Got it in Beijing. Didn't know what the bank situation would be like. See you back here in twenty?"

She marches off before I can say anything else. I glance around, taking in the high ceilings, the staircase. The openings to each of the various halls. People scurry around, chattering, busy with their day, not interested in me, and I stare up at the ceiling. At the peeling paintwork. I close my eyes, trying to block it all out. Then I take a deep breath, open my eyes, and paste on

51

a smile. The sooner we get this over with, the sooner we can go somewhere else, where I can ask Carrie more questions about herself, and tell her as little as possible about me.

The local crafts floor is just as you'd expect it to be. Lots of knitted or woven items — I touch a jumper and the wool is scratchy. The woman behind the table smiles at me but she can obviously tell I am not going to buy it. I wander through the aisles separating the various tables of trinkets, and come to a stand with hundreds of small woollen bags hanging off it. They are made of the same rough wool as the jumper, but it seems to work better for bags. I pick up a yellow one with a maroon rose, and a blue one with white stitching around the edges. "How much are these?" I ask a woman standing nearby, who I assume is the seller.

The woman frowns, then takes a small notebook and pen from the pocket of her tabard. She scribbles something on it and holds it up for me to see.

"20,000 MNT", it says. I pull the notes from my pocket. I have two 20,000s and a 10,000. Pink and green, orange and brown, respectively. Both denominations have the same face, which I recognise as Genghis Khan. Is he the only famous Mongolian? He certainly seems to dominate the guidebook.

I hope I'm not blowing all Carrie's cash, and I do, for a moment, think it's quite stupid of me to not have bothered to check the exchange rate — but things have been different since I met Carrie. I've somehow found myself swept along — doing what she's planned — acting as a substitute for her friend with the broken leg.

Perhaps I should get one of these bags for her, too. It would be a nice touch. Another reason for Carrie to trust me. I'm quite enjoying being a kept woman. It's such a nice break from having to do everything myself — like with Sam; if it wasn't for me pushing things along, I'd never have got with him in the first place.

There's an orange bag with a white flower on the front. I unhook it and hand it over for the woman to wrap. "Twenty-five thousand for the three," I say.

She laughs in my face. Not in a nasty way, in that same childish way that I had noticed in Beijing. She shakes her head. She understands me well enough now, it seems.

"Thirty thousand," she says.

"Twenty-five," I try, again. I'm confident now that I am dealing in pennies, not pounds, but what's the fun in buying this crap if you don't even try to knock them down? I think about all the stuff I haggled for in Bangkok. Better stuff than this. "Twenty-five," I say, dropping the money back into my pocket and making it look like I'm going to walk off.

Her smile dips to low beam. "OK, OK. Twenty-five." She thrusts the carrier bag containing the bags at me and gestures with her fingers.

I hand her the money, and she hands me another note in change. Pink. Still Genghis. She's already talking to someone else. I think about trying to say thank you in Mongolian, but realise I have absolutely no idea what the word might be.

Back in the lobby, Carrie is waiting. She has one large carrier bag, and I can see what looks like a huge bag of crisps sticking out of the top. She's leaning on the wall, and when she stands, there's the sound of bottles clinking together. I hold my bag up in front of me. "Got you a present . . . Hope the exchange rate isn't mental."

She laughs. "How much?"

"Twenty-five . . . for three."

She wrinkles her face in concentration. "Ten k is about three quid, so . . . seven-fifty. Three you said? Who's the third?" She takes the carrier from me, rummages inside and pulls out the orange bag. "Oh, these are perfect," she says. "Sort of rank, but actually nice."

"I got one for your friend . . . Laura? I thought, well, as I'm taking her place . . ."

"Oh! Nice work, love. This is exactly the kind of shitey tat that Laura loves. In fact, she asked for something just like this . . . You must be a mind reader!" She links her arm through mine and starts walking. "I was thinking we'd take this stuff back to the B&B first, but, actually, why don't we just head out? I'm quite up for a few bevs. You can tell me all about this ex of yours."

I just smile at that. I won't be telling her anything of the sort. I let her march us out of the shop, pleased with myself.

I'm doing well.

CHAPTER
NINE

The pub is full of wood panelling, green leather seats, gold-and-green patterned carpet. The walls are adorned with hundreds of signs — "Tipperary 200 miles", "*Clad mile fdilte*" — and various football and rugby shirts. I glance around; we could be anywhere in the world. Just like in the Hard Rock Cafe the other night.

"Wow," Carrie says, "it's like they went to Ireland-R-Us and bought the entire stock."

I laugh. "That really should be a shop. They'd make a killing on these Irish bars around the world." I think back to the Irish Bar I'd found in Beijing, the night before I met Carrie. I'd chatted to a pilot in there for a while. He bought me a few drinks and I'd thought he might be a good candidate for my new friend, but the more whiskey he drank, the more I started to doubt his story. He might have been a pilot once, but I wasn't convinced. Some people are pathetic when they lie.

Carrie heads over to a booth seat in the corner, close to the bar. A couple of lads sitting on stools at the bar glance over at us, throwing appraising looks, but I look away. I hope Carrie doesn't invite them over.

A pretty girl who looks about fifteen, wearing a green polo shirt with the bar's emblem in gold on her left breast, arrives at the table with a notebook and pen. She places two leather-bound menus on the table.

"Hi," she says. "I really recommend the cheeseburgers today. Can I get you a drink first? Some Guinness maybe?" She has the barest hint of an accent, but her words are precise, as if she has rehearsed this short speech.

"I'll have a lager, actually," Carrie says. She looks across the table at me expectantly.

"Same." The waitress opens her mouth, ready to reel off the brands. "You choose," I say, and she smiles and scurries off.

Carrie opens the menu and starts reading it out loud. "Homemade Irish stew, corned beef and cabbage . . ." She looks up and rolls her eyes, then goes back to the menu. "Irish cheddar cheese on homemade soda bread." She runs a finger down the page. "Burgers made with genuine Irish beef." She snaps the menu shut. "Really? They import Irish beef?"

One of the guys at the bar, who has clearly been earwigging, leans over to our table. "They have to import everything here. Vegetables from China, because nothing grows. Meat from Russia . . ."

"Thanks for your input," Carrie says, without turning round.

The other guy laughs, then slaps his friend on the back. "*Buuuurn*," he says, and gives me a wink.

I ignore him and open my menu. Why do men assume that all women want to talk to them? Sam and his irritating friends were exactly the same. Only difference was, I actually *did* want to talk to him, but it was hard to get into a proper conversation with the others around.

Carrie leans across the table and whispers, "Maybe later . . . Let's make them work for it."

I give her a small smile, hoping it masks my irritation. She is one of those women who craves male attention. I'd hoped she was better than that. I need to captivate her more, it seems.

"Oh!" She slaps her hands on the table. "I'm so stupid. You're thinking about Sam, aren't you? I'm so insensitive . . ."

"I'm not thinking about Sam," I lie. "I'd rather just talk to you, though. Not them."

She shrugs. "Fair enough."

The waitress returns with our pints and a basket of popcorn.

"Later for food," Carrie says, taking a handful and stuffing it into her mouth. She chews quickly, then licks the salt off her lips. "OK, forget Sam. Forget men." She lifts her pint then mouths a kiss at me over the top of it.

I decide to move on. "Do you think Geriel is expecting us for dinner?" One of the men from the bar looks over at us again, but his mate nudges him and mutters something I can't hear. Then they laugh, and I know they are saying something shit about us, because that's what these types always do.

"Oh, *Geriel* . . . sweetness and light — is that what she said?" "Something like that."

"I was named after the Stephen King character. My mum was a massive fan."

I'm about to take a drink and have to stop to take this in. "No way? Wasn't she a bit mental?"

Carrie laughs. "Not at all. Her *mother* was a religious whacko. Carrie was telekinetic. She wasn't bad — she just took revenge on the arseholes that tried to make her life hell. Including her mum. Thankfully mine is nothing like Carrie's mum. She just likes Stephen King. To be honest, I'm quite happy with the choice — it's a talking point." She shrugs. "Besides, could've been worse. She could've called me Christine . . . after the possessed car."

A girl in my class at primary school was called Christine. She was an annoying little whinger of a kid. One of those with a constantly snotty nose and horrible pink NHS specs. I wonder where she is now.

Carrie takes another handful of popcorn. "What about you? Violet is a *great* name. Was your mum a hippy? Flower child? Have you got sisters called Daisy and Tulip?"

"Well . . ." I take a long slow drink. She's gazing at me, waiting for an answer. "I actually wasn't given this name by my parents. I changed it when I left school. It's after the Hole song. You know it?"

She wrinkles her nose, drops her brows. "As in Courtney Love, Hole? Courtney who ruined your man's life, there?" She lifts her chin, gesturing at my T-shirt. Her accent has gone decidedly Irish.

"It depends whose account you want to believe," I say, sniffily. I loved Kurt Cobain, of course I did. But I loved Courtney too. They were the nineties' Sid and Nancy. Oh how I ached to be part of that lifestyle.

"Didn't their daughter disown her for being a terrible mother?" She takes another drink. "Maybe that was about the name though . . . Who the hell would be happy with *Frances Bean*, for fuck's sake."

"It doesn't matter. It's the song I liked. *Like*." I correct myself. "Do you know it?"

She looks up, as if trying to get the song to slot into place in the jukebox inside her head. She hums a few bars. "*Na nana, take everything . . . everything*. Something like that."

"Yeah." I'm a bit annoyed that she doesn't know it better than that, but it's my song, not hers.

"What's your real name then? Was your mum not pissed off that you changed it?" She turns away, waving a hand to attract the waitress.

"Violet is my real name," I say. Both of our pints are empty now. "Do you fancy some food yet?"

She shakes her head. "Two more," she says to the waitress, "and let's have a couple of sambucas too."

As we're waiting for the drinks, a short man wearing a pale-blue cap and beige slacks comes in from outside, handing out flyers. He slides one on our table. "Tour tomorrow, girls. Good price."

"Tour to where?" Carrie says. She peers at the leaflet.

"Into the Gobi. Authentic Mongolian experience. Stay two nights, see wild horses —"

"Let's do it." She takes a wad of Genghis notes out of her bag, and grins at me. "Don't look so shocked, V. Live a little, eh?" She turns back to the man, who looks slightly stunned that he hasn't had to try very hard at all. "Where do we get the bus?"

"Guide will pick you up. Where you stay?"

"Sunrise Guesthouse."

The man nods, satisfied. Then moves on to the next table. The lads at the bar wave him away, one of them slaps his back and says something I don't catch.

The waitress returns with our drinks, and Carrie hands me a shot glass, raises hers. "To adventures in the desert," she says, knocking the drink back in one.

"*Sláinte*."

Three more pints, and three more sambucas, and the lads from the bar are in the booth beside us. They've brought a large jug full of something lurid pink, and the waitress has brought four small glasses on a tray.

No one has had any cheeseburgers.

"I'm Rory," says the first lad. The one who tried to get our attention at the start. "And this boring fucker is Martin."

Martin is on my side of the booth, a respectful couple of fists' distance away from me. Rory is on the other side with Carrie, squeezed up against her. She doesn't seem too bothered, but she's not paying him any attention. She's looking over the jug, at me, and I'm trying to read her, but I can't. We're both too pissed.

"I'm not sure we should drink this . . ." I have to say the words carefully to avoid slurring.

"Come on, ladies. Got it made specially for you," Rory says. He fills two of the glasses and slides them across to me and Carrie.

"Why aren't you drinking it?" I ask. "Have you put something in it?"

"Rory . . ." Martin says, warning in his voice.

"Don't be daft," Rory says. "We're just sticking to the beer. We got this for you two. Just wanted to say hi."

Carrie picks up the glass and sniffs it, wrinkling her nose. She takes a sip. "It's not bad, *actshullly* . . ."

I take a sip. It tastes of Wham Bars. Those sweet, pink, fizzy chews we used to eat as kids. I knock it back.

"That's the spirit," Rory says. He winks across at Martin. I'm not sure what they're up to, but I know I don't like it.

"Carrie . . ."

Her head is lolling a bit, but it snaps up when she hears her name. I give her a hard stare, hoping I'm getting the message across. She gives me a half-smile and lifts her hand in a placating gesture. Rory is smirking now, but Martin looks annoyed. Carrie seems to slide back into coherence for a moment, glancing at me, then at both men. Then she pulls herself up straighter and shuffles along the booth seat towards the wall, so that Rory is no longer touching her. She slides the jug and the glasses along the table towards the end, and I feel Martin bristle beside me. Rory is still smirking, still thinks he's got the upper hand. But he hasn't.

Carrie leans across the table; she puts one hand on top of mine on the table, puts her other hand on my cheek, then leans in and kisses me softly on the lips. It's only a moment, but it feels like it is going to go on forever. I open my mouth slightly, press against her. She tastes of aniseed and salt.

Martin makes a small noise. Rory swears under his breath.

Carrie pulls away, but her hand is still on mine. She speaks to them without addressing them. Without taking her eyes off me at all. She smiles.

"You know what, lads? I think the two of yous need to *get tae fuck* right about now."

CHAPTER
TEN

Our guide, Sarnai, turns up at the guesthouse to collect us. She is early twenties, fresh-faced and smiley.

"Good morning, ladies," she says, in an accent that has been learned from MTV. "Are you excited about the trip?"

Carrie and I are at the kitchen table, eating toast and jam. It's the worst hangover cure of all, but stupidly, we ate all the supplies we got yesterday in the shopping centre, last night when we rolled in.

Geriel, our pissed-off landlady, says something to Sarnai and she looks over at us and hides a giggle behind her hand. Geriel woke us at 6.30am, and clearly hadn't expected us to still be drunk. The other guests had been up already, awaiting breakfast — and there is still a hint of what might have been fried eggs in the air, taunting us. Toast and jam it is, then. No doubt we'll get some decent food on the trip.

"How far is it to the camp?" Carrie says, with a mouthful of toast.

"Oh," says Sarnai. Smiley, happy Sarnai. "About four hours, hopefully. It's such a fantastic journey. We'll stop off once on the way, to see the wild horses, and we'll be at the camp before dark. We're going to have such fun!"

The front door slams shut and we hear voices in the hall. Two men appear in the kitchen, carrying rucksacks and grinning. One is broad and blond, the other wiry and bald. They look vaguely familiar, but I can't place them.

"Oh yeah? What're the chances," the blond says. "Knew you ladies wouldn't be able to keep away."

I hear Carrie murmur a "fuck" under her breath. Sarnai and Geriel are looking at us all expectantly.

"Did you already meet?" Geriel says. "The boys arrived after you last night, then went out for some food . . ."

"Food and a few drinks, yep," says the bald one. He winks at me. "Morning," he says. "All set for the trip?"

"These are the jokers who gave us that shady cocktail, V," Carrie says. "That pink stuff."

I remember now. The night coming back in small, uneven pieces. I put them together like a mosaic. The Irish Bar. Them sliding into the booth next to us.

"Shame we didn't get a chance to talk to you properly last night," the blond one says, winking. *Rory,* I remember. His name is Rory. The bald one is Martin. He has the grace to look sheepish. I remember him being reluctant last night too. Either he didn't fancy me, or he just wasn't a presumptuous pig like his mate. I remember the pink cocktail, and a wave of nausea washes over me. We got rid of them, but we drank the stuff anyway.

I glance across at Carrie, but she won't meet my eye. She's remembering the kiss. Does she regret it? It might've been a diversion tactic on her part, but it was something else for me. We'd stumbled out of that bar, then ended up in a tacky British pub with a perilous open manhole outside and an old Mini parked next to the front door. Carrie had tried to climb in, and the barman had come out and shouted at us. Rory and Martin didn't follow us there. Clearly too sensible to get wasted the night before a four-hour trip across the desert. *Shi-t* . . . Clearly they had this all planned. Did they want us to suffer, just so they could laugh? I wouldn't have put it past them. Rory, at least, seems the type to take the piss like this.

Sarnai grins and claps her hands like an excited child. "Oh it's great you already know each other. Come on, Erden has parked around the corner. Grab your stuff, and let's get going."

Geriel mutters something under her breath as we leave, but neither of us has the energy to get bothered about it.

For some reason, both Carrie and I had expected a coach. But our vehicle for this trip turns out to be a forty-year-old Land Rover Defender, the type you see in war movies. It's filthy, the seats need re-springing, and after a very short period of time, it's clear that there is minimal suspension. Our driver, Erden, is the man with the blue cap from the bar.

"I take it you had this booked before we did," Carrie says to Martin, as we bump along the potholed roads.

"We did . . . and we'd heard from a couple that we met in the shared taxi from the station that it was a bit full on. It was Rory's idea to get you drunk . . ."

Rory snorts, but Carrie ignores him. "We were doing pretty well at that ourselves, to be fair. Anyway . . . no harm done." She balls up her sweatshirt and rests it against the window, followed by her head. She closes her eyes and smiles. "Don't worry. We'll get you back."

"Good luck sleeping like that," Rory pipes up. He smirks at me and turns back to face the front.

I watch Carrie as she tries to sleep, wondering if she's really going to manage it, or if *she's* just closing her eyes to avoid talking to the others. Past the city limits and the rows of tumbledown houses, we're back in the landscape we saw from the train. I gaze out of the dusty windows, and the track seems to wind on forever. The landscape is pretty dull so far — that same sandy, hard-packed mud, sparse crops of bleached grass. A few piles of rocks here and there. Nothing spectacular. I pull the guidebook out of my bag and start flicking through.

"So where have you come from?" Martin says, swivelling around to face me.

Part of me wants to deal with my hangover in peace, but I realise very quickly that reading is not going to be an option with the constant bumping over the rough track. I put the book on the seat and give him my full attention. Who knows, he and his friend might be of some use to us out here. So far, Sarnai and Erden have not done much in the way of "guiding" — instead chatting to each other up front in their own language and leaving us be. The chat is punctuated by Sarnai's occasional giggles, and the attempted tuning of the radio every few minutes. Rory has copied Carrie and is leaning against the window, his head protected by his rolled-up fleece.

"Beijing. This is our first stop."

"Ah," Martin says. "Explains why you arrived in the morning. We're going the other way. We've been at Lake Baikal for a few days. Incredible place. Deepest lake in the world, you know —"

"Pity you didn't swim to the bottom," Carrie quips, her eyes still closed but a smirk now on her face.

"Funny. Are you going there after here?" Martin continues, directing the conversation back at me. "You should. Seriously, it's beautiful. We hiked, swam. Did some weird Buddhist stuff that I thought I was going to hate but actually was so chilled out." He reaches into his bag and takes out a bottle of water. "Want some? You look a bit pale."

Grateful for his hospitality, and deciding that they probably aren't as bad as I had them pegged — well, not Martin, at least — I take the bottle and a long, soothing sip. Why didn't we bring anything with us? Oh yes, because we drank it all last night. Two bottles of wine on top of the beer, shots and cocktails. I woke up with crushed crisps all over me in bed. The empty 1. 5-litre bottle of Coke on the floor. I don't know if it was me or Carrie who drank it, but I know I'd kill for some right now.

"Thanks . . . and wow," I manage, fuelled by the water. "The lake sounds amazing." I don't bother to mention that I can't swim. We're not going anyway.

"We're not going to the lake," Carrie mutters.

Martin gives me a "what can you do?" look and I smile back. Maybe I can persuade Carrie to change our itinerary. I'll work on her later.

"So what was the Buddhist thing like?"

"Hey, if you like to observe the different religions, you will love the camp," Sarnai chirps in from the front. She swivels around in her seat and grins at us. "There is a traditional festival happening tomorrow. There will be a shamanic ceremony later on. It's lots of fun."

"What's shamanism then," Rory says, sitting up. "Isn't that the thing with druids?"

Sarnai giggles. "Mongolian shamanism is a wonderful folk religion. It shares lots of elements with Buddhism too. We call it yellow shamanism — because of the links with the Buddhist colours. There is also black shamanism, but that's not what you will see here . . ."

"The black stuff sounds a lot more sexy," Carrie says. She's sitting up now too. All four of us are rapt, now that Sarnai is actually saying something interesting.

Sarnai giggles. "It's just an older form. Different. But really the roots are the same — in shamanism we worship the ancient deities, and nature. Tenger is the main god. He embodies Chingis . . ."

"Is that like Genghis?" Rory asks.

"You Westerners mainly call him Genghis, but in Mongolian it is Chingis . . ."

"Is he literally the only famous Mongolian?" Carrie says. "He's on all the banknotes. Most countries like to mix things up a little . . . a queen, a king, some inventor or whatever."

Erden says something to Sarnai, and she laughs. "Chingis is our king, our god and everything in between. You will love the ceremony. Trust me." She winks. "Oh, and Erden says you should buckle up now."

We've been so busy listening that we've stopped paying attention to the landscape, but when we look out, we see that it has changed dramatically. Dotted around are bursts of lumpen moon rocks. In the distance, huge craggy mountains. The road undulating towards them, before disappearing on the horizon. It's like the set of a Mad Max film. It probably *is* the set of a Mad Max film.

"Wow," Rory says.

And just as we've got used to the gentle, constant bumping of the truck on the uneven track, Erden swerves off it completely and onto the plain. The truck lurches to the side, and I feel the nausea from earlier threatening a reappearance. It wasn't obvious until we were on it, but the hard-packed sandy mud is like a never-ending surface of molehills. I think about skiing, and trying to traverse the moguls on the black slopes, getting it wrong and feeling like you're about to veer off the edge of the world. Erden is not trying very hard to traverse, and the truck bounces hard, over and over. We hastily clip our seatbelts on and use our hands to stop us from banging our heads on the roof, the windows . . . on each other. I look at Carrie and she has gone green.

"Sarnai," I call out, the clattering and bumping making it hard to be heard now. "Can we stop soon?" I have no idea how long we've been in the truck, or how long it is until the planned stop at the wild horses, but I know that if we don't stop soon, one of us is going to throw up — and the way that the truck is jumping, no one is going to be safe from it. I've done many things in my life that I'm not proud of, but I am not keen on puking over another three passengers — but judging by Carrie's face, she may beat me to it.

Sarnai holds onto the back of her seat and spins around. "Almost there."

I grab hold of Carrie's hand, squeezing it tight. "Breathe," I whisper. She squeezes back.

To: carrie82@hotmail.com
From: lauralee@gmail.com
Subject: RE: RE: RE: RE: RE: RE: Got a new pal, you're dumped

---

Why are you not replying? I missssss youuuuu!! Are you still in US? is there no Internet there? Have you found a Mongolian BBQ yet?

The *Halloween* film was shit, in case you were wondering.

Lx

P.S. Hope your new pal hasn't killed you and that's why you can't reply. HAHA!

★   ★   ★

To: carrie82@hotmail.com
From: sarah–and–dou9–osborne@btinternet.co.uk
Subject: Checking In!

Hello Darling,

Hope all is well and you're having a great time, wherever you are right now. Dad says he thinks you'll be on the train

71

at the moment and probably have no reception, and I expect he's right! Let us know you're OK when you can — you're probably having too much fun to be thinking about us!

I popped round to see Laura, and she's recovering well but she's a bit bored and obviously still so upset about missing the trip. She said she saw Greg, too. Still not sure what happened between you two — you seemed happy? I'm not trying to pry, just wondered what happened (your dad says I've to stop being so bloody nosey).

Rosie got a new job! Don't know if she told you? So proud of you girls and the things you're doing in your lives. Much more exciting than me and your dad, but we're happy with our lot (although your dad is still trying to get me to go on a cruise for Christmas but I've told him I don't want to leave you girls!)

Lots of love,

Mum and Dad xxx

★ ★ ★

To: carrie82@hotmail.com
From: rosieposie1985@gmail.com
Subject: news

Caz,

Dunno where you are. You're just as shit at keeping in touch as always. ;)

Got a new job — basically same job, but another company. Better money, hopefully no knobheads. Mum probably told you already.

Rx

P.S. Can I borrow your green cocktail dress? Marcus has been invited to some swanky awards thing and I can't find anything I like in Monsoon. Say yes, please. Mum will give me the key.

CHAPTER
ELEVEN

After another half an hour of the old truck battering across the lumpy ground, the nausea has miraculously passed. It has come to a point where we've got used to the vibrations, the jumping around, and it's become normal. I suppose it's like gaining your sea legs on a long voyage on a ship. I'm slightly concerned about how we'll feel when the vehicle stops moving, but we'll deal with that soon enough.

Thankfully, we're brought back to normal terrain in stages, with the bumps lessening and then like a mirage in front of us, a dusty track and a couple of large yurts, at the foot of a sparsely grassed mountain.

"Here we are!" Sarnai claps her hands excitedly, then unclips her belt as Erden pulls into a low-walled area that seems to be a car park.

"Where's here?" Rory asks. He yawns, stretches his arms above his head. "Is this the camp?"

"No, no," Sarnai giggles. "We are in the Hustai National Park. This is the home of the *takhi* — the beautiful wild horses that were brought back from near extinction. We will stop for a short while here, and you can see the horses and you can learn about their history —"

"And can we have something to drink? A Coke or something, maybe?" I ask, furious again that we've been stupid enough to come without anything. Apart from a few sips of Martin's water, we've had nothing for hours, and I'm starting to get the clamping head pain of a blood-sugar dip. I need something sugary before I pass out. Carrie looks over at me and gives me a slightly pained smile, and I can tell she's feeling exactly the same.

"Of course. We'll be having a lovely dinner with the nomadic family right after this, but of course we can have a drink now. I think there will be some water and some tea over at the visitor centre."

Carrie groans.

"Might have something for you in my bag, ladies, if you play your cards right." Rory winks, and picks up his backpack before jumping off the bus. Martin shrugs and follows him.

"We're such idiots," Carrie says, as we follow them off the bus and up the dirt track towards the biggest yurt, which is apparently serving as the visitor centre.

"I'm never drinking again." I mean it, at this point.

"So you might be wondering a bit about the nomadic family we will be staying with, right?" Sarnai says, as the truck bumps across the steppe again. "The buildings are similar to the ones you just saw — and I am sure you think you know these buildings to be called *yurts*, but actually these ones in Mongolia are called *gers* . . ." She pauses, grinning at us. She obviously enjoys this story. "Basically, these are exactly

75

the same thing." She giggles. "In Turkic, the word *yurt* means 'dormitory' . . . and in Russian, the word is *yurta*. But in Mongolian, the word is *ger*, and it just means 'home'. This is the home for the nomadic families, who will set up camp and live there for many months, until . . ." She's saying something about a circular wooden frame and a felt cover made from sheep's wool but I have mostly zoned out. As long as the beds are comfortable, I don't really care too much. I'm knackered.

I glance over at Carrie; she is using her sweatshirt as a pillow again, and she appears to be sound asleep.

"So are the nomadic tribes shamanic?" Martin asks.

"Of course," Sarnai says. "But I will let them tell you all about it. They are peaceful people, who tend to their livestock and live with nature. They are wonderful hosts, and they will be happy to answer all of your questions. If there are things that they don't understand, I will also translate for you." She turns back to the front. "Oh, we are nearly there."

I look out of the grubby window, trying to get a better view. In the near distance, I can see a cluster of gers, plumes of smoke snaking up through their chimney-holes.

"Thank God," Carrie says. "I'm not sure my arse can take any more of this bloody banger. Maybe I can knit myself a cushion for the journey back."

Erden stops the truck on the perimeter of the camp, and we all bundle out. I'm not sure what I expected, but it's small, and there don't seem to be any facilities other than the three gers. A little further away, there is a wooden structure standing on its own, and I have a horrible feeling that it is the toilet.

"Hang on . . ." Carrie says, dropping her bag on the packed mud floor. "Is this it? Where are the showers?"

"Oh, sorry. No showers," Sarnai says. "But we can boil some water. Only two nights so no big deal, right? Did you not read all the information on the leaflet when you booked? This is real, traditional camp. Not like the tourist camps — those are bigger, more expensive. They have showers, but not the true experience like here."

Carrie sniffs. "I suppose the toilet is a massive hole behind those wooden doors."

"That's right," Sarnai says. "You've seen one before?"

"Only in horror movies," Rory quips. "I'm pretty sure the leaflet didn't explain any of this . . . and I *did* read it before I booked.

"We're here now," Sarnai says, still grinning. "Will be a great experience. Live with nature, OK? It's only a couple of nights. You'll soon be loving it and you won't want to go back to UB. You know what? Just wait until you see inside your ger — you will just *scream!*" She leaves us while she goes off to get the woman from the camp, to tell her we've arrived.

Carrie drops onto the floor with a sigh. "I have died and gone to *hell*."

Rory sits down beside her. "Not a nature lover then?"

"I'm absolutely *fine* with nature. I'm all *over* nature. Nature is fucking *amazing*. I just like a few more home

77

comforts when I'm feeling delicate. After that journey, I'm pretty sure every bone in my body has been displaced. Not to mention all the brain cells that've been rattled clean out of my skull." She lies back on the ground and Rory laughs.

"What about you, Violet?" Martin doesn't carry the same mocking tone as Rory, so I don't feel like punching him right this minute — unlike Rory, who I'm tempted to kick in the shins as he sits beside Carrie, gently prodding her ribs, while she slaps him and tells him what she's going to do with his finger if he touches her again.

"I think we'll be OK," I say, hoping I can use positive affirmations to make it true.

I think Martin is going to say something else, but then Sarnai comes back and she's followed by a wide-hipped woman in a dusky red dress. She looks to be in her fifties, with shiny black hair tied back in a long, low braid and an open, smiley face. They are all very smiley, these people, and I feel myself responding in kind.

"This is Chinua and she is going to look after you here. Tonight you must relax, and have the wonderful food and drinks, and then tomorrow morning we will go off on a horseback trail and camel ride, and then spend some time at the festival. Make sure you have your cameras ready for the beautiful pictures."

Carrie is leaning on one elbow now; she's wriggled away from Rory and his poking finger. "Is there somewhere to charge our phones?" she asks.

"Oh . . ." Sarnai turns to Chinua and they talk in Mongolian for a moment. I'm pretty sure I know what the answer will be. "There are some chargers you can use, but not for too long as Chinua's husband must take these in the morning to be recharged at the centre ten kilometres away."

"So there's literally no electricity?" Carrie says.

Chinua grins. "Come inside, please. We will have milky tea."

We follow her into the ger. The door has been tied back with twine, and inside is a blast of colour and texture that is so at odds with the bleak landscape outside, that it makes me feel dizzy. Five narrow beds are positioned in a horseshoe shape, each covered with a colourful quilt. In the centre of the room, a large hearth, and up above, the hole that serves as the chimney, with smoke swirling and billowing up and outside. There are a couple of narrow bookshelves behind the beds, and near the roaring hearth, a low table and some colourful, fringed floor pillows — all set on top of a bright-yellow patterned rug. On the hearth, a huge pot is bubbling away, and next to that, a huge, deep frying pan, where Chinua is dropping small pieces of dough.

"Doughnuts! Excellent," Carrie says. She turns to me and whispers, "Might not be so bad after all."

"You can choose your beds," Sarnai says. "I'll take whichever one is left."

Rory races over to the one further back. He tosses his bag on the floor, then leaps onto the bed, just as Sarnai raises a hand and starts to shout a warning.

"Ow. Shit." He lands with a thud, and immediately starts pulling the covers out from underneath. "What's this made of? Cement?"

"It's a hard wood, with a thick woven mattress," Sarnai explains. "I was about to tell you . . . not very bouncy, like usual beds. But I promise you will be comfortable . . . and warm."

Rory makes a *hmmph* sound, and rubs his back as if he's been dropped from a height onto a hard floor.

"Thanks for testing that out for us," Carrie says, laughing.

We all choose which of the remaining beds we'd like, and Sarnai explains everything to us while Chinua serves up mugs of steaming white liquid, dropping a couple of pieces of the fried dough into them. Chinua hands them out to us with a smile and a small bow, as we all make *ooh* and *ob* noises of excitement over this new exotic drink.

I have the mug to my lips when Sarnai tells us that it is boiled ewe's milk and that the incredible-smelling doughnuts are salty rather than sweet. The smell hits, and I just know that I'm not going to be able to get this drink past my lips.

"Chin-chin," Rory says, putting on an over-the-top posh accent.

Carrie takes out one of the doughnuts and sniffs at it, like a dog smelling something nasty it's found on the pavement. She takes a small bite and pulls a face. "Um. Interesting," she says. She dips a finger into the tea and sucks her finger, then she turns away and I hear her retch.

80

Martin is holding his doughnuts like they're biscuits, and sipping contentedly at the tea. Rory has finished his and asking for a top-up.

"You might find it's an acquired taste," Sarnai says. She giggles again, and I have the urge to throw one of the doughnuts at her head.

"Maybe just a glass of water," I say, putting the cup down at my feet. I glance over at Carrie and she rolls her eyes at me, and mouths "What the fuck?"

Through the open door, I can see the light starting to change, from a pale blue to a dim orange, and I'm wondering how soon we can go to bed. Tomorrow will be fine. We just need some sleep.

As if reading my mind, Sarnai picks up a bag of carrots from the floor and starts peeling. "Not long until dinner."

"What are we having?" Rory says.

He's taken his shoes off and is lying down on his bed. Martin is looking at the ornaments and books on the small display case by the doorway. Carrie is sitting cross-legged on one of the cushions, rocking back and forth gently. A familiar smell fills the air, from the second pot that is now on the hearth, in place of the doughnut pan. I try not to breathe it in, but it catches in my throat. I should've guessed — the nomads are pastoralists — they tend sheep . . . the tea is made from ewe's milk. The gers are covered with felt, and the beds made of a tight woven wool. I have to try very hard not to gag, and realise it might be too late to pretend to be a vegetarian.

"Mutton stew," Sarnai says. "The nomadic speciality."

CHAPTER
TWELVE

I wake up to the sound of a cockerel crowing, and I can see through the chimney-hole that it is barely light. It had taken a while to get to sleep, with my stomach rumbling most of the night, and then having to make a trip out to the toilet shed in the pitch dark. I will confess that I didn't even go in it — I was terrified I would fall down the hole. So I went for a pee somewhere far enough from the ger, but not so far that I would get lost out there. The eerie silence and the sense of being watched were enough to stop me from sleeping another wink.

Chinua is crouched by the stove, presumably boiling more of that awful milk for us, and I feel simultaneously ungrateful and pissed off that I am here. But I *am* here, so I intend to make the most of it somehow.

Rory and Carrie have pulled the hoods of their sweatshirts up and over their faces in an attempt to stay asleep, but I can see that Sarnai's bed is already neatly made and she is nowhere to be seen. Martin is leaning on one elbow, reading a book by the light of a small torch attached to his head. If I'd realised he had that, I would've asked to borrow it for my middle-of-the-night bathroom break. I sit up, and try to stretch some life into myself.

"What're you reading?" I say, as quietly as I can.

"*Lonely Planet*," he stage-whispers back. "Why are we whispering?"

I smile at him, and pull myself out of bed. I am still fully clothed. I think we all decided that undressing wasn't really an option, under the circumstances. He sits up too, and mimes "walking" with his fingers. I nod.

"Here you go," Chinua says, seeing that the two of us are awake. She offers us mugs of milky tea, two small doughnuts in each. I'm about to protest, but Martin shakes his head. We take the drinks, pull back the felt doorway and creep outside.

"Here," Martin says, as soon as we are away from the get. He takes a small bottle out of his pocket and pours a couple of drops into my tea, then his. He spots my questioning look. "Vanilla essence. Read about it when I was back home researching the trip. Something on a forum. Vanilla essence for the tea and soy-sauce sachets for the mutton stew. Both strong enough to block out the flavours . . . unless you like things that taste of sheep, of course. Oh . . . and a sprinkle of sugar on the *boortsog* doesn't do them any harm." He hands me a sachet of sugar. "Purloined from Maccy D's in Moscow."

I sniff the tea, then take a tentative sip, avoiding one of the chunks of floating dough. "*Boortsog*? Is that what they're called? My God, you are a genius. Why didn't you tell us about this last night?"

84

He shrugs, and takes out one of his dough balls, biting into it. "Didn't want to offend them."

"Have you any idea how starving I was? I'm surprised you slept with the sounds my stomach was making."

"Ear plugs."

I roll my eyes. "Of course you've got ear plugs. And a head torch. And flavour disguisers. No doubt you have water-purification tablets and mosquito coils too?"

"What can I say? I was a good Boy Scout."

I watch him drinking his tea and wonder if I might fancy him a bit. I don't. Not yet. He is much too wholesome. Maybe that's where I've been going wrong. Sam was the opposite of wholesome. I want to check what he's up to right now, but I think it's better to try and conserve my battery. Besides, there's hardly likely to be a signal here.

The air still has an early-morning chill to it, and the sky is pale orange, leaking into lilac. The sun is rising slowly behind the mountain in front of the camp, and we walk a bit, trying to keep warm.

"You sounded interested in the Buddhist thing," Martin says, eventually. "I recommend it, actually. I'm thinking about trying to go to a meditation retreat in China. That's what I was looking up in the book earlier. Rory wants to continue with the plan — Beijing, Xi'an, Shanghai . . . then fly to Australia. I'm thinking a bit longer in China. I've been to Australia before. It's great, but I feel like I need something a bit more spiritual." He pauses, looks me in the eye. "Does that sound like utter wank?"

I laugh. "Whatever floats your boat."

"I've been looking on some forums, thinking about what I can do when I get back home. I don't want this to just be one of those trips where you do stuff, then you go home and everything just goes back to the same old shit. I really feel like this is a chance to change my life. I work in IT, for fuck's sake. I've been contracting for years. I've no mortgage. I can work anywhere, do what I like. But . . . I just feel like something is missing."

"Deep," I say, draining the dregs of my tea. It's not at all bad with the vanilla in it, and the sugar hit has given me the boost I needed. "Sorry. I didn't mean that to sound patronising. It's just . . . well, I've had these conversations with so many people. Ultimately, everyone you meet while travelling is the same. They're all trying to escape something. All looking for answers to some unknown question."

"I get it. You're a cynic." He looks down at my skirt. "You look . . . I don't know. I thought maybe you were a bit alternative."

"Oh I am . . . but not in the way you mean."

"See. You just disproved your own point there. Not everyone you meet when travelling is the same."

"Touché," I say. "Shall we head back?"

We've walked quite far, engrossed in our conversation. The doors of the gers are all tied back now. Chinua is outside ours, shaking out a carpet.

"There's this place in Cambridgeshire. Rosalind House? It's a commune, set in an old asylum. They're very selective about who they allow to live there. Only a

86

small number of people, and the guy who runs it was brought up in various communes so he knows his stuff —"

"Knit-your-own-yogurt types, is it? Or devil worshippers? Aren't those the two main types of commune?"

"You can mock all you like. Just wait until you go back home to your shit job and your normal boring life, then you'll wish you'd listened to me."

"Who says I'm going back home?"

He opens his mouth to say more, but is interrupted by Rory running out of the ger at full pelt, a pained expression on his face, clutching a toilet roll. He throws himself at the door of the toilet hut, almost yanking it off its hinges.

"Oh dear," Martin says to his retreating back. "Did someone forget they were lactose intolerant?" He turns back to me. "To be honest, I thought he was making it up."

"Surprised you haven't got any lactase tablets for him, in your bag of tricks."

He shrugs. "Maybe I'm not such a good Boy Scout after all."

After a decent breakfast of dark bread rolls and blackcurrant jam, and more milky tea — which I am actually growing to like now, with the vanilla enhancement — we are introduced to Batu and Gan, who are going to take us on a horseback tour around the mountain. I haven't ridden a horse since I was eleven and had begged my parents to let me try it out at the stables near our house. They refused, but my friend had convinced her mum to let me go with her instead. My parents had handed over the money without any fuss. They weren't short of cash — they lived off the inheritance that my grandparents left — and were abundant in indifference, a trait that I used to my advantage many times in later years. Anyway, half of the time at the stables was spent learning to groom and muck out, and I realised then that I was never going to be a horse person. When I did finally get to ride, I found it uncomfortable, and vaguely terrifying, and I never asked to be taken again.

"Oh, I love horses," Carrie says, surprising me. "What breed are they?" She chatters away to the guides as they take us around to the far side of their ger, where the horses are roaming around, seemingly oblivious to us.

"They are Mongol horses," Batu says. "They have been here for many, many years. Since times of Chingis, our great leader. These horses helped to build our empire. You know there are three million of these animals . . . more than the humans here, in Mongolia."

The "horses" are more like ponies. Short and stocky, with long manes and tails. They don't look like they can carry our weight. Batu sees our expressions and nudges Gan, and they both laugh. No doubt they are used to this reaction.

"Very strong," Gan says. He throws a blanket over the horse nearest to him, and it nods its head as if in agreement. Then he places a very small, multi-coloured saddle on top. The seat — I think it's called the pommel, from vague memories of that day at the stables — seems very high, and the stirrups very short.

Gan pats the horse on the hind and gestures at me to mount it. Why the hell he has chosen me to go first, I have no idea. Perhaps he can sense my reluctance.

"Er . . . do you have any with longer stirrups," I ask. "I'm not sure I'll be able to get my feet in unless my knees are at my ears."

Batu and Gan laugh. "All same," Batu says.

Gan has dressed a second horse and is gesturing to Carrie, who shrugs and sticks her foot in a stirrup. Gan shoves her up and over, and she manages to land correctly on the saddle. Her knees are bent at almost ninety degrees. "You can stand if better," Gan says.

"This is so cool," Carrie says. "It's like a racehorse. I can guide with my knees, right?"

"Of course," Gan says. He demonstrates how to use the reins to stop and start the horse, and regulate the speed. "And knees," he says, patting her knees. He slaps the horse gently on the hind again, and it takes off at a gentle trot.

Eventually, we are all on the horses, and the guides head off to the front. I am not at all comfortable on the saddle. It is so high and tight, and I don't like the way my horse keeps stopping to chew on grass, forcing me to keep yanking on its reins and squeezing it with my knees to get it going again. I'm pretty sure it's taking the piss.

I try to keep up, but the guides have to keep circling back to check on me, while Carrie leads the pack like a seasoned pro, with Rory bounding after her. We're only half way round the mountain, when my stupid horse decides to eat more grass, dipping its head and neck so low that I feel myself sliding off. I end up tangled in the stirrups and on the verge of tears.

"Maybe we should swap?" Martin suggests, seeing my distress.

Batu agrees and helps us swap over. "Be firm," he says to me. He rides with me, side by side, until he is sure that I am OK, then he canters off to the front.

As soon as he's gone, my horse slows, and does exactly what the other one did, this time causing me to tumble over its bent neck and land on the hard ground.

"Oops," Rory calls, turning round at my cry of frustration. I'm not hurt, other than my pride, but I do not want to continue riding these ridiculous horses.

I take the reins and start walking it, pulling a little harder than necessary. The others aren't going particularly fast anyway, and when they see that I am walking they slow further. Carrie appears beside me, a look of pity on her face. "Poor V," she says, "not having fun?"

"You carry on," I snap.

She says something to the horse, and then slaps it and takes off at as much of a gallop as the short, stocky legs can manage.

I think back to my attempts at the stables, and my mum's unsurprised face when I'd told her what had happened. How difficult I'd found it. "We can't all be good at everything, dear," she'd said, barely lifting her head from the Jane Austen she was pretending to read. "Maybe try something a little less taxing for your next

90

hobby." I'd hated her then, for her lack of care. Her lack of encouragement. But it was always the same, no matter what I did. I tried playing the cello, tap dancing, ice skating, athletics, gymnastics, embroidery — you name it, I tried it — but nothing was good enough to interest either of my parents, who spent their own time hosting lavish dinners for people they didn't like, trying their hardest to fit into a world that didn't interest them at all. I would've jumped off a cliff if I'd thought it would provoke some sort of reaction.

"Come on Violet," Martin calls and I snap out of my daydream. Up ahead, I can see multi-coloured tents, hear the sounds of car engines, shouted instructions. Children are running around, while hundreds of men and women in nomadic dress are attempting to set up what looks like some kind of fair. Of course — the festival — Sarnai mentioned this on the way here.

We just need to get these horses back to base, and then we can relax here — maybe even have some decent food. And drink . . . I really hope this isn't a dry affair.

Batu circles back to me again. "Jump back on horse now. We go to camp . . . then later on, we come back to festival. Lots of food, wine. Have fun, yes?"

"Yes," I say, climbing back onto the horse. This time I slap it hard, just as I saw Carrie do, and it takes off — and soon I am in line with the others. I glance over at Carrie, and she is grinning, her hair blowing in the wind. She turns to face me, gives me two thumbs up. Yells, "Well done, V," Before giving her horse another little tap, and galloping off ahead, back towards our camp.

She is so effortless, so graceful. So fearless. I realise my mistake now; realise that sometimes, you just need a little encouragement — and then you can get exactly what you want.

To: lauralee@gmail.com [DRAFT]
From: carrie82@hotmail.com
Subject: Random Nomadic Camp

Hiya,

Writing this to you from my bed in the ger (like a yurt, but it's Mongolian) because even though I really, really want to sleep, I can't. Totally minging sheep's milk tea and nothing but boiled mutton to eat. I am hank. I think my rumbling stomach is going to keep everyone away! We're here with two lads we met in the pub (no, neither of them, before you ask, but one of them definitely wants it). They were clever and researched the trip so they have had a day *sans* hangover, while me and V are absolutely hanging and don't even have one can of Coke between us. Saw wild horses, which was pretty cool, and tomorrow we're going to be riding horses (and camels) and going to a shamanic festival ceremony thing (I know, WTF?)

Cx

P.S. Miss you!

P.P.S. Dunno when you'll get this. No Internet.

* * *

To: lauralee@gmail.com [DELETED]
From: carrie82@hotmail.com
Subject: Greg

———————————————————————

Still cannae sleep.

Been thinking about Greg a lot I'm writing this but I know
I'm never going to send it. But it might help sort things out
in my own head. Maybe I'll tell you one day, face-to-face, I
mean, it's not the kind of thing I want to have in writing.
Maybe I should though, because if it's there in black and
white, I can't pretend it didn't happen.

Fuck.

You know when you see those people on telly and they're
fuzzed out, voices distorted, all that. Talking about stuff
that's happened. Stuff someone's done to them, or stuff
they've done to someone else, and you just think WTF and
imagine . . . and you think "that'll never be me", and "that
would never happen to me" and all of that.

And you know sometimes, it just does. And that is the
whole point.

* * *

94

To: iauraiee@gmail.com [DRAFT]
From: carrie82@hotmail.com
Subject: RE: Random Nomadic Camp

Started writing you an email in the middle of the night but have deleted it from drafts. Luckily I couldn't send it anyway cos no Internet. It was just me being a fanny. Think I was alcohol poisoned, to be fair.

There's a mountain sort of right in front of the camp, with this thing on top called an *oovoo* . . . some kind of shamanic sacrificial altar — basically a pile of stones. Apparently it's a sort of worship thing, rather than a place where they disembowel goats, but I'm not entirely sure to be honest. Anyway, we went round it on horses today . . . I say horses, but they were like miniature ponies and they were bloody uncomfortable — I am walking like John Wayne, and not after a shag, for once — starting to get a bit horny actually, dunno why, will have to seek out some sexy Mongolian goat-herders at this festival thing we're going to tonight (unless of course they're planning to slit our throats and dance around us on top of the oovoa — FFS, that would be just my luck).
    EXPECT A LOAD OF MESSAGES WHEN THE INTERNET IS BACK.

Sorry for caps.

Cx

P.S. No, V has not killed me — haha — more like the other way round! She's annoying me a bit. She was telling one of the lads all these bonkers stories today and I don't know if she's having a laugh, or she's lying, or if she actually believes the nonsense she's spouting. Also, she is wearing my top and I swear I never actually gave it to her. I did let her borrow stuff in UB but this isn't one of the things and I've got a feeling she's been raking in my bag, but maybe I'm just imagining it. I'm probably just being grumpy, cos she is actually a laugh . . .

CHAPTER
THIRTEEN

There are certain people who you meet in life, who you just know have been given to you by The Universe. I'm not wildly into all that stuff, so in theory the law of attraction shouldn't work for me — apparently it only works if you truly, deeply believe, not just if you want to. I want to, and I try to visualise the things I want, but I find it difficult to see them through my own eyes. It's as if I am looking down on myself, at my life, at my interactions with others — that I am not in control of my own destiny. When Carrie smiled at me in the bar — no, when she rolled her eyes in the travel centre, there was an instant bond. For me, at least. I recognised it because it's not the first time it's happened.

I think back to the moment that I first saw Sam. He was sitting at the bar, pint in front of him, chatting easily with the barman — I heard snippets of the conversation, something about United's latest signing, and the state of the Champions League. I have no interest in football. I can't even bluff it, like some girls can — knowing just enough to keep a man interested. Men are stupid when it comes to football. As soon as a girl fires off a useless nugget of information that is even remotely accurate, they hook on to it, and the entire game, the money behind it, the reasons for it all, are meticulously mansplained — making him feel superior, like he has explained a universal truth. While the girl smiles and nods and knows she's achieved her goal, pardon the pun, as a brand-new shiny cocktail appears in front of her, and he slides his stool ever so slightly towards hers.

I've seen this happen so many times, and I've considered learning a small nugget of my own, just to get the reaction. But I've found it easier to go with my own plan — which is to feign absolute ignorance of all sports and to look positively bored when the man has floundered for another way to reel me in. I prefer my way.

I watch Carrie as she interacts with Rory. They are sitting on cushions, outside the ger. Smoking. Giggling. Martin is leaning back on his cushion, his face pressed into the guidebook again. I'm happy for a bit of quiet time to reflect, to watch.

Carrie is fascinating to watch.

Sam was fascinating to watch, too. I sat at a table in the corner, just far enough away so that I could see him, observe his mannerisms, hear snippets of his conversation. I liked his accent. I definitely have a thing for accents, especially on men. He sounded like he was from Essex, but trying to hide it. He wasn't going for that over-the-top exaggerated take on the accent that most of the new wave of tedious reality stars are fond of affecting. I was interested in how his accent might change when his environment did — if others like him were to appear. It sounds like I'm watching wildlife —

observing baboons in their natural habitat — but really, humans and animals aren't so different at all. I know this. I watch them a lot. Watch, listen, learn. You have to know what you're dealing with before you can try to infiltrate.

Sam didn't notice me that night. Why would he? I did my best to blend into the background. I watched as others approached him. Men, women. Some that he clearly knew, some that he was only just getting to know. He was an interesting creature. I watched him snake a hand around the back of a thin blonde girl in an electric-blue shift dress, her spaghetti straps falling off her tanned shoulders. I watched as others gave him admiring glances from afar. The thing about Sam was, he wasn't even my type.

Neither is Carrie.

I haven't had many close friendships, with men or women. They seem to burn intensely like an oil fire, and then they are doused hard and fast, with barely a flutter of ash to remind anyone that they ever existed.

I need to do things differently this time. I don't want Carrie to be extinguished too quickly. I need to feed this one more carefully, stoke the coals, add in just the right amount of accelerant to keep things exciting.

I lie back on my cushion, arms behind my head, staring up at the sky through the chimney hole. It's a deep, bright blue, with perfect puffs of white cloud moving slowly away from us. I think of that song that all the stoners used to play in the nineties. The Orb's "Little Fluffy Clouds" with that piece of hypnotic sampling about the skies in Kansas, and I feel myself drifting into a trance. Somewhere in the distance, I can hear the rhythmic sound of drums. The party is starting.

CHAPTER
FOURTEEN

The sun is still high in the sky as we set off across the sparse grass and packed mud towards the festival. I feel strangely excited, a weird fluttering in my chest that could in other circumstances signal the start of a panic attack; but in this case it feels like something big is about to happen. Something significant.

Or maybe I'm overreacting.

I'm tired and a bit wired from lack of sleep and food, and there's a painful ache in my muscles from the awful trek with the horses.

Carrie has changed into a dress, with leggings and her hiking boots. Her hair is pinned up roughly with clips, she says to hide the greasy roots, but it looks sexy and tousled and I get a squirming jolt in the pit of my stomach when I see Rory staring at her with undisguised lust.

I've changed, too, wearing a pale-blue vest that I took out of Carrie's bag before we left UB. She looked at me a bit strangely when I took off my jumper to reveal it, but I smiled back — giving her a "you said I could borrow it" look, and she obviously decided not to question it. I should be a bit more careful though. I don't want her getting annoyed with me over something so insignificant.

Martin appears at my side, matches my pace. "You looking forward to this?" he says.

"I am. I've never been to anything like this. I went to a full-moon festival in Thailand, but that was just a bunch of drunk stoners stumbling around on the beach. I'm sure it was spiritual once."

"I've heard that," he says.

I don't know why I said that. I never went to the beach in Thailand at all. But I've seen YouTube clips and I know from some of the idiots I met in Bangkok that this is exactly what the thing is like.

"Apparently you can have a reading from one of the shamans," he says. "I really want to, but I'm also a bit scared. I've never had the guts to go to a fortune-teller or a psychic or anything like that. Part of me thinks it's all nonsense, but the other part of me is scared about what they might say."

"They aren't going to say anything bad to you," I say, not that I have any direct experience. "All that 'something terrible is going to happen' is only in bad horror films. Besides, didn't you say you were becoming more spiritual since your Buddhist experience?"

"That's not the same; that's a proper religion."

"I think the nomads think the same about their shamanism," I say. "Let's just wait and see, shall we?"

A giggling behind us makes us both glance around. Carrie has linked arms with Rory, and their heads are tipped closely together. I can't hear what he's saying. I ball my hands into fists, feeling my nails cut into my palms.

"Is he always such a lech?"

Martin shrugs. "I don't think Carrie is complaining."

I frown, and ignore him. Then I pick up the pace and march further ahead.

Sarnai is walking along with a couple of boys I haven't seen before. I don't know if they've come from another camp, or if they just turned up for this, but she also doesn't seem to be complaining. Her skills as a guide are quite lacking, and usually it doesn't bother me, but I need something to take my mind off randy Rory and compliant Carrie.

If only I fancied Martin, it would be so much simpler.

"Hey," I shout, "Sarnai!"

She turns around, her MTV grin already in place. "Oh, hey guys. This is going to be so much fun!" The boys keep walking and she slows down a bit, waiting for us to catch up. "You've got free time to do as you please here, guys. You can watch the wrestling, the archery . . . there are lots of fun stalls and great food and drinks . . ."

Martin butts in: "I heard we can talk to the shamans — is that right?"

Sarnai laughs. "Of course! There will be a ceremony later on, and we can all join in. And then if you want to have a private meeting, you can arrange this and you can go to one of the gers. Are you thinking about this? I really recommend it."

Martin shrugs. "Maybe." He glances at me, hoping for guidance and I nod.

"Sure. Why not?"

Carrie breaks away from Rory's side and comes up to me, throwing an arm around my shoulder. "We should do it together, V! Let's see what they have to say about us both."

I glance around at Rory, who looks like someone just puncrured his football.

"That sounds perfect," I say. My cheeks tighten. I can't stop the grin.

Carrie grabs my face and gives me a hard, wet kiss on the cheek, making an exaggerated "mwah!", then she skips off ahead, towards the stalls and the drums and the smell of smoke, and we all traipse along behind her, like the Pied Piper's children: excited and mesmerised, and ready to follow her anywhere.

The drums get louder as we reach the epicentre of the festival. Redfaced, happy children run through the crowds, while the adults watch the entertainment — smoking, drinking, chattering. I feel my chest constrict as we squeeze our way into the crowd. A flutter of panic beats its tiny wings deep in my stomach. Then I feel a hand, clasping mine, a gentle squeeze. I turn quickly, to see Martin's concerned face.

"Let's get a drink." He leans close to me, and I smell his sweat, leaching upwards through the open neck of his shirt. It's not unpleasant. Perhaps it's the rhythmic banging of the drums, the vibrations from the crowd dancing in time to the beat, but I feel a tingle spread through my body as I let him lead me through the throng.

He drags me into a small ger where they are serving drinks in wooden cups. The woman behind the trestle table that's been set up as a make-shift bar hands us a cup each and smiles and nods.

"Where are the others?" I say.

"Never mind that right now. Cheers," he says, holding his cup aloft. We smash the cups together and knock the drinks back in one.

"Jesus, what the hell is that?" I cough, and the swirl of herbs and strong alcohol makes my throat tingle.

"Bloody good stuff," Martin says, grabbing my cup and offering his and mine over the bar for a refill.

The woman behind the bar pours in dark-brown liquid and says, "Very strong. Be careful."

Martin laughs. "I reckon we can handle it."

I sip my second drink, but I'm pleased. I hadn't seen this side of Martin before. He's broken out of the serious and let his hair down a bit.

The woman comes out from the other side of the bar, holding two larger cups. "Try these now, longer drink. Not so strong."

I take a sniff, and it has a yeasty, hoppy smell. Some sort of beer, I expect, which isn't a bad thing after the other stuff. I don't want us to peak too soon. Outside the tent, the sun is still high in the sky and the drums carry on their steady beat. The crowd is chanting something hypnotic, and the smell of wood smoke and the effects of the alcohol make my head swim. Martin stands close to me, sharing my trance, and I feel the

105

warmth of his skin against mine, and right now I want the night to last forever.

"Hey! There you both are. We've been loolting everywhere for you."

Carrie's skin is glowing, her cheeks flushed. Rory has an arm draped around her shoulders, and he's grinning like the cat that got the cream.

A rush of pure rage surges through me.

"What have you two been up to?" I hiss.

Rory smirks. "Wouldn't you like to know?"

"I couldn't think of anything worse." I push his arm off, harder than I realise, and he stumbles back.

"Hey . . ." he starts.

But Carrie just laughs. "Wow, V. Miss me, did you?"

Rory's face glows red, his eyebrows knitted. But he says nothing.

The tingling in my body seems to grow more intense. I throw my arms around Carrie, just managing not to spill my drink down her back.

She pulls away, startled at the embrace. Then she looks Martin and me up and down, and laughs. "Oh, wait . . . it's more like what have *you* two been up to, eh?"

I open my mouth to speak, to correct her, but she carries on.

"Where did you get the drinks? We have been hunting high and fucking *low* for a drink." She squeezes past me and into the tent, Rory following behind like the little pet that he's become. He throws me a dirty look, but I ignore it.

I down my beer. It's warm, and it's not very nice, but I just want to get wasted now.

"Hey . . ." Martin puts a hand on my shoulder and I shrug it off. Then I have a change of heart, and spin around to face him, grinning. "Let's have some fun tonight, OK?"

He looks wary of me now. He's seen the way my moods can shift up and down like loose gears in a manual transmission. I don't wait for him to answer — I head straight after Carrie.

Carrie and Rory are leaning on the bar, having their second shots of the weird herbal schnapps. The woman serving them gives them the same warning.

"Oh don't listen to her," I say, grabbing Carrie's arm. "She'll try to give you the beer next and it's awful." I address the woman directly now. "I'll have another of the small ones, please." I sense Martin at my shoulder. "And one for him."

"Woohoo!" says Carrie. "Violet wants to party?" She squeezes me, then nudges Rory, who's looking a bit more excited now that he's had a drink. "If Violet wants to party, then we will *all* party." She grabs a bottle of the schnapps from the bar. "How much?"

The woman looks uncertain. "We like to give in small cups."

Carrie waves the bottle in front of the woman's face. "How much?" She turns to Rory. "Pay the woman, *Roarster*. A few Chingis."

Rory starts pulling notes out of his pocket, handing them to the woman. She nods when she's decided it's enough, but we've no idea what we're paying. I've already forgotten the different colours and the exchange rate, but it doesn't matter because it's not my money. I still haven't paid for a thing. And it doesn't matter because Carrie has linked arms with me and we're running out of the tent, the boys following behind. The sun has dipped a little now, and the wide, cloudless sky is turning a shining gold and shimmering shades of peach.

The drums are getting faster now, reaching a crescendo, and people are all huddled together in the middle of the festival space. "I think the shamanic ceremony is about to begin," Carrie shouts into my ear.

The games are over. Now it's time for the real party to begin.

CHAPTER
FIFTEEN

The drums slow down their frenetic beat, and the crowd begins a low, monotone hum. Little fires have been lit in a circle, and something fragrant has been thrown on them with the wood — some kind of incense, heady and intoxicating. We stand, transfixed by the show.

Out of one of the small gers near where we've been drinking, three shamans in full ceremonial dress appear, and walk slowly in a line, into the circle, where they stand together, facing out at the crowd, which has now formed a semi-circle around the lower part of the circle of fire.

Carrie grabs hold of my hand, and I glance at her, but she's staring straight ahead. I squeeze her hand, and we stay like that while the shamans begin their ritual.

By the time it's over, we're both feeling the effects. The boys are forgotten now, the two of us are hugging each other, damp-faced from crying.

The crowd starts to disperse, heading back for more food, drinks. People stamp on the fires. "Bloody hell," Carrie says. "That was mental."

I pull away from her, and give her a small smile. "I'm glad I experienced this with you. I don't know if it's too much alcohol, or the chanting or what, but I feel like . . . I don't know. I feel like I'm somewhere else right now."

Carrie laughs and takes a swig from the bottle, seemingly snapping back into reality. "It was wild. I'm not keen on all that milk-throwing though." She mimes retching, sticking her tongue out and crossing her eyes. She hands me the bottle. "We need to get another one of these . . . Also," she glances around, "there's definitely something being smoked here that's not cigarettes." She gestures towards a bank of gers people seem to be flocking towards. "Shall we?"

I finish the bottle of schnapps without even a grimace. It's funny how you can get used to something vile so quickly, especially when it makes you feel like you're floating off the ground. For a moment, I'm concerned about smoking something too. My past experiences with weed haven't been particularly pleasant. I usually throw a whitey and pass out after the first puff, but maybe this stuff will be different.

Carrie is still grinning, and I have her all to myself.

"Let's do it," I say. "Oh . . . and let's do a private reading after it. Can we?"

"Not sure about that." Her face darkens. "Might be mumbo-jum-boing it a bit too far, eh? Let's go and check out the other stuff first."

As we walk towards the tents, I think I hear someone calling my name, but I ignore it.

110

We follow a trickle of revellers into the first tent. Inside, fairy lights have been strung around the wooden beams, and there are people sitting on floor cushions in small huddles, some chatting quietly, others staring straight ahead, peaceful expressions on their faces. The tent is filled with smoke, but it gives the space an ethereal, mystical feel — unlike the dense, cloying fog that I'd expected.

The aromas are strong, yet delicate. Sweet, yet sharp. Whatever they're smoking, it doesn't smell like the weed I've been offered anywhere else. Not even in India.

"Good evening, ladies." A good-looking young Mongolian man appears in front of us. I'm not sure where he came from. We haven't even touched the stuff yet, but I feel disorientated. I turn to Carrie, and she looks as bewildered as me. We both gaze at the man, wondering if he is actually there.

He laughs, revealing perfect white teeth. "I'm Altan," he says. "I can be your guide. You'd like to try some?" He turns, gesturing at the smokers. "It will be nothing like you have ever experienced. You cannot get this anywhere else in the world." He winks. "I think you'll love it."

"I, um . . . we were thinking about having a reading . . . with one of the shamen."

This seems to bring Carrie out of her trance, and she giggles, before turning to me and mouthing the words to "Move any Mountain".

Altan doesn't know what's going on now, but he keeps smiling. "Of course," he says. "Let's get you prepared."

"Prepared? We don't have to, like, get our kit off or anything?" Carrie giggles again, and I find myself doing the same. I think the smoke is affecting us.

"Come," Altan says. He gestures to a space on the other side of the tent, where cushions have been arranged, seemingly for us. They are plump red-and-yellow velvet, and they look a lot more comfortable than the hard beds we've been forced to sleep on. Altan holds out a hand for us to take, to help us sit down. And when we're ready, he tells us to close our eyes and breathe deeply. He chants something, slow and soothing. Then he clicks his fingers.

We open our eyes, and a small boy is standing in front of us. He can't be more than eight years old, but he has eyes that make him look like he's seen a hundred years. He's offering a small wooden tray.

"Go ahead," Altan says, still grinning.

Carrie looks at me and raises her eyebrows. I shrug. Then I take one of the small wooden cups and she takes hers. The boy mutters something and then nods, and we knock the drinks back in one. It burns like fire down my gullet, and I feel an instant awakening inside my head. This is not the same drink as before.

The boy leans forwards with the tray and we see that there are two small wooden pipes lying on it. In the murky darkness, and with the colour of the tray, we hadn't seen them before.

We tentatively select a pipe each. They are slim with a small cup at the end, already filled with something that I don't recognise. A dark, crystalline substance that

112

bounces the glow from the fairy lights as I turn the pipe from side to side, inspecting it.

"This will help you prepare your truth," Altan says. He gives us a small bow.

I glance around, wondering if everyone in here has had this same treatment, or if they're more casual about it all because they probably do it all the time. But I can't tell. Carrie puts the pipe in her mouth, and the boy leans forwards, flicking a silver lighter. The crystal glows red, and then dulls to a sparkling amber as Carrie sucks on the pipe, drawing it in. She coughs once, waves a hand in front of her face, and then goes again. She turns to me and exhales soft, purple smoke. Then she blinks, and her eyes turn glassy in the dim light.

"Fuck . . ." she mutters, then sinks down into her cushion.

I put my own pipe into my mouth, and the boy grins at me as he leans in to light it. He says something to Altan, and the two of them laugh.

"We'll leave you to it," Altan says. Their figures blur as they walk away.

The smells and the sounds in the tent swirl together inside my head, and I feel a deep pulsing in my temples, a *thump thump thump* like a drumbeat. I feel Carrie's hand in mine, soft and warm. And then we both sink further and further until we disappear.

To: lauralee@gmail.com [DRAFT]
From: carrie82@hotmail.com
Subject: Festival

OH, OH NO. My head is spinning, I feel sick, the battery is nearly dead but I have to write this down before I forget. The shaman said bad things, Laura. He says there's a dark cloud hanging over us. There's bad energy. I don't know if he meant me or Violet because then he said he wasn't doing our reading anymore and then we smoked more of that crystal shit and I don't even know what it is, it might be crack. Have I smoked crack? My head . . . my head . . . and I did something else. Not tonight. I did do something else tonight but it wasn't a bad thing, just a mad thing, a crazy thing, but I DID DO A BAD THING but I can't. I can't. No. NO. NO I can't tell you. I just need to sleep now then it will be OK. Won't it?

Help me, Laura, I'm scared.

CHAPTER
SIXTEEN

The voices are coming from far away, mumbled and jumbled and incoherent, as if they are underwater, or else I'm in a dream. My body is being shaken, and I feel everything rattle inside me. There's a sharp chemical taste in the back of my throat, and what starts with a cough soon turns into near choking as my eyes fly open and I try to sit up.

"Jesus Christ! Earth to Violet! Thought you were never going to wake up."

The face swims into my vision, and I squint. I open my mouth, "Martin?" My voice is a hoarse croak. I cough again.

"Wow, your breath stinks. What the hell have you been drinking?"

I lick my lips, and they are dry and cracked. I try to sit up, but my head protests. Everything goes black and red and spins around and around, until I close my eyes and lie back down again. "Carrie?" I manage.

"Carrie has managed to throw up whatever it is that you two space cadets took last night. She's outside, waiting. We're all waiting. We need to get back to UB."

"UB?" It takes me a long time to work out where I am and where I am meant to be going, but then I open my eyes again and I recognise the internal walls of the ger. The colourful hangings. The smoke hole at the top. I need a drink.

Martin reads my mind. "You're in luck. One of Sarnai's friends brought supplies for the next tour group. Apparently we could've had stuff like this too but it wasn't offered. Anyway, we were more authentic. I can get you some milk tea if you like." He's holding a can of Coke, and he pretends to take it away again, just as my hand goes to grab it. He lets me have it, the ring-pull already popped, and I drink it greedily. It's freezing cold and it burns down the rawness of my throat. I feel like I might stop breathing, but at this moment, I don't even care.

"Don't know what happened to you two last night. We lost you in the crowd after the ceremony. That was something else, wasn't it? I'm definitely going to pursue the spiritual connections I've made on this trip. I'm quite excited about going home. Getting started on my new plans for life." He leans down and rubs my shoulder. "I had thought that maybe . . . you know, yesterday . . . that me and you . . ."

"Please stop talking. My head can't cope right now."

He sighs, stares out of the open door. "I tried to get it out of Carrie, but she reckons she can't remember what you two got up to last night either."

Good, I think. I don't want to remember right now. My body aches from head to toe, and what I'd really like is another Coke, a handful of heavy-duty painkillers, and maybe a hot bath. I realise that this combination would likely kill me on its own, never

116

mind whatever it is that is still in my system from last night. I close my eyes again, trying to remember last night, but the last thing that's stored in there is watching the ceremony. Everyone chanting and throwing milk in the air. After that is a yawning chasm of complete blank.

It's far from the first time I've had a blackout after drinking and drugs — I am assuming I have taken drugs, smoked something hard core, because my throat is in ruins, and I can smell the stale, cloying scent on my clothes. I know that bit by bit, the fragments of lost memory will come back to me, haunting me, shaming me — and I know that some bits will never come back at all. Between me and Carrie, I imagine we'll be able to piece most of it back together, but there's no guarantee.

"Come on, get packed. We're leaving in ten." Martin puts another can of Coke on the floor beside my bed and disappears back outside. He's pissed off with me, which is fair enough, I suppose. He probably imagined some tantric sex on top of that miniature mountain with the pile of stones on top. If *he's* pissed off, Rory must be fuming.

I sit up slowly, and notice that Martin has also left me a packet of painkillers next to my second can of Coke. Even annoyed, he's a good Boy Scout. I feel bad for leading him on, but it'd just been one of those things, caught in the moment. There was never a hope that I'd sleep with him. I take a sip and lick again at my chapped lips. They don't just feel dry, but cracked at the edges, and a bit swollen and bruised. A memory hits me. Carrie's voice: *Close your eyes.* Carrie's touch: her fingers on my lips.

The sound of the Land Rover starting up knocks the rest of the memory away. It's so close to the surface, I know it'll come back. I pick up my backpack, and, ignoring the pounding in the back of my skull, I throw everything inside. There's something stuffed into the side pocket, taking up the space where I usually put my smaller toiletries, so I shove them into the main section instead. I don't bother to see what it is. I can sort the bag out properly later, before we get back on the train.

They're all waiting for me in the van.

"Morning, Violet," Sarnai says. "I think you had a good time at the festival last night?" She giggles, and I manage to give her a small smile.

Carrie is wedged up against the window, her head against her rolled-up hoodie. She has her bag beside her on the seat so that no one can sit next to her. She doesn't speak but a flash of her eyes tells me that she's just as messed up as I am right now. She looks grey and clammy. I imagine I must look the same.

"About time," Rory mutters. He's in the same position as Carrie, one seat in front. I ignore him, and take the single seat behind Martin, who, at least, manages a proper smile.

"You look a bit better than you did half an hour ago."

"I don't feel it."

None of us says anything else for a while. The atmosphere is heavy. Subdued. And I wonder if Carrie or me did something embarrassing — something that the others know about but we don't. I have no idea how

118

we got home, so I suspect someone must've helped us. But I don't want to ask any questions. I don't want them to think that I have no idea of what happened in the last few hours. I realise that I don't even have any concept of how long a period of time is missing from my memory.

The Land Rover humps hard across the dusty steppe roads, and it's all I can do to take small sips of water from the bottle that Martin gave me when I sat down. Rory and Carrie are asleep, which I think is miraculous under the conditions — but sometimes sleep overrides everything.

"It's been quite an adventure," Martin says to me, at last. "I'm glad we met up with you two. Shame we're going in different directions now."

We were always going in different directions, but I don't tell him that.

"Any tips for Beijing?"

I can see the high-rises of UB on the horizon. We're still trundling across the harsh earth, barely a thing around us except for sparse grass and the outlines of the mountains far away on either side. "Well, it's got a lot more people in it than this place."

"Nine million bicycles," he says.

"At least. Oh, that's a song isn't it?"

He starts singing, and he's not bad. Shame we didn't get to go to karaoke. "Is the smog as bad as they say?" he asks.

"Worse. You think you can see it but you can't, really. It just looks like thick, grey skies. But you can feel it. You can taste it. It squeezes your head like a vice. And there's so much noise, and colour and everything is just . . ."

"Frenetic?"

I nod. "Yes, frenetic. I'll tell you where I went for a bit of quiet time — weirdly. There's a shopping mall under the Hyatt with a food court, with loads of brilliant food. It's called the Oriental Plaza. Amazingly, it's not really a tourist kind of place, and you can just eat and chill and no one will bother you in there."

"Sounds great." He twists around in his seat to face me. "Anything else?"

"There's a great dumpling shop off the Wangfujing pedestrian street. I think they have about fifty different fillings and it's so cheap. They're completely addictive and I recommend having at least five portions." I feel saliva building at the back of my mouth at the thought of this. I wish I'd stayed a little longer, now. Not got so hung up on getting the train when I did. But I was lonely. It's easy to forget that now, with these people that I have formed a strange and intimate bond with. If I'd stayed, I wouldn't have been in the travel centre that day, and I wouldn't have met Carrie.

Carrie is what took my mind off Sam.

I wonder what he's doing right now, but I don't even bother looking as I know my phone is dead. As soon as we get back to the hostel, I'll charge it and have a look. It's only been a couple of days since I checked his feed — but a lot can happen in a couple of days.

I rub at my face. It feels itchy, like something is crawling on it. "Go to Qianmen Quanjude for Peking duck, too. They present the head on a little plate — it's

120

meant to be a delicacy. I had to keep it covered up with a napkin I could eat the rest of the thing."

"Bloody hell, stop talking about food. I could eat a scabby horse." Carrie's voice is as rough as mine feels.

"You could've eaten that stupid little horse that kept throwing me off. Best thing for it."

"You two are revolting," Rory says, joining in.

"You're going to China now, you idiot," I say. "You can eat anything there. You probably will."

"I think I'm becoming a vegetarian," he says. "Well, maybe after a final burger in that Irish Bar before we leave. What do you reckon, ladies? Want to join."

Carrie rolls her eyes at me then leans back into the window. "The only place I'm going tonight is bed."

"Game on," Rory says, clapping his hands.

Carrie pulls her hoodie over her face. "Not with you. Ever."

Another memory hits me. People clapping. Carrie pulling her dress up over her head, spinning around, unhooking her bra. I close my eyes and lean my head against the window, waiting for more to resurface. Trying to bring it closer.

Trying to push it away.

CHAPTER
SEVENTEEN

Ulaanbaatar–Irkutsk

Despite the pounding headache and the bone-weary tiredness, I barely slept a wink back in the guesthouse. Geriel tried to coax us into the sitting area to chat about our trip, but neither of us had the energy, and I had the feeling that Carrie didn't want to talk to anyone about what had happened. I wasn't sure yet if she remembered more than I did, but I heard her tossing and turning in the night, crying out a couple of times — mumbling things that were incoherent and nonsensical.

Luckily I remembered to charge my phone as soon as we got back, so I spent most of the sleepless night scrolling through Facebook, reading about Sam's exploits. There is definitely a girl on the scene now. A vacuous blonde is with him in several of the photos, her comments beneath full of heart emojis and kisses. I fought the urge to hurl the phone across the room, but then I heard Carrie snuffling in her sleep and I remembered that Sam was in the past now. I have more important things to think about.

More memories of the night at the festival have tried to force themselves to the front of my mind, wanting

122

me to deal with them — but I'm not ready for that yet. We're about to embark on a ninety-hour train journey. There will be plenty of time for us both to dissect the night, and our feelings for one another.

Because I know now that Carrie has feelings for me. The first memory that came to me was of the kiss we shared on the way to our readings with the shaman. I'm savouring it for now, not yet sure where it will lead.

The train is already waiting for us when we reach the platform. Geriel has given us each a little bag filled with jam sandwiches, fruit and bottles of water. She tried to be kind, despite us ignoring her goodwill, and I feel a little bad about that, but if it had been up to me I wouldn't have booked such intimate accommodation. I prefer hotels, where things are a bit more impersonal. The last thing I want is someone pushing me to be friendly and communal, wanting to share everything about my day with them. Even in the hostels I've been in, I've managed to avoid this for the most part, so I really hope that our accommodation at the next stop is something more to my liking. I suppose this is what happens when you tag yourself onto someone else's trip. It's the first time I've done something like this, usually preferring to choose my own accommodation, although I have to admit that Sam chose well, and I had no problems staying with him. He has money, though, and he's not afraid to spend it. Which I suppose is why people generally flock to him. Yes, he is good-looking and charming and generous and funny. Sexy and current and the perfect person to be around.

123

But he's also a little stupid, and quite vain, and he was an idiot to let me go.

"Come on, let's get on." Carrie hoists her backpack on and starts walking along the platform, glancing at her tickets and the stickers on the doors, looking for the right carriage.

I stub out my half-smoked cigarette and follow behind her. A female guard is gesturing, and Carrie stops to talk to her. Eventually I catch up.

"We're in first-class," Carrie says. "Whoop!"

I frown. "Weren't we in that before? From Beijing?"

"Yes . . . but we didn't really make the most of it. It was only one night. I spent most of that in the standard-class buffet car while you slept through it all. We're on here three nights now. We can live it up." She throws her bag onto the train and clambers up the steep metal steps after it. Then turns to me. "Although . . . I am actually pretty wrecked after that mad festival. Could probably do with laying off the drink for a while. Maybe I'll make this a detox trip. I'm sure they'll have loads of herbal teas."

My laugh comes out as a snort. "We're travelling to Russia. You really want to spend your time drinking chamomile and peppermint? Do you realise that Russians drink alcohol literally *all* the time? All of them?"

"Aye, you're right. Not the best time for a detox, right enough." She laughs, and picks up her bag. I grip onto the handrails and pull myself up the steep steps, my bag still on my shoulders. I'd debated the safety of this, seeing the size of the gap between the train and the platform, and considering my still-fragile state. But thankfully I make it onto the train unscathed, and without losing anything into the abyss.

I poke my head around the open doors of each cabin that I pass until I find her, three down. Good — not too far from the toilets, but far enough that we'll avoid the constant annoyance of the sliding doors. She's sitting on one of the beds, her rucksack already open, contents spilled across the covers.

"What you looking for?" I throw my rucksack onto the other bed and sit down opposite. The cabin is pretty much the same as the last one. I'm assuming it's the same class of train. The colours and the fittings all look familiar.

"Speaker," she says. "Haven't had a chance to use it yet. I had it in my bag when we went to the nomad camp, but there was no point seeing as my phone battery died after the first night."

She's not looking at me when she speaks, and yet I know she's lying. A memory swims into my vision. Carrie tapping furiously on her phone. Me trying to grab it off her. Her laughing. Dancing. Pulling me close to her.

Carrie plugs her phone into the charger under the small table that separates our beds, and then plugs the speaker into her phone. She jabs at it for a moment longer, and then the music starts playing. I recognise it from the first three bars. It's "Move any Mountain" by The Shamen. She climbs up onto her bed and starts doing some rave moves that I haven't seen anyone do since the nineties.

125

"Aww, I miss this music," she says, still moving her arms in jagged little movements. "Remember when all the clubs played this stuff? Those were the best times. All the club music is shite now, and all the clubbers are rubber-lipped posers. Not proper ravers. Not like us." She jumps down, then picks up the phone and switches the music off. She's breathing heavily, her face shining from her exertions. She sits down hard on the bed and looks away. "Maybe not that song though, eh? I'll find us another classic instead."

She glances up at me, and I know she remembers what happened at the festival. I'm about to say something, when the engines start up, and the doors are slammed. A whistle blows, and there's a lurch. Then we're off. I lean over and place a hand on her bare knee, and she lets me, just for a moment, before shrugging me off and standing up, turning away so I can't see her face.

"Carrie . . ."

"We're not talking about this right now. I'm getting a pack of cards out and I'm heading down to the first-class lounge car, see what's what. It's a shame that Steve and Marion aren't on this train. They'll be in Moscow now. Be good to catch up when we get there."

"I didn't really speak to them."

"No. I know. But we'll contact them when we get to Moscow, arrange a night out. They'll have a head start so they can tell us the best places to go. I think they were doing a river cruise, but then they were coming back. We looked at the dates. They'll be there when we arrive. I made a mad plan, just in case we don't manage

126

to email or whatever. Outside Lenin's tomb in Red Square — Tuesday at midday." She pulls more things out of her bag, tossing them on the bed. "I can't find those damned cards!" She picks up the bag of sandwiches and water from Geriel and dumps it on the table. "We should've brought some supplies. Proper supplies. Vodka. Crisps . . ."

I stand up, and I watch as she freezes, sensing me behind her. She doesn't turn around. I take a step closer. Lay a hand on her arm. Then I turn her around to face me, and put both of my arms around her, resting my head on her shoulder. She stiffens. Then her shoulders drop, and she puts her arms around me, and I take the opportunity to pull her closer. "About what happened . . ." she starts, but I *shbh* her, and keep her in my arms. She's warm, her body toned, yet soft. I long to be close to her again. I didn't expect any of this, but it doesn't mean I don't want it.

"Just relax, Carrie," I say. "We don't need to talk about it now, but when we do, well . . . just know that whatever you want is fine with me. If you want to forget it —"

She cuts me off, her voice is a whisper. "I can't forget it. I want to . . . it's not. It's not something I've done. Not something I ever thought I wanted to do."

"Me, neither," I say, into her neck. She flinches, and I blow gently on her ear, then give her a series of tiny, soft, butterfly kisses. "You don't need to worry about it, Carrie. You don't need to make it anything more than it is."

She unlocks her arms and pulls back. We're exactly the same height, I realise now, and she stares right into my eyes. "And what is *it?*" she says. She sounds scared. Vulnerable. And for the first time in my life, I want to protect someone. I want to protect her. Maybe I've been wrong all these years. About what's right for me. I keep looking for men to look after me, but all they do is use me. Maybe I'm supposed to be the protector. Maybe it's not a man I should be looking for.

But I can't push too far right now. I don't think she's ready.

I lift my hand and move a lock of her hair away from her face, pushing it behind her ear. She has small, dainty ears, pierced three times on each side and decorated with different coloured gemstones. Everything about her is beautiful and exotic. I want to lick her, taste her sweet, salty skin. I want to drink her up, just like that cocktail I craved on the night we met.

"Let's go down to the lounge," I say. "I think we could both use a drink."

To: lauralee@gmail.com
From: carrie82@hotmail.com
Subject: Choo-Choo(n)!

_____

Hiya!

Bloody hell — Mongolia was MENTAL! I had a load of emails in draft but I deleted them off my phone. Total rambling shite — count yourself lucky there was no wifi or phone reception or you'd have been sending out a UN rescue mission to find me. Is Mongolia in the UN? You might still get some of them, they might be floating around in the cloud or something. Anyhoo . . . I'm feeling OK now (ish), but it was touch and go for a while — I'm trying to be positive but I keep having these little flashes of stuff that I'm not sure I actually want to remember.

I'm in the first-class lounge, writing this on the laptop. It's nice to just sit here and chill out, actually. I wanted to play cards but I can't find the bloody things, and Violet's planning to read up on Moscow, because apparently I know all about the place where we're stopping off next, so she's not going to bother researching that. I thought we were on the herbal tea but V's at the bar and I don't think it's tea that the soor-faced cow behind the bar is making!

We're on our way to Irkutsk, which is in Siberia. Isn't it funny, places like Outer Mongolia and Siberia always seemed totally made up and a bit legendary, and not the kind of places that anyone could ever actually GO to, and here I am!

Shit, sorry — that was a bit insensitive! You should be here. I do wish you were here. I miss your face and your dull chat. Haha.

How's your leg? Are you out of the stookie yet?

What news??

Cxx

P.S. [link to YouTube: The Shamen — *"Move any Mountain" https://www.youtube.com/watch?y=SpjnzxtZ6Og*]

★　★　★

To: carrie82@hotmail.com
From: lauralee@gmail.com
Subject: RE: Choo-Choo(n)!

Fucksake, I was starting to get worried, you daft cow. That video is brilliant! Was that actually you at the mad festival? Did you meet an actual shaman? Or lots of shamen? What are they like? Did you get your fortune read or something — is that what they do?

130

I am getting the plaster off next week, and then some bandage and sexy-boot combo, which will at least be lighter to drag around and give my skinny wasted leg a chance to grow some muscle again. You know, I keep thinking about that night, and I still can't really work out how I fell. I know I was wearing those stupid heels, but you were there, and I remember holding on to your arm. I wish I could remember! I might hobble back round to the steps and see if there are any loose cobbles. Maybe I can sue the council — haha!

Oh, don't know if you know, but I think Greg is seeing someone.

Lxx

CHAPTER
EIGHTEEN

"We'll have two Brandy Alexanders," I say to the stern-faced woman behind me bar. I'm expecting a further look of disgust, as she chooses not to understand me or know what I'm asking for, but instead she takes two martini glasses from under the counter, picks up a cocktail shaker, and starts to add the ingredients.

"Ooh," Carrie says. "*Fancy*. I thought we were off the drink for five minutes?" She laughs, and nudges my arm. Then she heads over to an unoccupied table and slides into the window seat.

I watch her while the woman prepares our drinks. She didn't find the playing cards, but she's brought her laptop and the guidebook, and some paper and pens instead, and she's got some idea for a game. I'd rather just stare out of the window, when I'm not staring at her. We can chat. She can tell me more about everything, and I can tell her more about Sam — although maybe that's not the best idea. She thinks I'm forgetting him. Getting over him. I suppose I am, but it still hurts.

A quick look on Sam's Facebook while Carrie is busy setting up the game, and it's much of the same. For the first time, I feel a little detached as I scroll through the photographs. He's still checking in to every place he goes, still hanging out with the beautiful people, still partying like he's a student on a gap year. Surely he'll tire of it all soon? Think about heading back home? I'm planning to keep looking at his posts for the foreseeable. If things don't work out with Carrie, I do think I'll be looking to track him down again. What annoys me is the rejection, I suppose.

It's supposed to be me who does the walking away.

"Enjoy." The woman behind the bar plonks the glasses in front of me unceremoniously.

I give her a smile, but she doesn't return it. I can't work out if she is genuinely pissed off, or if this is just the way she looks, but so far most of the female staff I've seen on the train have had similar expressions of woe. I expect she goes into the kitchen when we're not there and laughs at us — the travellers — thinking we know what's what in the world because we've taken a few trips. She's right to be cynical. Most travellers I've met have been vacuous, or self-important, arrogant rich kids. That's why I liked Sam . . . loved him, I mean. Because he was different. He had a good job, he had ambition — all he wanted was an extended holiday. But look at him now. He's not who I thought he was. Carrie is different, too. Another one with drive — she saved that money for this trip, and she's making the most of it. Sam . . . Carrie . . . these are my kind of people.

I've made a few mistakes along the way with some of the other friends I've made — but I don't want to dwell

133

on that now. Not when things are heading in the right direction.

Carrie grins at me as I place the drinks on the table. Beige, creamy liquid in proper martini glasses, with a litrle chocolate straw placed on the top. I hadn't expected the woman at the bar to make such an effort but, as I'm finding out, things often surprise you when you least expect it.

Like Carrie — at the festival. Like that kiss, and her grabbing my hands and placing them on her naked body. I grin back as I take a seat opposite her, and I think my eyes must flick down towards her chest — unintentional, but the image is there in my mind. A shadow passes across her face, and I look away, out of the window, and wait.

After a moment of silence, she says, "It's so weird being here."

I turn back to face her, watch as she takes a sip of her drink. "What . . . on this train? In this country?" I pause, take a sip of my own drink. It's creamy, but there's a hard bite of alcohol in there. "Being here with me?"

She picks up the chocolate straw and starts nibbling on it. "All of the above."

I take another sip of my drink. Memories of the night at the festival have been coming back to me all day, jabbing at me like random, tiny pinpricks. One minute I want to blurt something out, and the next I want to keep it locked away inside my head. From Carrie's up-and-down mood, I sense she is getting the same reminders.

134

"You know . . . you said something the other night. About Sam . . ."

It's as if she's read my mind.

"I don't really want to talk about him, actually." I drain my drink. The problem with these types of glasses is that they hardly hold any liquid. I turn around towards the bar, and catch the woman's eye. "Can We have two more, please?"

"Are you sure that's a good idea?" Carrie is ripping corners off a piece of paper, dropping small, rough confetti onto the table. If she had a bottle of beer, the label would be in shreds by now.

"Of course it is. We're in first-class, aren't we? Let's enjoy it."

The bar woman brings us another two drinks and planks them hard on the table, with another emotionless "enjoy", then leaves us to it.

Carrie picks up the chocolate straw and holds it like a cigarette, sucking the end. She turns to face me, looks me straight in the eye, and I can't look away.

"We should talk about the festival," she says, "what happened . . ."

"Which bit?"

"Which bit do you remember?" She slides more of the straw into her mouth, bites it in half with a snap. Then nibbles at the remaining piece, small tiny bites, like a little animal. Her eyes flash a warning at me, and I wonder if she wants me to tell the truth or lie.

"I remember some of it . . ." I say. This is the truth, at least.

"I remember running out of the shaman's tent. I remember colours, flashing everywhere. My head spinning. I fell onto the floor, and someone picked me up —"

"That was Rory."

"No." She shakes her head. "We didn't see Rory or Martin after the reading. They said so in the van. They'd been looking for us . . ."

I take another drink, trying to buy time. I thought I remembered, but now I'm not so sure.

"I was scared, Violet. I don't know what of . . . but I remember the feeling. The panic. My heart racing." She puts a hand to her chest. "I can feel it now . . . something happened in the reading, didn't it? He said something bad was going to happen . . ."

A small burst of laughter comes out of me, but it's forced. I am trying to quell my own panic. The memory has come back now. Not a pinprick anymore. More like a long, thin blade, right to my heart.

Carrie is shaking now. She is looking at me in sheer horror. "He said you had a bad soul, V. We laughed, but then his face changed, and it wasn't funny anymore. He said something was wrong with you . . . he said —"

I lean over and lay a hand on top of hers. Her skin is hot and clammy. Her hand is shaking, and I press down on it to make it stop.

"It's all a load of rubbish. A bloody witch doctor — that's all. I bet they do it to all the tourists, after plying them with their weird herbal highs."

She picks up her drink with her free hand and drains it. "You're probably right," she says. "I'm just mixing things up in my head."

She bites her lip, and looks away.

CHAPTER
NINETEEN

We've had too many drinks. There is a small part of me that is trying hard to keep control of the situation, but a larger part wants to give in to it, just to see what's going to happen next. Carrie is free and fun when she's drinking. When she's hungover or coming down, she's moody and paranoid. More than that, she's too inquisitive — and I'm scared that sooner or later she's going to get to the truth about me.

I'm not ready for that.

I manage to keep it together enough to get us back to the cabin. The first-class carriage had started to fill up — a bunch of older people on a tour, just like on the China-to-Mongolia train — but this time, Carrie hadn't been so ready to talk to them. She'd been probing me for information about the festival, one minute saying she was scared, the next laughing it off. Plus, her endless questions about Sam. I had to shut her up, and the alcohol wasn't hitting her fast enough, so I slipped something into her drink when she went to the toilet. Just a tiny bit. Just enough to loosen her up and stop her asking so many questions.

She started to slur after that, and I realised I needed to get her out of there.

We've got three more days on this train — we can't piss off the staff, and we don't want the other passengers getting annoyed with us. Annoyed people tend to be nosy people, and I don't want any of them sticking their beaks into our business. This is my and Carrie's trip. I need to keep it going, keep it fun — or else she'll tell me she's heading off on her own, and to be honest I'm not sure I can take another rejection so soon after Sam.

I checked his Facebook again when Carrie was in the toilet. I couldn't help myself. He looks happy, as always, and I feel small angry feet stamping across my heart.

Carrie pulls away from me and slumps onto her bunk. She's in a worse state that I realised. I definitely didn't plan this. She curls herself onto the bed, pulling her knees up to her chest, trying to make herself safe in the foetal position.

Does she think I would hurt her?

I pull a small bottle of water out from under the table by the window and lay it on the bed beside her head. She's already snoring quietly, and I could kick myself at my own stupidity. I wanted to talk to her tonight about what happened between us. I know she's been trying hard to avoid it, but the chemistry is there. That fizzing, squirming feeling deep below — transferring itself from me to her and back again, like the fluttering of a butterfly's wings. I close the door, and lock it, then I slowly undress — never taking my eyes off her as I peel off my clothes and let them fall to the floor.

Then I start on hers. Even more slowly, even more carefully. She barely stirs. She's completely out for the count. This wasn't what I had in mind at all, but I take a moment to stroke the soft skin of her naked back, down to the curve just above her perfect, pert buttocks. A sprinkling of goose pimples flit over her skin, and I know that she can feel my touch. She can sense me. She knows that I'm here.

Watching her.

Longing for her. I stay like that for a long time, and then climb into my own bunk, and pull the cool sheet up over my chest. My breathing has quickened, and the butterflies are beating faster, faster, further and further down my body. I slide a hand under the sheet. Carrie lets out a small moan, and I close my eyes, aching now. Desperate for release.

When is she going to realise that I love her?

To: lauralee@gmail.com [DRAFT]
From: carrie82@hotmail.com
Subject: RE: RE: Chaa-Chaa(n)!

Oh, Loz — you know we were both pissed that night. All I
remember is one minute you were holding on to me, talking
shite, and we crossed the cobbles in Cockburn Street, and
the next thing you'd taken a header down the steps of
Fleshmarket Close. If you weren't so drunk I think you
might've smashed your head open, but you were like rubber
. . . you just flipped and bounced — it all happened so fast.
I puked with the shock before I could even come and help
you up, and you were greetin' and shouting and I couldn't
get you up, but then they heard all the commotion down at
the Halfway House and a couple of old boys came up to
help — they were as pished as us but clearly more used to
it, thank fuck! Just one of those mental drunken accidents,
doll. No point keeping going over it.

Anyway, listen — I woke up naked in my bunk this morning. As if I would sleep naked on my own? You know what
I'm like. Violet was asleep in the other bunk, facing away
from me, but I dunno, I had this feeling — like I could
sense that just a moment before I moved, she'd been watching me. I was all bare under the covers. Mortified!

141

I've decided not to mention it, TBH. I think she might have a bit of a crush on me, but she's too intense. I think she thinks we had a "moment" at the nomadic festival, but I was so off my tits I can't remember a thing . . .

Love you, doll. Can't wait to see you.

Cx

P.S. Good for Greg. I told you, I don't want to talk about him, and I don't even care! I wouldn't even care if it was you he was seeing. You'd be welcome to him. I was pissed off for a while, but I'm over it. Totally. OK?

CHAPTER
TWENTY

When I wake up, Carrie is gone — her bed unmade, rumpled clothes tossed in the corner next to her rucksack, which is spilling its contents over the bunk — as if she has dressed and left in a hurry. I'd spent most of the night lying here, watching her. She was a restless sleeper, maybe more so because of the train than the alcohol, and part of me was watching to make sure she didn't throw up and choke to death in her sleep.

But mostly I was watching her because I like watching her.

I know I've become a bit obsessed, and I think I should pull back a bit — but she seemed to be enjoying our friendship and getting closer. Maybe I've misinterpreted her, but I don't think so. I am usually good at knowing if someone likes me or not. I know that Michael did, and Sam — until things went wrong. But when relationships are so intense, things do go wrong — I realise that. I just don't want to blow it with Carrie.

I decide to leave her to it for a bit, wherever she might be.

I sit up in the bunk and pick up my phone from where it's been charging on the small table beside me. I open Facebook and have a scroll through my feed, but there's nothing much of interest on there. I don't have enough friends for it to be particularly interesting, preferring instead to look at individual profiles, especially those who have everything set to "public" — which is a surprising number of people, despite all the warnings about online safery. Sometimes I send random friend requests, if I find someone intriguing, but I usually delete them before they get accepted or ignored. I'd prefer not to be rejected, but also I prefer not to have them question why I am sending the request. I have had that a few times. I've learned my lesson.

I check a couple of my usual profiles, but nothing much is happening. Maybe because of the time-zone differences, I'm missing out on the new stuff. I consider ignoring him, but I know I can't stop myself looking at Sam's profile for updates.

He's at a street market. Him and two of those German lads, gurning, grimacing faces holding insects up to their mouths. I click on a video clip and watch one of the Germans eating a live cockroach, his face joyous at first and then a look of sheer horror, before he turns away from the camera and vomits, while the others laugh. I don't think it's funny. I stab a finger on the app, shutting it down. I should delete Facebook from my phone. It really doesn't make me feel good.

I get dressed in a pair of leggings and a long T-shirt, tie my hair back with a band, and then I set about tidying Carrie's stuff. I sort and fold the clothes that have spilled out of her bag, and when I see anything that takes my fancy, I hold it against myself and check my reflection in the window. It's not the best, with the train moving quite fast and the background colours changing so quickly, but it's enough. I open each of the side pockets of her rucksack and have a quick rummage inside, but there's nothing too exciting. I was hoping for maybe a notebook or a diary, but she seems to store all of her information on her laptop, and she always has that with her. I might ask to borrow it later — tell her I'd like to write some proper emails. She'd hardly believe that I literally have no one to send any emails to.

Eventually I get bored being on my own, and it's clear that Carrie is not coming back, so I push her rucksack over to the far side of her bed, the neatly stacked clothes lined up beside it. It doesn't look like I've been snooping, and she can hardly complain about my folding her clothes. I open her toiletries bag and take out her deodorant — a roll-on — and use it to freshen up under my arms, then I take a squirt of her toothpaste and rub it over my teeth. It'll do for now.

I hear her voice before I even get to the dining car — laughing loudly, regaling with an anecdote. Just like in UB, in the Irish Bar — playing to the crowd. I paste a smile onto my face and walk in to the carriage.

"There you are," I say, forcing a jolly, carefree tone into my voice — one that I definitely don't feel. "Thought you'd jumped off." I laugh.

She swivels round in her seat, and I see the laptop on front of her, closed, a glass of clear liquid beside her. Is she drinking again? Stupidly, I'd thought we could spend some time together today, catching up, but I see that she's already making her own entertainment.

A young couple are sitting opposite her, and they smile when they see me.

"V! Come and meet Jared and Leia. They've been travelling for six months — can you believe it?"

Jared and Leia look like the type of know-it-all travellers that I've spent my entire trip avoiding — and I've been travelling a *lot* longer than six months.

"Oh hey," says Jared. He holds up his fingers in a peace sign, and I want to punch him in the face.

"Carrie says you're from Nottingham," Leia chimes in. "Guess what? We're from Nottingham, too! What school did you go to?" She peers up at me through her too-long fringe. It makes her look like Dougal from *The Magic Roundabout*. I want to grab it and yank it off.

"Oh I didn't go to school there," I say. "Besides, I'm a few years older than you two, I think."

"No way," Jared says. "You look like our age, if that. I guess we're a bit weather-beaten though, right? You know, when we were in Bali, we —"

"What's everyone drinking? Shall I get us another?" I walk across to the bar, trying hard not to look at Jared or Leia so that I don't feel the urge to grab both of their stupid heads and smash them together until they break. "I'll just nip to the toilet first," I say, and I keep walking, past the bar, and the grumpy barmaid, and through the next set of connecting doors — where I slide the window down and stick my face out into the fresh air. I close my eyes and try to slow my breathing,

146

feeling my heart rate gradually return to normal. I haven't felt this level of rage for a while, and I need to be careful. A moving train, several hours from its next stop, is not the place for me to lose my shit. If Carrie wants to spend the day hanging with those two losers then I'll just have to let her.

I decide to steer clear, by walking the length of the train, seeing if there's anything more interesting to do, but after a couple of carriages of being buffeted back and forth, I lose patience and head back.

When I get back to the table, there's a bottle of vodka sitting on it. Four glasses, three of them half filled. There's a plate piled high with cream-cheese blinis, and I feel a roll of hunger in my stomach.

Fuck it.

"Oh you're back," Carrie says, winking across at the couple. "We wondered if you'd got to the end of the train and fallen off." They all laugh, clearly pleased with themselves for twisting my own attempt at humour back at me.

"Pour us some, then," I say, sliding into the seat next to Carrie, nudging her until she moves up closer to the window. I grab two blinis and sandwich them together and shove them into my mouth. "God, I am starving. When did we last eat?"

"Eating's cheating," Leia says, in her distinctly non-Nottingham accent. I think these two went to private school and that's what they were trying to catch me out on. Idiots. I went to private school too. One of the most exclusive in the country. Thinking about it now, I have no idea why I lied to Carrie about

Nottingham, of all places. I'm not even sure I've been there.

I pour a large measure of vodka into my glass and raise it briefly before knocking it back and refilling it. "Damn right it's cheating. Let's get on with this, eh?"

Carrie turns to me, amused. "Get on with what, exactly?"

"We're going to play a game, aren't we?"

"Oh yes," Leia says, clapping her hands. "Let's play 'Would You Rather?' "

I slam my glass down on the table and Jared flinches. "Bo-Ring."

Carrie downs her own drink, then refills mine and hers. "I think 'Never Have I Ever' is more what you're after, V? Yeah?"

I turn to her and smile. "Yeah." Then we both turn to Jared and Leia, and I feel that frisson of connection with Carrie again, and it tingles right down to the pit of my stomach.

"I'll start," Carrie says, grinning. "Never have I ever . . . stolen something valuable."

Jared and Leia give each other a look, and then Leia gives Jared a small shrug, and they both take a drink.

"Oooh," Carrie says. "Go on, then, spill!"

"Well," Jared says, "I'm not sure if it was truly valuable or not, but . . . when we went to Easter Island, we both picked up some pieces of crumbled rock from the base of one of the statues . . ." He goes bright red, and I realise that he truly believes he has done something awful. I want to wind him up, but Leia is shifting uncomfortably, and I decide to leave it.

148

"Naughty," Carrie says. "I hope you're not cursed." She laughs, before turning to me. "Got to say, V, I am not at all shocked at you not drinking. Proper goody-two-shoes, aren't you?" She winks, and I give her a half-smirk. We both know that's not true.

"Me next," Jared says. "I've got an excellent one."

I bet it isn't.

"Never have I ever . . . had sex with more than one person at the same time." He grins, ridiculously pleased with himself, but his face falls as neither me nor Carrie lifts a glass — but Leia does, and goes even redder than he did before.

"Leia," I say, cocking my head to the side in faux wonderment. "Aren't you a dark horse."

Jared is staring at Leia with a strange mixture of lust and revulsion. "Lee-Lee?" he says.

She shakes her head. Then barks out a laugh that is obviously fake. "Just kidding. I'll take another drink to make up for it."

Carrie side-eyes me and I smirk again. That pair are going to have some interesting discussions back in their cabin tonight. "Right. I'll go. Never have I ever . . . bullied someone at school."

Jared and Leia both let out sighs of relief. Of course they haven't. I turn to Carrie, "Bugger, *I'm* going to have to drink and then pick another question now, aren't I?"

She slowly shakes her head, then takes a sip. "It was a long time ago. I'm not proud of it. We all did it." She takes another sip. "Apparently he's not a very nice person now, but that doesn't mean it was OK."

The table falls silent. Even the barmaid, who has been chattering quietly to a man perched on a bar stool, stops talking and glances over. I don't think she has heard us, but she has sensed the atmosphere. There's nothing but the sound of the train hurtling along the tracks. *Badum. Badum.*

Leia lets out a nervous giggle. "Oh come on, we all did stupid things when we were kids, right? I know I did."

I don't believe her, but I appreciate her attempt to lighten the mood.

"Let's all drink," Jared chimes in. "Because we were all little buggers once upon a time."

I lean in closer to Carrie, lay a hand on her knee and give it a little squeeze. She jumps, knocking her knee against the table, and all the glasses jilt and roll and we all grab them, and the tension is gone.

"Fucksake," she mutters. She holds up her glass. "Cheers. Down the hatch."

We all drain our drinks, and Jared refills them, and we carry on — playing more fun questions for a while. Never have I ever . . . pissed behind a bin; told someone a lie about their new haircut; borrowed someone's something and lost it; given someone a fake phone number; cheated in an exam.

The day fades to dusk, and we're on the second bottle, when the questions take a darker turn once more.

"My turn," Leia slurs. "Never have I ever . . . had sex with someone of the same gender . . ."

150

Carrie snorts. "Hang on — that means your threesome was with two blokes? Did they get it on with each other, or did they both just do you?

Leia shakes her head and laughs. "I told you. That was just a joke."

"Yeah, right," I mutter. I turn to Carrie. "I'm not really sure if I should be drinking right now or not . . . I'll need to follow your lead."

"Wait, what . . . you two?" Jared perks up at my hinted confession, even though I haven't drunk anything yet. Why do men do this? What happened between Carrie and me was for us. Not for someone else's entertainment.

Leia looks pale, and I suspect there is a lot she's done that Jared knows nothing about.

"How long have you two been together?" I ask, taking a sip of my drink and trying to make it vague as to whether I am still playing the game or not.

"Since we were sixteen," Jared says, his voice a mixture of smugness and pride. "We went to different unis, but we met up every couple of weeks and we were both totally faithful . . . weren't we babe?" He turns to Leia, who shrugs. Her eyes are glazed and she is swaying slightly in her seat, despite the train being relatively smooth at this point.

"Course," she says.

She won't meet his eye, and I can see that he is hurt, but he's also too scared to probe further. This is not something he is going to benefit from digging into.

"I'm bored with this game," Carrie says, pouring more vodka into her glass. She fills it to the brim and a bit slops over the side. "Oops." She turns to me. "Let's talk about our exes. Tell them about Sam."

I shake my head. "I don't want to talk about Sam."

Carrie laughs. "You never do, V In fact, despite the fact that you claim to be checking his Facebook fifty times a day, I'm not entirely sure that he exists."

A rush of anger heats my cheeks. "Why would I make it up?"

"Whatever," Carrie says.

Leia and Jared are ignoring her. They're leaning in close, Jared whispering something to Leia that we can't hear, and she is looking increasingly uncomfortable. Serves them right for trying to play drinking games with the big boys. I'm intrigued about why Leia has chosen to start confessing her sins right now, though. Perhaps their perfect relationship isn't quite so perfect after all.

"Can I get out please, Violet? I'm going for a walk."

I slide out of the booth seat and Carrie comes out after me. "Where are you going?" I say as she wobbles down the aisle. "Should I wait here for you?"

"Do what you want," she calls back.

"We're crossing the border soon, aren't we? Don't we need to be in our rooms for the customs inspection?

She ignores me, and disappears out through the sliding doors. When I turn back to the table, Jared and Leia are gone, the door on the far side of the bar slides shut, and I'm alone.

Again.

CHAPTER
TWENTY-ONE

Irkutsk

As we pull into Irkutsk, I notice that the view around the station is mainly comprised of miserable concrete buildings and a car park full of men waiting expectantly for our arrival, just like in UB. There is a barely perceptible hum in the air, a feeling that this place is infinitely more threatening than Mongolia. Most of the Russian men are younger and somehow that makes them more dangerous to us. All of them are either smoking or chewing on matchsticks, staring us up and down, and I stare back at them and try to decide which of them looks the least likely to rape and kill us.

One of them catches my eye and comes ambling over towards us. He is wearing a shiny pair of tracksuit bottoms and a grey T-shirt, the sleeves rolled to display his sculpted biceps. He spits a chewed matchstick onto the floor and leans forwards, ready to pick up our bags.

"You have hotel? I know good hotel," he says, grinning. "Or maybe tour? You want to go to lake? Tell me what you want and I can do it." He pauses, sensing our reluctance. Carrie hasn't spoken to me since we woke this morning, and after last night's carry-on, I have no idea what she is thinking.

"We need to go to the Rachmaninoff Hotel," she says, offering him a piece of paper.

"OK, good," the man says, lifting both of our bags as if they are full of feathers. They are both at least 20kg each, despite my backpack being half the size of Carrie's proper backpacker's rucksack. "I am Ivan," he says. "I am at your service, and I am not so terrible." He does a little bow and I burst out laughing. Eventually, Carrie laughs too, and she leans over and squeezes my arm as we climb into the back of the car — which, I'm glad to see is a Lada. It's good to find out that they do actually drive their own brand of cars, despite them having a slightly dubious reputation back home.

He starts the engine, then leans over and rummages in the glove-box. Then he turns round to us and offers a business card between two fingers. "In case you need my services again." I take it, without really thinking, and he winks at me. Carrie looks out of her window.

We're clipping our seatbelts in as he releases the handbrake and shrieks across the car park, causing us both to flop forwards then back.

"Oi . . ." Carrie starts, but he just turns on the radio and drowns us out with loud, heavy techno.

I look across at Carrie, but she has her eyes shut tight.

As we leave the area around the station and enter the main body of the city, I stare out of the windows at the dirty, grey communist-era architecture, mixed with the over-the-top fancy structures that are peppered throughout. We pass through street upon street of

154

blocky high-rises, and we pause at traffic lights at an impressive gold-painted church with a huge statue of Lenin outside.

I'd only planned to look up Moscow in the guidebook, but after Carrie did her disappearing act last night, I had little else to do, so now I know that there is little for us to do here. We should've stopped at Ulan-Ude, and gone to Lake Baikal — from what Rory and Martin had told us, there were many things we could've done there — but on the other hand, it's probably just as well we didn't go anywhere near water. Besides, Carrie planned to come to the city instead, wanting to see the wooden houses and learn more about the Decembrists, but with us barely speaking, I'm not sure what we're actually going to do for the next couple of days. I just hope the hotel is nice, and that the food here is better than in Mongolia — which really shouldn't be much of a stretch.

The car slows, and Ivan points out of his window.

"This hotel," he says. "Hotel Irkut. Very nice hotel."

Carrie sits up straight. "No. We're going to the Rachmaninoff. I showed you." She leans forwards and tries to pick up the piece of paper that the driver has tossed onto the passenger seat.

"No problem," he says, "I cancel this one for you. I take you to best hotel in Irkutsk. Best food. Caviar. Anything you like, ladies." He stops the car and gestures again at the hotel to his left. A man in a dark suit is standing outside, and he starts to walk towards us.

155

"No," Carrie says, more forcefully now. "Take us to the Rachmaninoff Hotel."

The suited man approaches the car, and Ivan winds down the window and starts talking to him in rapid-fire Russian.

Carrie leans over to me and whispers: "I've read about this. It's a scam. They have an arrangement with this place, and they'll take our money but then the other place will get all shitty and they'll try to throw us out and make us pay for both."

"Fuck."

"Exactly. I'm not falling for it." The suited man steps away from the car and Ivan closes the window. Carrie leans over the seat. "Take us to the Rachmaninoff Hotel. Now." Her voice is hard, full of venom. I am terrified, but I stay flat back against the seat, and try not to give any indication of how scared I am. Once again, I am impressed with how she handles things. I'd thought I knew what I was doing before I met her, and yet she continues to surprise me.

Ivan sits still for a moment. The suited man shakes his head, just a fraction, but enough to indicate that we're possibly going to get our way.

"Now," Carrie says again.

Ivan blows out a stream of what I assume are Russian expletives, then he jams the key into the ignition and throws the car into reverse. He hangs back over the seat, causing Carrie to bounce back towards me, and then he reverses down the middle of the road at full speed.

156

My heart is hammering now, and I'm far too scared to turn around, convinced that at any moment we are going to crash full-on into a car coming the other way — the correct way — down the street. Carrie is holding onto the handle above the door with one hand, and she grabs mine with her other and we both squeeze tight, bracing for impact.

But just as I think we're going to crash and die, the car slows, and swerves and then he's driving the correct way again, down another street, still far too fast. Then he slams on the brakes and points out of his window again.

"Rachmaninoff Hotel," he says. "Shithole."

I glance out at the dull grey block with a faded red canopy over the door. There's a dingy-looking alleyway running along the side, and I dread to think what might be down there. There's no doorman at this place. We might've made a mistake, after all.

"Are you sure this is the Rachmaninoff Hotel?" Carrie says, grabbing the piece of paper.

I lean over to read it, and it does indeed have the correct name on it. But I've done this before, in much nicer cities than this — sometimes there are hotels with the same name. Sometimes one is much nicer than the other. Naming it after a famous composer doesn't mean it has to be nice, obviously.

"I try to tell you," he says. "I not rip you off."

Carrie sighs. "OK," she says. "Maybe you were right. But I've booked this place and I know the price, and they're expecting us, so . . ." She glances over at me,

157

giving me an uncertain smile. "Are you OK here, V? Should we go back?"

I take another look at the miserable place that we've apparently decided to spend our time in, and then I make a stupid, ridiculous mistake. "I reckon we should go with this one, Carrie. You chose it. I bet it's lovely inside. That other place was probably all front."

Ivan catches my eye in the rear-view mirror, and shakes his head sadly. He mutters something in Russian, and then opens the car door and climbs out. He disappears around the back and lifts our rucksacks out of the boot, then walks silently over to the hotel, and up the three steps to the front door.

"I hope we're not being mental," Carrie says.

"How bad can it be? It's all just part of our adventure."

"You're right," she says. "Also . . . I'm sorry, V. I was a total dick on the train. Can we just forget it?"

I'm about to tell her that I'd already forgiven her, when Ivan appears back down the steps.

"One thousand rubles," he says.

Carrie hands over the note she has taken from her purse, folded up in her hand, ready. Knowing how much it should be. Yet again, not letting us be ripped off.

The hotel will be fine. The main thing is, we're together.

CHAPTER
TWENTY-TWO

The reception is small and cramped, with a chest-height, dark, wooden desk on one side and a tired-looking red-velvet sofa on the other. The floors are polished marble, and a quick glance around suggests that the place is clean, if not luxurious. I squeeze Carrie's hand and she gives me a small smile. We're here. We're still together. But we do have lots to talk about. I'll let us get settled before broaching it though.

"Room seventeen, on fourth floor. Lift is at end of corridor. Restaurant is at end of corridor also. No food now. Breakfast eight until ten. Dinner five until nine. No lunch." The bored-looking receptionist rattles off the bare minimum of information needed without even the hint of a smile. She hasn't asked for any money yet, so maybe Carrie has pre-paid, but I don't bother to ask her.

The lift is tiny and instantly claustrophobic, without even a mirror to make it look bigger. We squeeze in with our bags, and I try not to breathe in Carrie's direction as I'm sure my breath is stale from the journey, despite brushing my teeth every day. Now that we are in here, the smell of us both is overpowering.

The taxi had its own sweaty aroma, and it was hard to know if it was us or Ivan who smelled the worst. Now I'm starting to think it was us. But we have been on a train for nearly four days, and no amount of cat washes can deal with that kind of sweat. There was a lot of drinking. A lot of other stuff too. I get a thrill as well as huge waves of embarrassment when I think about it.

After what seems like an age, we arrive on the fourth floor and almost tumble out into the corridor to escape the confines of the lift.

"Jesus Christ," Carrie mutters, heaving her bag onto one shoulder. "We fucking stink, V."

I burst out laughing, glad that the tension has snapped at last. Although she'd held my hand in the taxi and apologised outside, there was still something unspoken between us, and there still is — but at least we're laughing again. I have a flashback to Carrie, last night — her sharp vodka breath in my face:

"You need to fuck off, Violet. You're a leech. A parasite. Fucking worming your way into my life. Into my pants . . ." She'd actually grimaced when she said that. "I don't know what the hell I was thinking. I fancied experimenting, but why the hell I chose you, I do not know."

Then she'd disappeared from the cabin and I hadn't seen her until she'd come back this morning, half an hour before we were due to arrive. Smelling of sex. She'd tossed things into her backpack in silence, and I'd gone through so many options in my head of what I could say to her, wound myself up so much, that I couldn't say a word.

160

Today she is subdued, and judging by the tremor in her hands, which she's trying to hide, I think she's coming down from something more than just the vodka.

I find my voice as she's turning the key in the door. A huge brass thing on a red leather fob. "Where did you go last night, Carrie? I missed you."

She sighs hard, and the door swings open, as if she has blown it in.

"Not now, V. I need a long soak in the bath. I need to sleep in a proper bed. I need some food. Jeez, when did we last have some food?"

"We had those cheese blinis . . ."

It's her turn to laugh now. "I think that was around twenty-four hours ago." She tosses her bag into the corner of the room. "Please, please can there be a bath? What time is it? Do you think Cruella de Vil downstairs will take pity and send us some room service?"

"I doubt it. But I can go and get us something as soon as the kitchen opens."

"Fuck's sake, V. You don't have to keep . . ." She lets the sentence trail off. "Forget it. I was being a bitch. Again. That would be great, obviously. I feel like I haven't slept in days." She looks at herself in the narrow mirror on the wardrobe door. Turns to the side, sucking in her stomach, pushing it out. Standing up straight, letting her shoulders sag. Then she turns back to the front and pulls her vest off over her head. There's a huge waft of B.O. with the movement, and I have to force myself not to gag. "I think I've lost weight." She sucks in her stomach again, then pushes out her breasts. "Oh fuck." She pulls at one of the cups of her bra, peers down, then unfolds it and stares at herself in the mirror, pulling a face. "That is rank." It's a large purple bruise, with teeth marks around the sides. "That fucking prick I shagged on the train has probably given me rabies." She yanks off her shorts then disappears through to the bathroom. "A bath," she shouts back. "Thank fuck." She slams the door.

I peel off my own dirty clothes and lie down on top of the covers of one of the single beds. The cover is shiny and floral. Polyester. Absolutely not safe in a fire. I listen to the sound of running water. Then I sit up, anxious. I can't relax right now.

The room is decent enough. Two beds, wardrobe, desk and chair. Sliding glass doors out to a small balcony. I unlock the doors and step outside, taking in the view: another building across the alleyway — the side of it though, just concrete, no windows. No one to see me here in my underwear. I look down and see nothing of interest. The alleyway doesn't seem to be used for much, with cracks running down it filled with proliferating weeds and random pieces of rubbish — cans, packets and who knows what else that people have thrown out of their windows. I close the doors and go back inside.

On the desk, there's a small leather stationery holder, with paper and envelopes with the name of the hotel and a logo stamped on them. Maybe this place isn't so bad. Maybe it was grand, once. I pull out the deep drawer beneath the desk and a small plink of excitement runs over my arms like goose bumps. A kettle, lots of tea and coffee — hot chocolate . . . I rummage further in the basket next to the cups and saucers . . . and find some biscuits. I never thought I'd be so excited for some home comforts, as basic as they might be. I give the kettle a little shake, to make sure there is some water in it — and thankfully there is, as I don't want to disturb Carrie right now — then I flick it on, and sit down in the chair to wait for it to boil.

There's a large lamp on the desk, one of those heavy-based ones with an elaborate shade. It's a bit out of place in the stark room, but I assume it harks back to a time when there might've been a few fancier things in here. Curtains, maybe. And less hazardous bedspreads. I pull the little gold chain and the room is basked in an amber glow. Relaxing, at last, I tip a hot chocolate sachet into a cup, and fill it with water. Just the smell of it makes me want to cry. I can't say that my mum ever brought me hot chocolate in bed as a child. I'm pretty sure I had to make it myself — but there is something comforting about it all the same. I associate it with reading with my glow-worm lamp and imagining myself in another place. I might've lived in a fancy old mansion, but it was a lonely place with just me, the neglected only child, and my parents, and I longed to go to a boarding school, like Mallory Towers in the books I loved to read. I wanted to be around other girls. I wanted to be part of something.

I pull the chain on the lamp again, flicking it off. Then on again. Off. I listen for the splashing sounds from the bathroom that tell me Carrie is still alive in there — you hear about these things, you know, when someone full of vodka, and who knows what else, gets into a hot bath. Because she definitely had something last night. She was wild, her eyes rolling around in her head. It was worse than the night at the shamanic festival, and that's saying something — although I was off my head then too, so it's not the same. I hope that whatever it was she took, we can get past that now — I don't want this to turn into one of those drug-fuelled trips that no one even remembers. There is such a lot that I want to remember. I flick the lamp back on again, then I go over to my bag and take out my phone.

Sam is on a beach. There's a selfie of him and one of his stupid mates drinking out of coconut shells. I enlarge the photo, looking for girls, and don't see any in close proximity. I click on the comments. "Top night, bro." "Sundowners at the Kiki Club, girls are HOT." There are a series of blazing-sun emojis on that one. I toss my phone onto my bed, and ball my hands into fists. Screw you, Sam. You predictable tosser.

I'm poking around in Carrie's bag, getting ready to have a look at her laptop, when I hear the click of the bathroom door unlocking and have to quickly rethink my plans. She comes out wrapped in a towel and smelling of something sickly and floral.

"Not sure what the shower gel is meant to be but I think I smell better than I did before I went in. My clothes are absolutely reeking. I'm soaking them in the bath. Want to chuck yours in?" Finally she spots what I've been doing. "Oh . . . what're you —"

"Thought you looked tired," I say, sliding a silky top onto one of the few hangers in the wardrobe. "I was

164

just unpacking for you. I know you packed in a bit of a hurry this morning . . ."

Her eyes flash with something that might be annoyance, but then her shoulders sag and I know I've got away with it. "Thanks, V. I am bloody tired. I felt myself drifting off in the bath, but I didn't want to be in there all night. You must be desperate for a wash too. Listen, thanks again for this. I think I'll just lie down for a bit, while you're in there. I think I've even gone past hunger."

"Let's see how you feel later," I say. I hope she has a nap, then changes her mind. I want to go out tonight, just the two of us. I feel like it hasn't been just the two of us for so long. I want to go somewhere nice. Have good food. Drink some wine, and talk . . . and talk . . . and get it all out there in the open. I want her to put her hand on mine, like she did that first night in the Irish Bar in UB. I want her to kiss me like that. Softly, full of promise. I want to forget about what happened at the camp. I want to forget about what happened on the train. I want us to start again. I know I pushed it too far, and I'm close to blowing it — but I can't let that happen. I can't give her a reason to not want to be with me anymore. We're only just beginning.

I look across at her as she lies on the bed, towel still wrapped around herself, and her face relaxed at last. I want to stroke her hair. I want to lie beside her. I want to touch that horrible love bite on her breast, and wish it away.

I want to curl in to her naked body.

I want to whisper in her ear, "I love you, Carrie."

165

But instead, I take the extra blanket from the wardrobe and lay it gently over her. Then I wait until I hear her soft snores, before I take her laptop out of her bag and lay it on the desk. And without making a sound, I carefully open the lid.

I'm not doing anything wrong. I just want to know more about her. Sometimes people don't tell you the whole story, they like to present the version of themselves that they want you to see.

But it's amazing what you can find out about a person from their deleted items folder.

To: lauralee@gmail.com
From: carrie82@hotmail.com
Subject: Never Drinking Again (NDA)

Writing this from bed in a random town in Russia. It's called Irkutsk and it's where all those poor fuckers got exiled to about a hundred years ago. Apparently there's a huge rate of depression and suicide in Siberia, and to be honest, from what I've seen so far it's not much of a shocker. Not that I have seen much, as the taxi journey was absolutely mental and I had my eyes shut most of the time, thinking we were going to die. Then the driver tried to take us to a different hotel and I was sure it was a scam, but now I'm not sure as this place is a bit shit. The view out of the balcony is the wall of another building, and I'm sure I can hear the sounds of wolves pacing and growling outside. Do they have wolves here? I don't actually know, but it's all just a bit shady and I realise we should've just gone to the bloody LAKE that people insist on telling us about all the time . . .

Siiiiiiigggggghhhh.

Anyhoo, how are you? Did you get my message from the Gobi? I've got a LOT more to tell you about what went on out there, but I'm still trying to process it all myself. I had a

167

reading (if that's what they call it) from a shaman (yeah I know), I have now planted an earworm — "Move Any Mountain" has been in my head ever since the word shaman was mentioned . . . and we did meet more than one, so I guess that means I have actually met the shamen . . . OK, not The Shamen. I wonder where they are now — do you think Mr C is still alive? I always fancied him in the 90s.

Fuck, I'm rambling. So we had some weird shit in the desert. Magic mushrooms in a pipe type shit. Some weird tea. I am ruined. Things went a bit mental with Violet, and then we were stuck on a train together for NINETY HOURS. But we survived . . . God. I'll go into it later. I'm still knackered. She's gone out somewhere — probably doing the bit of sightseeing that I'm not going to get round to, despite it being the entire reason for coming here and not the bloody lakes . . . but she did leave me a very nice breakfast: cheese and ham and bread and yogurt all wrapped up in a linen napkin.

I started to think we were going to have to go our separate ways, but I've had a kip, and I'm clean again after being a stinking cow for about five days, so maybe I'll just see it out with her to Moscow and then piss off after that. I've stuck rigidly to our plans up to now, for no reason other than I just wanted to do the trip we had spent so much time talking about — but maybe that's pointless, I don't know. I think I'll head to Germany after Moscow. I feel like I need some proper European reality for a while. Sausages and pretzels.

168

Btw, I wrote a couple of rambling messages to you when I was off my head, but thankfully I was still coherent enough not to actually send them — haha! Deleted now and never coming back. Hallucinogenics and vodka are not a good mix.

I need to come back home and go on a detox.

Love you lots — tell me all your news!

Cxxx

★ ★ ★

To: lauralee@gmail.com [DELETED]
From: carrie82@hotmail.com
Subject: Freeeeee

Oh, man. I don't know what was in that tea, but it has done mental things to me. I don't know if Violet even drank it. She totally freaked us all out anyway. I feel fuzzy. I keep looking at my hands on the keyboard as I type and they don't look like my real hands, they look like muppet hands -furry and fat and they seem to be moving by themselves, or else someone else is moving them. I keep getting stab-bing pains in my head and I have to close my eyes, and when I do remember all these things, all these memories just flash into my head and I can't make sense of them and I don't even know if I am dreaming or awake now and I don't even know if I am typing this at all or if I just think I

169

am. The desert is scary. It's empty and dry and there's this big fucking sky and these mountains and little lumps of things that look like moonrock and it just doesn't feel like anything is real anymore. The shamen were banging drums and throwing milk — yes, milk, I don't understand — and they said things to me that made sense and some of it didn't, but Violet . . .

Oh, Violet.

I am scared of her now.

I just want to come home. I'm not going to send this email. Forget it. Forget it. Forget it. I brought some stuff with me in a little bag and I've hidden it but I can't remember where.

★   ★   ★

To: sarah_and_dou9_0sborne@btinternel.co.uk
From: carrie82@hotmail.com
Subject: RE: Checking In!

Hello!

You're right, I was on the train when you emailed. There was reception now and again but I don't think all my messages were coming through. I'm having a great time! Obviously it's not the same at all without Laura, but I've made a new friend — she's called Violet, she's about my age. Comes from Nottingham but has lived all over. I think

170

her parents are super-rich from what she's been saying but she hasn't paid me for anything yet . . . aargh. I know, I know. I'm going to ask her for some money today. I don't really mind about the train ticket as I was resigned to losing that cash anyway, but she's quite good at evading the subject of cash! I know that sounds dodgy, but to be honest I just needed someone to hang about with — I was getting a bit lonely on my own, despite all my chat before I left saying it would be an adventure and that all women should travel on their own for the experience. I know you tried to talk me out of it, in your diplomatic way, but anyway, you and Dad can enjoy saying "I told you so" when I get back. Haha!

We are doing so many amazing things though — the train journey itself is a huge experience, but we've been in the Gobi Desert and ridden horses, we've been to a nomadic festival, drank sheep's and horses' milk (not as bad as you imagine), and now I am in Siberia — mental! I am looking forward to Moscow -I'll make sure I buy you the biggest Russian doll I can find (and now I have Kate Bush singing "Babooshka" in my head . . . hope you have too!)

Having a chill-out day today, catching up on emails and reading. Probably just have a quiet dinner tonight and then we're off on the train again tomorrow.

Rosie emailed me about her job — good news. I think I might look for something different when I get back. I've been a bit bored for a while, and I think this trip has opened my mind a bit (don't worry, I have not gone "all

NEW AGE" -I can actually hear Dad saying that right now when you read this out to him).

Love you lots,

Carrie xxxx

* * *

To: rosieposie1985@gmail.com
From: carrie82@hotmail.com
Subject: RE: news

Gypsy Rosalie!

I am in Siberia! Well done on the job. I am totally ditching mine when I get back. Life is too short for boring offices and that freak Danny who keeps bringing me peeled oranges with his fingerprints dented into the flesh. He is OBVI-OUSLY a serial killer trying to perfect his knife work (and he has a long way to go). Of course you can borrow the dress, my darling sister who has never ruined any of my clothes, ever (I assume you have already worn it -IT IS DRY CLEAN ONLY).

Cxx

P.S. I will bring you back one of those big hairy Russian hats with the ear flaps. You and Marcus can share it.

172

To: lauralee@gmail.com
From: carrie82@hotmail.com
Subject: RE: Freeeeee

I am trying so hard to be normal right now. Somehow I have managed to email Rosie and my parents and not sound like I am on the tail end of an epic bender, but Rosie probably knows even if I write two sentences. She's probably on the phone to Mum now, telling her they need to book me into rehab. So much crap is swirling around my head, Loz. It's like my brain has expanded, and all the memories I've kept locked up have pushed their way back to the surface and now they won't go away.

I keep thinking about school and all the stupid things we did. That I did. Do you remember when that new boy started in P7? I think his name was Keith, or Kevin or Keegan. Something like that. But remember when we all chased him in the playground, and the boys battered him and we threw stones at him until he cried? I can't believe we did that, Loz. I think about it all the time, and I think about where he is now, and I hope he's got a good, successful life and I hope he never thinks about that day and how we bullied him for no reason at all, other than he was new. Why are children so cruel? I don't think I'm cruel now, but I don't know.

I still need to tell you about Greg.

My head really hurts, and I'm shaking now. I'm fucked, Loz. I'm still coming down from that weird tea shit, and whatever it was that we smoked . . . and the vodka and the pills I took on the train. I've drunk four coffees but it's not helped. I just need something to take the edge off.

CHAPTER
TWENTY-THREE

Carrie didn't wake up at all last night, so I spent the time reading her emails, which was enlightening, to put it mildly. She's very trusting to leave her laptop lying around without a password, but then she's very trusting to allow a total stranger to share a room with her. These are things that people do when they're travelling — but you'd think when you passed the age of thirty that some of the naivety would disappear, along with the youthful roundness and flawless skin. Not that there's anything wrong with Carrie's skin. Quite the opposite. It's as smooth and pale as alabaster. She looks at least ten years younger than she is. It surprises me that she's so trusting in some ways, and yet so on the ball with other things — like knowing the currency and the costs and not letting us get ripped off. I've been ripped off a few times, but then I suppose, when you've never had to work a day in your life, never had to want for a thing, it's easy to play fast and loose with a few quid.

Just like my little game of not paying for anything.

I'm sure Carrie has realised by now that she's paid for all the accommodation, food and tickets since she met me, but she hasn't commented yet. Well, unless you include her drunken rant on the train. To be honest I'm getting a bit bored with the game now. I'll draw some money out and pay her back today.

I ate breakfast alone, which wasn't the plan, but Carrie barely stirred when I asked if she was getting up, so I suppose she needed that sleep after all. Being the good friend that I am, I took her up a little something from the dining room. Some bread, jam, ham, cheese and what I think was a raspberry yogurt — it was difficult to tell from the picture on the carton. The maid was on our floor when I left, and I asked her for a few extra coffee sachets and some fresh milk. Perhaps I'll take Carrie out for dinner tonight too, to say thank you for everything. Partly because I want to, but also because it will knock her off guard and give me the upper hand again. I sense she is starting to tire of me, and I'm not ready to move on just yet.

The street that our hotel is on is quite dull and grey, but a few streers on, heading towards what I think is the historic town centre, things start to brighten. The place is fairly quiet, on the whole, but I'm glad of a little downtime for a while. I can see the brightly coloured rounded turrets of a church in the distance and feel myself drawn towards it. There is something very beautiful about the over-the-top gaudiness of the Russian Orthodox churches. This one is called Kazanskaya Tserkov — and it looks like a cross between a gingerbread house and a children's painting of a castle, all red brick and green chequered turrets. I stop at the entrance and take a few photographs, but I decide not to go inside. The sun is shining, and I need to stretch my legs and blow away the cobwebs.

176

Carrie was interested in finding out about the Decembrists — those revolutionaries who were exiled to Siberia in the 1800s, but as I've no idea when she's likely to surface, I decide to visit the area myself and report back. It's not my fault that she slept in and missed the chance to do the only thing she came here for. I take out the map that I picked up from the surly receptionist, briefly checking that I am going the right way, and it's not long before I come across the streets filled with ramshackle wooden houses where they set up their new community, under much suspicion from the locals. It's interesting enough for a while — I try to imagine what it must've been like, although it's hard to believe that it's almost 200 years ago. But without anyone else to talk to about it, I get bored fairly soon. I'm not particularly interested in the history, but at least I can tell Carrie that I have been. For both of us.

Back in town, I pass another fancy church but I don't bother taking a photo of this one as it's not as impressive as the one that I already have many photos of. I'm craving some human interaction now, and I consider heading back to the hotel to see if Carrie has woken up yet, but then I see a sign for a market and decide to pop in there first. I didn't eat a huge amount for breakfast, spending more time wrapping up a pretty little parcel of food for Carrie — I hope she's eaten it and not let my efforts go to waste.

My thoughts today are uncharitable, and I feel irrationally irritated, for no real reason that I can put my finger on. Maybe it *is* time for me to move on. Perhaps Carrie isn't what I'm looking for after all. Or maybe I'm just feeling a bit out of sorts and in need of another adventure. I've always had a short attention span. I tend to spend a lot more time coveting what I think I want, than I do enjoying it when I have it. I used to beg my parents for things when I was younger, and they used to hold out for as long as possible, just to see me suffer. Then they'd relent, and I'd be fed up with whatever it was I had campaigned so hard to get: everything from the newest trainers, to fancy dresses, overnight stays in fancy places, and eventually a car. They bought me a pale-blue Saab 900, wrapped it in a red ribbon and left it on the driveway. I didn't even bother to learn to drive it. For reasons that no one could ever understand, my parents and I played a constant game of cat and mouse — with each of us taking turns in both roles. I suspect it was because we were all extremely bored. What's the point of getting all the things you want if you don't even have to make an effort?

The market turns out to be one of the covered, permanent types, in a huge building taking over an entire block. This seems to be where everyone in the town hangs around, as there are more people just at the multiple entrances, hovering around, smoking, chattering and doing nothing, than I have seen in any of the streets up to now. On a bench outside, a youngish man in a tracksuit sits swigging from a can of beer while jabbering away on his phone — at the other end of the same bench, an elderly woman is knitting. A small bottle of vodka rests on the ground next to her handbag. Behind them both is a kiosk, about the size of

178

two telephone boxes jammed together. It is glass fronted, and all that is on display is about five hundred different kinds of alcoholic spirit. On the counter itself are several different brands of beer, cans and bottles.

So this is what people get up to in Russia. The guidebook did suggest that drinking plays a significant part in their daily lives, but I hadn't expected it to be quite so blatant. But then, we are in the depths of Siberia. It's a nice enough day right now, but I hate to think what winter might bring.

As I enter the market, I am assaulted by the strong smell of fish. I walk quickly past the stalls with their frightening-looking underwater creatures — which I assume have come from the lake — and I'm subjected to many calls in Russian, presumably telling me which of their wares are the best and trying to get me to buy them. I head down another aisle and am smacked in the face with the intense aroma of cheese. I slow a bit here, and allow them to tempt me — taking small cubes on cocktail sticks and making appreciate noises. I don't buy anything. I pass the salivating scents of bread and cakes, the meaty stench of the butchery section, and then I get a strong hint of hops, and I follow my nose down a narrow aisle that leads to the prize.

A series of narrow aisles join a wider open area, where lots of men, of various ages, and a few women, are standing at high tables, drinking from plastic cups of beer. All around the tables are small stalls with one or two beer pumps, and some with snacks: blinis and pretzels and nuts and olives. The sounds of the chatter are echoed and magnified, and I glance up and realise

179

there is a huge glass-domed roof that wasn't visible from outside. I look around, and see that while I had initially thought that most people were here in groups, there are lots of people on their own too, some sharing tables, some looking like they want to chat and others not. For a moment, I wish that Carrie was here. She would be in her element. She'd be scouting around for the liveliest table, asking for recommendations for the best beers. She'd be in the thick of it. Not like me. Hanging back, those familiar feelings of being overwhelmed coming to the surface. I can hear my mum's clipped voice: "You're too dull to make friends. It's no surprise that they all get bored with you." I've tried though. I have. I shake my head, trying to get my mum's face out of my mind. Her patronising voice. What did she ever do with her life? Her friends are all fake, only sticking around for her over-the-top parties and her too-expensive gifts. She's bought all her so-called friends, and I don't want to be like her.

Thinking about money, I remind myself that I wanted some cash to take back to Carrie. There's a cash machine across the room and I head over and withdraw 50,000 rubles. I've no idea how much that is, but it'll do for now. I push the money deep into the pocket of my denim cut-offs, and head to one of the small bars. I frown at the pumps, not knowing which one to go for, and then something makes me turn around. That feeling when there's someone in your presence, a shift in the air that grabs your attention. He's at the next small bar, the one I had almost chosen before this one. His head is dipped, turned away from me, and I can't see his face, but suddenly I can't breathe.

It can't be.

"What you like?" The man behind my bar is holding a glass aloft, head cocked slightly. Waiting.

"I . . ."

I can't stop staring at the man at the next bar. It's something in the way he moves his head. The way he runs his hand through his thick, sandy hair. His hair was one of the first things I noticed — well cut and styled, but natural; not one of these stupid hipster haircuts full of wax and cream. The shape of his shoulders, too, and the perfectly sculpted arms, fitted perfectly into his T-shirt — not straining and bulging like those idiots who spend too long in the gym.

I'd stood behind him at the reception desk, waiting to check in. The man behind the counter was flustered and taking too long. He was serving a couple who seemed to be making a number of requests that he wasn't used to dealing with.

He was standing behind them, seemingly un bothered by the delay. Head bent slightly as he scrolled through his phone. He smelled of citrus aftershave and the underlying hint of coconut sun cream. I'd taken a couple of steps towards him, and I could see his phone screen though the gap in the bend of his arm. Pictures of him and friends. Active, happy people. I think he must've sensed me then, in his personal space, and had taken a step forwards, just as the harassed receptionist finished with the couple and beckoned him to the desk.

181

I'd stepped forwards too, but kept enough distance this time. I dropped my rucksack onto the floor and started to rifle through the top pocket, making it seem like I was busy looking for my passport or something.

"Miss — you want beer?" The man behind the pumps speaks loudly to me, as if he thinks I haven't heard him.

"I . . . uh." I shake my head and step away from the bar. Another man slides into my space and he and the bar man start talking in fast Russian.

The man at the next bar points to one of the pumps and the man behind the bar nods and starts pouring the beer. Dark liquid and a thick foamy head that spills over the sides. He slices the foam off the top with a long, flat knife and places it on the bar. The man with the sandy hair hands over a note and he must sense me staring, because he turns around to face me, and I feel a whoosh of relief. Of disappointment.

"All right?" he asks. Australian. Quite a bit younger than I'd thought. He lifts his pint up and says, "Cheers, then," and gives me a look that says he's not really sure what I am staring at him for. Then he walks away, and I watch out of the corner of my eye as he joins a table of similarly young travellers, all shorts and sunglasses and empty glasses all over the table.

It's not him. Of course it's not him. I checked his Facebook a few hours ago, and he was still in Thailand, so he's not likely to be here in Siberia now, unless someone has stolen his phone and is continuing his trip updates for him.

182

I start laughing. I can't help it. Then I have to pretend to look at my phone so that I don't look insane, and I go back to my little bar and point to the pump and drop a note on the bar, and smile . . . and take a huge drink of the beer, barely tasting it — enjoying the fizz as it burns down my throat.

"I'll have another," I say, pointing at the pump again. The man behind the bar says something I don't understand, and then he grins, and hands me my drink.

I'm shaking slightly, as the adrenaline leaves my body, and I walk over to a high table where two men are drinking and chatting expressively with loud voices and gesturing arms, and I say "Hi." Then, "*Dobryj den*" — which I memorised from the guidebook and I hope means "good afternoon". They glance at me, and then back at each other, and then back to me again.

"Hello, lady," the first one says. They look practically the same — dark hair, cut in the same, blocky style. They are both wearing tracksuits, which is what most of the younger men seem to wear.

"Another beer?" the other one says.

"*Da, spasibo*," I say. *Yes, thanks*.

They both laugh at this. "Your Russian is very good," the first one says.

I giggle at this, because it's what I think they expect. "That's about it," I say. The second one goes off to one of the little bars to get more beers, and I smile and try not to look like I feel — which is utterly out of my depth.

It was easy to talk to Sam, I realise now — but it felt almost impossible at the time. I glance around at the table where the Sam-lookalike sits with his friends, and I think about going over there, giving them my biggest grin. Trying to merge in with their plans. Act like I'm just like them.

But I can't.

Russian number two comes back with our drinks, and I know I've chosen this path now.

"*Za zdorov'e!*" says Russian number one. We all smash our glasses together, but they don't chink, because they're plastic. I take a long, slow drink. I can feel their eyes on me, so I smile. They grin back, and there's a hint of something else under the surface. Something dangerous. I like it.

Russian number two moves around the small table until his arm brushes against mine. "You want to go to party?"

"Fun party," says Russian number one. "We look after you." He points to his chest. "Sergei —"

"And Lev," the other one cuts in. They're both grinning, delighted with themselves for managing to ensnare me. Or so they think.

I drain my drink, and grin back. "Sure. Why not?"

CHAPTER
TWENTY-FOUR

I manage to convince my two new friends — Sergei and Lev — that I have to return to the hotel first, to freshen up, and also to collect my friend. Their eyes light up at the second statement, and I'm quite sure that Carrie and I are in for a wild night, in their eyes at least. They give me an address, and when I check the map on the way back to the hotel, I see that it's up in the area of the historic wooden houses. Carrie will get to see them after all. I'm feeling nicely buzzed from the beers and the compliments, and even though I have no intention of letting things go any further with either of these men, I feel a bit better than I did earlier.

Thoughts of Sam are pushed firmly to the back of my mind, for now, at least.

When I get back to the hotel, Carrie is up and dressed, and looking a lot better than she did this morning. I notice that she's unpacked my bag and hung everything up. I want to say something but I can't, because I did the same to hers, didn't I? A fleeting memory passes — something stuffed into the side pocket of my bag in the ger. Did she put something in there?

"Having a look through my stuff? Go for it, you won't find anything." I try to make it sound light, jokey, but from the expression on her face, I don't think I've succeeded.

She recovers quickly. "I was just doing you a favour, V. Like you did for me. It's nice to hang everything up once in a while, to let the creases fall out. This room has the most coat hangers I've ever seen." She turns away, and stuffs something into her make-up bag. I decide not to question it.

"Maybe they get lots of customers wearing dresses."

She laughs at that. "Ladies of the night, you mean? I guess that would explain why the receptionist seems to be studiously avoiding looking anyone in the eye. I went down and asked her for some Coke, and she got quite flustered. Although the non-liquid kind might've been welcome when I finally managed to get myself out of bed. I had the shakes so bad I could've churned butter from a carton of milk."

She must've been on more than vodka on our last night on the train. There's no way she'd have got in that state otherwise. But then again, there was a lot of vodka, and not a lot of anything else. We're probably both lucky we didn't die of alcohol poisoning. Carrie's lost weight since we first met. Drinking more than eating will do that to you.

"Well, if you're up to it, we've been invited to a party tonight. Up at the wooden houses."

"Oh, cool. If you'd come back and said this a few hours ago, I'd have told you where to go, but actually, yeah. Why not? Whose party is it?" She wanders over to

186

the dressing table and lays her make-up bag down, then picks up a powder compact, starts dabbing her face with the little sponge. She looks at me in the mirror. "Where have you even *been*?"

I shrug. "I went for a wander around town. Saw some fancy churches. Went to the houses. Saw some old cars. Then I ended up in this market . . . oh God, I nearly forgot — I saw this guy and I thought it was Sam —"

"Please tell me you're not still thinking about Sam. Jeez, V. You weren't thinking about him much at the festival . . . or on the train."

I stand beside her and pick up a mascara. "You're going to bring this up now?"

"When, then?"

"I think you made it pretty clear that you're not interested." She picks up a black eyeliner, starts expertly running it across her lids. Her hand is steady and the line is neat. I have never been able to do it like that. She places the eyeliner back down, then rummages in her make-up bag and a small, plastic wrapper slides out. She grabs it quickly and looks away, but I've already seen what it is.

"Fucking hell, Carrie. You brought that over the border?"

She won't look at me. "Forgot I had it."

I grab her shoulders and spin her around to face me. "What do you mean, you forgot you had it? You took that from the tent — the one we were in before the private ritual? Was it not bad enough at the time? Jesus, why would you want to take it again? Where did you even hide it?" I understand then. She'd hidden it in my bag. It would've been me who'd been arrested if it'd been found, not her. I'm fuming, but I'm also quite impressed at her clever move. I decide to store this information for later.

"Don't say it's been in your make-up bag all the time, because I don't believe you. That's exactly the kind of place the border guards would look."

"Yeah, well they didn't look, did they? I distracted them. I told them you were ill."

I'm confused by this. I can't even remember the border crossing. I'm sure I didn't wake up — but the guards must've come into the cabin. Surely they've heard all the tricks before. She's a decent liar, it seems. Well, well.

"They like pretty white girls, V. Hardly a shocker. I made sure the stuff was hidden and I didn't involve you. I thought you'd be pleased. You know what happened last time we smoked that stuff."

I've really tried hard to stay calm, throughout everything, but I can feel the anger bubbling in me now. "Stop it, Carrie. Stop playing with me. Everything's just a big game to you, isn't it? You gave Rory the come-on then you blocked him at the final stage. You're messing about with me, and you think it's OK because it's just a bit of fun, but I'm telling you now, this is not that. This is more than that —"

"Christ, Violet. Keep your hair on. I'm sorry, OK? I shouldn't have brought it. I shouldn't have messed with your feelings, either. I never meant to. I just thought that —"

188

"Don't you get it?" I scream at her. I want to grab her and shake her. Her eyes widen at my raised voice and she sits down hard on the end of her bed.

"Violet —"

"No. You need to get it, Carrie. You need to understand."

She closes her eyes. "Understand what?"

"I love you, Carrie."

She falls back onto the bed. "No, you don't, Violet," she says, gently. She flips onto her side and faces me. "You just think you do, because it's all been so intense. We've been in each other's pockets since we met. You know, I've been thinking . . ." She pauses, sits up again, swinging her legs back round off the bed. "I think maybe we should go our separate ways after this. You need to carry on with your trip how you want it, and I —"

Tears spring to my eyes, making them itch. "No. Please. That's the last thing I want." I take a few deep breaths, trying to calm myself down. I don't want to do this. I don't want to sound desperate, or make a fool of myself. "This is just like what happened with Sam. I can't believe I've been used and let down again."

Carrie sighs. "Look, you're blowing this all out of proportion. Let's go to the party. Have a laugh." She comes over to me and puts an arm around me, squeezing me into her side. "We've had so many laughs. We've made so many memories. Let's not spoil it though, eh?"

I swallow down salty tears, then I nod. I don't want her to see me like this. I want to be the fun, sexy Violet that she's been hanging out with.

"Come on then," I say. "Let's go." If I've only got one night to convince her that we should stay together, then I need to sort myself out fast. "You know, I think I've got PMT."

She laughs, then grabs her bag, and heads for the door.

I follow her, because that's what I always do. She can kick me as many times as she likes, and I'll still want her. I'll still love her. Won't I?

The thumping bassline leads us to the right door. I knock, hard, but I don't expect anyone to hear it. I'm about to tell Carrie we should just go in, when the door swings open and the smiling bulk of Sergei stands in the doorway. He's holding a bottle of Baltika lager in one hand, and a cigarette in the other.

"Ladies . . . you made it." He seems genuinely pleased, even more so when he clocks Carrie, standing a little behind me, hidden in the shadows. She steps out into the light and his eyes seem to darken immediately. He grins wider, looking her up and down. "This is your friend? Hello, friend," he says.

"I'm Carrie," she says, stepping forwards and taking the cigarette out of his fingers. She takes a drag, then blows a perfect smoke ring into his face.

He turns to me. "I like your friend."

Carrie follows him into the house, and I follow her.

190

The house is packed with people, lots of men lounging on chairs in tracksuits, and ridiculously glamorous women in tight dresses and high heels, faces Botoxed and made up like drag queens.

Carrie turns to me and raises her eyebrows, and I'm glad that we're still bonded over this. We are not like these women.

The women are drinking champagne, or vodka shots. Sergei disappears into the crowd, but we keep walking, looking for a place to sit, or even just a place to stand. I feel overwhelmed, all of a sudden. Despite the things we've done already on this trip — the people we've met — the situations we've been in, when it comes to something like this, I clam up and I need guidance, or else I have the urge to flee back to safety, where I don't have to try to fit in. Luckily, Carrie steps up to the challenge. She grabs my hand and drags me through gyrating bodies.

She turns to me, grinning. "Thank fuck you made us come out," she shouts. I can barely hear her above the din. She jostles us past various party-goers, some dancing, some huddled in groups, shouting into each other's ears. A thin girl with long dark hair almost as long as her buttock-skimming dress is gyrating against a fat man in a grey tracksuit, who looks old enough to be her dad.

Eventually, we find the kitchen, where people are huddled around worktops littered with bottles and cans. A couple of people are in a corner, squashed close together, leaning down, heads together. The woman lifts her head and turns to me, wiping her nose. She glares at us, then the man lifts his head, and she looks at him and tips her head back and laughs. They move apart just enough for me to see the granite chopping board in the space behind them, two silver straws sitting there next to a credit card and their one remaining line.

"Here." I spin around at the sound of Carrie's voice, and she holds out a champagne glass, filled with pale liquid — bubbles still fizzing up to the top. "Cheers," she says, and downs her drink. Then she picks up the bottle from where she's left it nearby, and tops up her glass. Downs it again.

"Steady," I say. "We've only just got here."

She laughs, and gestures around the room, using the bottle as a pointer. "We've got a bit of catching up to do."

I finish my drink, and I'm about to say something else, when I feel strong arms grabbing me around my waist. I try to squirm free, but I'm trapped.

"Hey there," he whispers in my ear. "It's Lev. Remember?"

He releases his grip and I wriggle free, turning to face him. "Hi."

He lets me go and takes a step back. "Oh, not so much fun tonight, maybe? I think your friend is having all the fun though."

I turn back to see Carrie laughing hard, swigging from the champagne bottle. Sergei has a meaty arm draped over her shoulders, and he is leaning in, whispering in her ear. He's stroking her cheek.

192

A burst of annoyance pops inside me. Why can't she just be here with me? Why does there always have to be a fucking man involved in her fun? Does she have so little self-esteem that the only way she can enjoy herself is to have male attention? I think back to the Gobi trip, and how she led Rory on — all for her own amusement. He was all mouth, when it came to it — all over her but not brave enough to see it through and make a proper move. I watch Sergei, at the way he is hulking over her, and I think she'd better be careful. I don't think he's going to be a fan of her little games.

I snatch up a bottle of lager from a cooler box on the worktop and take a long drink. Lev has gone. Disappeared into the crowd — I was clearly not up for the kind of fun he had in mind, and to be honest I'm glad he's left me to it.

When I turn back, Carrie has gone.

Panic washes over me for a moment. I don't want to be here. My heart thumps in time with the bassline that's still pulsing through from the other room. I should go back to the hotel, forget this place. Leave Carrie to it. I don't like the way she's trying to play my emotions — one minute my best friend, the next she's off with whoever takes her fancy. Why am I not enough for her?

Why am I not enough for anyone?

I down the beer and take another one from the cooler, then I wander back through to the main room, where all the action is happening. Maybe I should go with Lev — he's keen enough for us both. But there's something about this place, this party, the whole set-up, that makes my insides itch.

I hover on the edges, observing with disgust. Why are these girls so interested in these hideous men? I don't believe that they can't find any better options. Sergei and Lev are far from the worst here, but I'm just not feeling it. I take another mouthful of beer then push myself through the crowd. I spot Carrie on the other side of the room, near the DJ. She's huddled close to Sergei and I can't make out if they are kissing or doing drugs as I can only see the backs of their heads. An angry-looking, harshly bleached blonde elbows me out of the way as I walk further towards Carrie and Sergei, and I feel a rush of blood threatening to burst out. I need to get Carrie and get the hell out of here.

"Hey." I touch her shoulder, and she turns slowly to face me, and then I see what she's doing.

"Oh, hi," she says, the "i" long and drawn on her smoky outbreath. "Have some."

She thrusts the small pipe into my face, and I snatch it away, peering at the lit end, not believing what I'm seeing.

"What the fuck? Didn't we just talk about this?" My cheeks burn with fury. How could she do this — it could've been both of us banged up in some Asian prison, not just her. She snatches the pipe back from me and rolls her eyes.

"Jesus Christ, lighten up, bitch."

Sergei laughs, and I feel the rage boiling deeper inside me.

"Carrie, this is insane. Don't you remember what this stuff did to us?"

It's her turn to laugh. "Not really, V. But I think it was something good, yeah? Anyway, thought you'd be pleased. I had to suck both of the guards' cocks to get this stuff over the border without a fuss. You're so fucking ungrateful." She turns away, and her and Sergei start laughing again. She whispers something in his ear, and then he leans across to the DJ, moving the guy's headphones and cupping his hands around his ear.

"Fuck you, Carrie."

I push through the crowd again and this time it feels like I am shoving hard through crashing waves. Faces swim at me, laughing, drinking, kissing. Voices saying words I don't understand. I see the woman who pushed me, and I push her hard out of the way. I hear shouts of "you fuckeeing beetch" as I ignore the cacophony and stumble through the room, desperately searching for the way back out. I see Lev lurching towards me, and I have to dodge past a couple who are practically having sex against a bookcase in the corner of the room. I slide round the edges, until I find the door, ignoring the calls, ignoring Carrie's voice in the distance, coming towards me, somewhere above the din, as I realise now what the DJ is playing.

It's my song. "Violet" by Hole. Courtney Love is shrieking her beautiful, grungy tones, telling me to take everything — she wants me to.

I think that might be my problem. I *do* want everything. But I can't always get it.

To: carrie82@hotmail.com
From: lauralee@gmail.com
Subject: You're freaking me out!!

Fucksake, Caz! I hope you've come down from whatever that shit was you were taking, and I REALLY hope you didn't find your stash. Maybe Violet took it? I think you need to lay off the drink and the partying for a while. I think you're right to be thinking about leaving Violet too — she doesn't sound like a good person, Caz. Or, at least, she's not doing you any favours. I've seen you like this before, remember? But that was a long time ago and you seemed to have really sorted yourself out, and now it's going a bit mental again . . . Maybe you should come home? It doesn't matter about the rest of the trip. If it's not doing you any good, then sack it off and come back.

OK, I know you don't want to talk about Greg, and that's fine with me. You need a new job too — I know you weren't happy before you left. But just come home, and we can sort you out, OK? I'm worried about you over there.

I do remember Keith, actually. You obviously don't remember what I told YOU about him. He left our school when he was fifteen and got sent to a boy's home — juvie, or whatever you call it. He burned his house down . . . his

196

mum nearly died. There was a big article about him — all about the things he'd done as a kid. There was something wrong with him, Carrie. You didn't bully him. He hurt us, and we tried to get him back. You seem to have stored this a bit differently in your head — or maybe the drugs and the trippy shamanic thing just made you mix things up.

Sometimes, people are just bad apples.

You're not the bad one, doll.

But I think you need to come home.

Lxxx

★　★　★

To: lauralee@gmail.com
From: carrie82@hotmail.com
Subject: dffdijingfig

Ohhhhhhh shit. At a eird party, dunno whatshapening. This bloke wantstofuckme. Violet is being a mental. I don feel good.

Wishouy were here . . . xxxxxxx

CHAPTER
TWENTY-FIVE

The walk back to the hotel passes in a blur. A blur of tears, humiliation and anger. I thought I was getting to know Carrie, but I don't know her at all. Not only did she push me away, but she laughed at me, and made the others laugh at me, too. The song is still swirling around in my head. My song, spoiled now, by her. Carrie screaming it across the room. Laughing. Smoking. I felt like I'd been stabbed in the heart. The last thing I saw was her face, pink and sweaty, hair plastered to her forehead, mouthing the song lyrics at me. Sergei laughing, arm around her neck. Saying something in Russian, and the other men laughing.

Then she disappeared. Sucked back into the crowd.

The other men tried to get me to stay, but they were rough-looking, wearing tracksuits, drinking too many beers. Chattering and nudging each other. Staring at me with hunger in their eyes. I know what they wanted. They smelled wrong. It felt wrong. They called my name, tried to get me to stay — and for a moment I worried that they would try to stop me from leaving, but they gave up pretty quickly. There were plenty of other girls there to entertain them. Girls in short, tight dresses. Too much hairspray, and no time for the likes of me. Carrie seemed to fit in with them better — she is like a chameleon; she can adapt to any environment, get on with whoever she's with: the old folks on the train, the Mongolian farmers, and now these people. These people that I don't trust at all.

I don't even care where she is now.

The streets are quiet, eerie. This is not a town filled with revellers. I wish I could grab my stuff now, and jump on a train out of here, but I know there are no trains tonight. I think back to our arrival, my time in the market where I had fun, felt alive. I'd been so excited about the party.

I pass a café that still has its lights on, but there is no one inside. I'd like to sit somewhere on my own, have a drink. Maybe try and speak to the person working in there. Someone who hasn't humiliated me. The people in the market were friendly, but the ones at the party weren't. They might've been, if they hadn't been taken in by Carrie.

Like I've been.

I should've known it was too good to be true — meeting her like that, having her bring me along on this trip. Who does that? Impulsive people? I'd always thought I was impulsive — ready for anything, excited by new experiences — but Carrie is something else. She's used me up and spat me out.

I wander the streets for a long time, trying to calm down. I lose all track of time, as things rattle around in my head. Taunting me. I lose my bearings, ending up in several unfamiliar streets, but I keep going and somehow I find myself back at the hotel. I glance down the alley, and I pause for a moment, thinking that someone is down there. A noise. Did someone cry out? I take a step closer, but it's too dark. There are no lights from the balconies. I shake my head. A fox, maybe. Or a wild dog. It's late, the sky already changing hue as the sun starts its ascent. I need to get inside. I need to sleep.

The receptionist doesn't lift her head as I walk past. She has headphones in, and I can see the flickering light of a TV show reflecting back from her computer. I take the stairs instead of the lift, trying to prolong the journey. I don't expect Carrie to be in there. I don't care if she is or she isn't. First thing tomorrow, I'm out of here.

I hear the voices before I get to the door. Muffled grunts, the *thump, thump* of the bed post against the thin partition wall. I can't tell yet if it is coming from our room or not. I pause outside the door for a moment, dredging my keys from the bottom of my bag. I am completely sober now. Any happy buzz I'd felt from the drinks I'd had early on at the party are long gone, and now all I want to do is curl up in bed and go to sleep. If that noise is coming from the room next to us, hopefully I can block it out with a pillow over my head.

The scream comes as I turn the key in the lock. I freeze. What do I do now? If someone is being hurt, then I should help them. But what if I'm wrong. Was it a scream or was it a cry of pleasure? And which room is it coming from? I push open the door, and then I realise.

200

It's coming from our room.

Carrie is lying face down on the bed, her face towards me. The man is on top of her, unbuckling his jeans. Pressing down on her. She cries out again, and I know for sure it's a scream, not a cry of pleasure. Her eyes find me there and widen as big as saucers.

"Violet . . ." she whispers.

"Shut up," the man says. "You want me to hit you again, you filthy bitch?"

My heart is thumping hard now, and I feel like I might throw up.

Carrie tries to shake her head, to signal that it's OK, but I know it isn't. But I also know that the man hasn't seen me yet. He's too engrossed in what he's doing.

The red mist descends. I have been on my best behaviour. I have let her take centre stage. I've reined myself in, tried to be who she wanted me to be. But I can't maintain this facade now. Not when this is happening right in front of my eyes.

Her eyes plead. *Don't come in. Don't get involved.*

He's up on his knees now, pinning her with one arm, holding his bulging cock with the other. She's stopped struggling. She closes her eyes.

He still hasn't seen me. I walk slowly into the room, glad that I am wearing flat shoes — good drinking shoes, I think, with a smile. They make no sound on the lino floor. I pick up the lamp from the desk and carefully pull the plug from the wall. I notice there's a bottle of vodka sitting there that wasn't there before. I hesitate. Bottle or lamp?

Lamp.

He's back on her now, grunting. Thrusting. Her eyes are now tightly closed, and he has. one hand around her neck. I watch for a moment longer and then I raise my arm — the lamp is not as heavy as I thought, or perhaps adrenaline really does give you superhuman strength.

His breathing is faster now. His grunts are like the squeals of a disgusting fat pig.

But he's not a pig. He is a wolf. A predator. And no matter what Carrie has done to me, I will not allow this to happen.

I take another step, and Carrie's eyes fly open as I bring the base of the lamp down on the back of his head. Again. Again.

Again.

Carrie screams, and I throw myself onto the bed, pushing him off her onto the floor. I put a hand over her mouth. Blood is still coursing through my veins.

"Shhh," I say. "You have to be quiet."

Her eyes dart to the side, and I see what she can see.

He's moving. Trying to pull himself up. He puts a hand to the back of his head, then looks at it quizzically. There's a lot of blood, but head wounds tend to be like that.

Carrie opens her mouth to scream once more, and I launch myself back towards him, lamp in hand. I hit him in the face this time, and he staggers back, tripping over his own feet. Out of the open door and onto the balcony. He is trying to speak, but only bubbles of blood come from his mouth.

Carrie grabs hold of my T-shirt from behind.

"Stop," she says. "Stop!"
But I can't.

To: carrie82@hotmail.com
From: lauralee@gmail.com
Subject: RE: dffdiiingfig

Carrie . . . email me back, please.

I don't even understand your last email.

I'm worried about you!!

Lxx

★ ★ ★

To: carrie82@hotmail.com
From: sarah–and–dou9–osborne@btinternet.co.uk
Subject: Just your mother!

Hello Darling,

Just a quick one as I know you're busy gallivanting. Dad was wondering if you were thinking about getting a new car when you come home — Maurice at the office is selling a lovely little Fiat.

Check in soon, please? We miss you!

Lots of love,

Mum and Dad xx

CHAPTER
TWENTY-SIX

When I wake up, there is a brief moment when I think that everything is the same as it was yesterday. I lift my head slowly, and it feels fuzzy and heavy, and a pulsing starts behind one eye. I wince, dropping my head back on to the pillow.

"Carrie? Are you awake?" I turn my head towards her bed, but it's empty. Not just of her, but of her sheets, duvet and pillows too.

I turn back, close my eyes. I take a long, slow breath, in through my nose. Trying to calm my heart, which has started to thump hard in my chest. The usual smells of the room have gone, replaced by the sharp tang of bleach.

Shit.

I sit up fast, and regret it immediately. My head spins, and I feel myself lurching to the side. I have to hold on to the sides of the narrow single bed to stop myself from falling onto the hard, tiled floor.

"Carrie?"

I call her name again, hoping that the memories slotting into place inside my drink-addled brain are dreams. Nightmares. Not something that really happened. Drinking that vodka was a mistake, but I was never going to be able to sleep otherwise.

Slowly now, to prevent the spins, I climb out of bed and take in the room. The floors are sparkling clean, all my stuff is bundled onto the chair next to the wardrobe. I see a strappy pink vest top that I know is Carrie's, and have a brief moment of hope. But it's a waste of energy. My shoulders slump and I sit back down on the bed. There's only one rucksack leaning against the wall now. One pair of boots next to it.

Carrie is gone.

I'd like to just stay in bed now, forget about it all. It's not long until I can get the train out of here, keep going with the journey. I'll have to buy a new ticket of course, but I don't think I have any other choice now.

The clock under the TV says it's 12:43. The train to Moscow left at 9.37.

Carrie is long gone. Off to Moscow alone, after all we've been through. It was obvious last night that she felt nothing for me. I gave her my friendship. My love. But it was nothing to her.

My head buzzes from the sleeping tablet that I washed down with the vodka, only a few hours ago. I'd been too wired to sleep after what happened with Sergei. Most of the memory is intact, but there are parts that are blurred at the edges. I should feel more, I know this. But I suspect the drugs are taking that from me too, and I'd prefer if it stayed that way, for now, at least. I need to deal with the practicalities before I deal with the emotions.

A quick glance around and it's clear that he's made a decent job of cleaning the room, but I suppose it's his job. Or one of them, at least. He'll be on his way to Moscow now too, I assume. Six-hour flight, he told me. Incredible that this country is so vast.

And I am here alone.

Calling Ivan last night was an impulse decision. A risk. When he'd handed me his card in the taxi and told me to contact him for anything I needed, I'd assumed he meant sex. But as it turns out, he's much more versatile with his services. He was more than happy with my roll of emergency dollars too.

I wander out onto the balcony and peer down at the alleyway behind. There's a large, dark stain directly beneath me, but it looks like it could be anything: water from a leaking drain, oil from a clapped-out engine. So far, no one seems to have noticed it.

Why would they?

I head back inside, leaving the balcony doors open to air the room. I imagine the cleaners will be surprised at how spotless the place is.

Perhaps I should tell them not to come in.

I planned to check out today, but I'm going to have to stay for another night at least. I hope Carrie settled the bill.

I throw on cut-offs and Carrie's vest, pick up my shoulder bag with the guidebook inside, and head down to reception.

The receptionist, as usual, is plugged into headphones, glued to the TV.

I have to bang my hand on the desk to get her attention, and she jumps slightly, then just looks pissed off.

"Yes." It's not even a question.

"Did Carrie . . . did the other girl check out already?"

"Your friend, yes. Very early. Walked out fast. Didn't pay."

"She didn't pay when we checked in?"

The receptionist shakes her head. "Didn't pay. You pay, OK?"

"I need to draw out some cash."

She makes a *pfft* sound through her teeth and sits back down. Headphones are in, face turned back to the screen. She doesn't want to know, or she is used to pretending not to care.

Damn it.

Looks like I'm going to have to start paying my own way again. I pull out my purse and riffle through the contents. A few notes left. I've no real idea what I've done with the money I withdrew yesterday. I think I might've given Ivan some of that cash too. I'm starving, and my head is fuzzy, and I think the only thing I can do right now is get myself something to eat and drink, then think about what I'm going to do next.

The market is quieter than yesterday, and I'm glad. I don't really want to start drinking beers with strangers at this point. I head through to the stalls I'd passed yesterday, selling meats and cheeses, and find one further into the maze, where people are sitting outside drinking coffee and eating from plates filled with salami, and boiled eggs and hard rolls. A young woman with a ponytail so severe that her eyes seem to be stretched wide is tapping on her phone, sipping her coffee. I gesture to her table and try to tell the stout, motherly woman behind the counter that I'd like the same.

I sit down at the table opposite the ponytailed woman, and she glances up briefly, then frowns, and looks back down at her phone. I'm not really bothered. I'm not looking for a new friend today. I'm still in shock, after last night and the way things ended with Carrie. I still can't believe that she's actually gone.

I'm still trying to keep the events of last night at the back of my mind, because if I let them affect me now, I know I won't be able to cope. There's definitely still alcohol in my system, mixed with the remnants of the sleeping pill; it's clouding my mood. I roll up a piece of salami and pop it into my mouth, then I stir milk and sugar into my coffee and take a sip.

My mother always said I was cold, but I like to think that I'm just good at compartmentalising. I had to be. Besides, if anyone was cold, it was her. I'm not sure she was given the "show your emotions" gene; I think it skipped a generation, because I have no such issues. I can control my emotions, sure, I suppose that's where the compartmentalising comes in. I can put things into their separate boxes, and only deal with what I need to. Right now, I need to deal with my plans for what happens after this. As long as I am out of the hotel room, I can keep the box with last night's nightmare safely locked away.

210

I finish my food and coffee. The young woman still hasn't looked up from her phone, and her food remains mostly untouched. For a brief moment, I wonder what her story is — why is she here alone, why has she ordered food and not eaten it, who she is texting with so frantically — her expression fixed and stony, giving nothing away. I thank the woman at the counter and disappear back into the maze of the market. I spot the cash machine that I used yesterday and, realising that I actually do need to start paying for everything myself now, I head towards it.

The machine takes its time, whirring away, and then a message pops up on the screen. It's in Russian, because I hadn't bothered to change the language at the start, confident that I would be able to work my way through it as I did before. But now I don't know what it's saying. Annoyed, I stab at the red button to cancel the transaction and start again, but then the whirring starts again, and another message appears. Frowning, I wait for my card to appear in the slot, but it doesn't. I press the red button again, and now the screen changes back to the home screen — the logo of the bank, and the images of the different types of cards accepted: Visa, Mastercard, American Express.

Shit.

I pull my backpack off my shoulders and grab my purse, pulling out another card. I shove it into the slot and silently pray that I know the pin for this one. It's not my usual card and I usually just tap it on contactless readers. I scour my brain, trying to visualise the four numbers. *Incorrect pin*. I try another one,

211

swapping round the third and fourth, but no luck. I don't try again for fear of this card being swallowed up too.

My mind starts to race, my limited options whirling round like a Roulette wheel. I have several other cards, but I'm going to come up with the same issues unless I can remember the pins . . . but, yes. Thank God! I slide all the cards out of the little wallet and find the folded piece of paper at the back. I know it's stupid to have all the pin codes in the same place as the cards, but I'm very careful with my stuff and I've never been mugged yet. I have the list of pin codes with a little symbol beside each one that only means something to me — anyone who did try to work out which was for which card would lose the cards to the machine before they did. I run a finger down the crumpled piece of paper, until I find the one I'm looking for — there's a tiny stick-drawing of a crab, and I smile at my own ingenuity at this foolproof reference system.

I take out another card and slide it into the machine, then I tap in the pin. My heart does a little leap in the split second before it takes me to the next screen, and then I quickly type in the maximum withdrawal limit and hold my breath while the machine clicks and whirrs and counts my cash. Part of me is surprised that this card is still working — I'd assumed it would have been cancelled long ago.

I leave the market, not wanting to repeat yesterday's performance. I need new pickings today. There's a decent-looking bar on one of the streets off the square. I need something to take my mind off things.

Something, or someone. Preferably someone with no links to Sergei or Lev.

A woman in a strappy floral dress is leaning against the wall outside the bar, smoking. She eyes me up and down, then turns away. Not her then. I go inside. I won't stay long, I tell myself. There's nothing to worry about. Ivan has sorted everything for me. Carrie is gone, but I am safe. I can relax.

It's just a couple of drinks to take the edge off.

Messenger

TO: Laura [04:59]

Something's happened. I need to speak to you. Please pick up!

. . .

[One missed call 05:00]

. . .

TO: Laura [05:02]

PLEASE pick up!!!!

. . .

TO: Carrie [06:32]

Call me now, I'm here! Why are you using Messenger? You said you couldn't use Messenger because someone was bothering you on there???

. . .

TO: Carrie [06:40]

I'm here now! Don't leave me hanging!!

. . .

[One missed call 06:42]

[One missed call 06:45]

[One missed call 07:05]

[One missed call 07:18]

. . .

TO: Carrie [07:30]

Carrie — please call me! Or just message . . . Let me know you're OK?

. . . [One missed calf 07:56]

[One missed call 08:31]

. . .

TO: Laura [09:01]

Check your work email.

CHAPTER
TWENTY-SEVEN

A blindingly bright light wakes me up, the harsh rays slicing through my eyeballs and a piercing sharp laser beams directly into my skull.

"You go now. I work, OK?"

I blink, trying to stop a multitude of stars from flashing in front of my eyes, trying to focus on whoever is standing in front of the window, silhouetted by the sun. It takes me a moment to realise that there is no balcony. I sit up too quickly and my head spins. The sheet that's covering me slips down, and I realise three things, all at once: I'm naked, I'm not in the hotel, and I have no idea where I am.

"Fuck," I mutter. My voice is a rasp. My throat burns. "Could I have some water, please?"

The figure walks towards me, bottle outstretched. The man is fully dressed, suit trousers and a crisp white shirt. He has a handsome face and neatly gelled dark hair. He's not like any of the Russian men I've met so far.

I've no idea who he is.

I take a greedy gulp of the water. It's cold, and soothing as it flows down my throat. I pause, then take a couple of slow sips. I'm trying to buy time, trying to work out what I'm doing here, and whether I can somehow get back to the hotel, where I want to curl up in bed and forget that the last few days have happened.

He picks up a jacket and slides his arms into it, and I notice them bulge against the unyielding fabric of his shirt. He glances around the room. "This place is shithole. I drive you home."

I sit up further, pulling the sheet up to hide my nakedness. Judging by the chafed feeling between my legs and my raw, stinging nipples, I'm pretty sure he's seen it all already. Unless there was someone else on this mattress with me. At the moment, I'm not willing to place any bets.

He tosses a pile of clothes at me, and I hastily pull them on. Wafting the sheet releases the fetid stink of dried bodily fluids, and I have a sudden urge to vomit, but I manage to hold it back and finish getting dressed.

He mutters various things in Russian as he walks through the flat, me trailing behind him like a lost puppy. He's right. The place is a shithole. Paint is peeling off the walls, the floors are mostly bare or partly covered with dirty, fraying rugs. There's a stale, musty smell throughout, a mixture of mould, spilled drinks and old smoke. I have to breathe through my mouth, taking small, shallow breaths until we reach the fresh air outside.

"Whose flat is this?" I ask, at last, as if it has only just occurred to me. In truth, I've been racking my brains since I woke up. As for my suited saviour — I don't even know his name.

He turns round, and sneers. "You don't remember?"

I say nothing.

"We met in bar. You were with other men. I helped you. This place . . ." He sighs. "My brother owns this place. It's not nice place, but you said no hotel."

"What about *your* place?"

He holds up his left hand, and his gold ring sparkles in the sun.

"Fuck's sake," I mutter. I'm about to say more, but he's already in the car. I climb into the passenger seat, and I'm considering asking him more questions, when his phone rings.

He hesitates for a moment, then swears under his breath and picks up the phone. I look out of the window as he starts the car and pulls out of the gravel driveway, yammering away on his phone in rapid-fire Russian. I don't pick up any of the words, but the tone is clear, from the tinny voice on the other end, someone — a female — isn't happy. He ends the call then throws the phone into the central console, accelerating onto the main road, swerving around other cars. They are all driving too fast, weaving in and out, and I feel a wave of nausea hit me again. I swallow back bile and cling on to the seat.

Maybe it would do everyone a favour if I died right now.

I consider grabbing the steering wheel and ploughing us into the path of a lorry, and the thought of it triggers a memory that I've tried hard to supress.

Six months before. Pondicherry, India. Faded French colonial grandeur with hordes of people sleeping rough in the middle of the streets. So pretty, everyone told

218

me. Fine if you don't go out alone. Don't go out at night. It had been fascinating watching how people travelled around there — open-backed trucks stuffed full with men, old British cars, clapped out but still full of charm. Tuk-tuks. Motorcycles with Mum, Dad and Junior piled on top — only the driver wearing a helmet. I'd told Michael that I didn't want to go on the back of the ancient, whiny little scooter, so he'd forced me to drive it instead.

I remember the dusty roads, lined with people walking barefoot, laden with packages and baggage. Skinny cows and goats weaving in and out of the traffic. Horns blaring in the blazing sun . . . and Michael, gripping on to the seat, shouting In my ear, telling me to slow down, to be careful. I was careful though, Michael, I wasn't the one who got caught coming out of someone else's room after an all-day, all-night party, fuelled by potent cocktails and too much coke. He thought I'd been asleep, but I'd woken in the night, mouth parched and head pounding — and I'd gone to the kitchen, hoping that the party-goers were long gone, and I could down some water in peace. Ignoring the mess of the place, knowing we'd lose the deposit on the small apartment that we'd rented together for the month. It had been a blissful month, for me, at least. I didn't sense that Michael had grown bored of me . . . or perhaps he hadn't — perhaps he was just another man, lured away by the siren's call when his mind wasn't working at its full capacity.

He didn't know I'd seen him sneaking out of the bedroom and into the living room. I'd gone through at midday, after a few hours of fitful sleep, and I'd tried to act like everything was normal.

"Man, that was some night," he'd said. "I must've passed out."

Sure, he did. After spending a few hours with that whore, Melissa. The bikini-clad Aussie with the too-white teeth and the too-even tan, and the voice that cut right through me.

If I'd had the chance, it would've been Melissa who had the accident — but she took off as soon as she woke up that day and I never saw her again. I think about her sometimes — I hear a voice, or I see a flash of expensively highlighted hair, and I think it's her, but it isn't.

I saw someone I thought was her when we were on the motorbike that day. My head snapped around, watching her disappear into the crowd, and I lost control, just for a moment.

But then I righted myself, and it was all going to be OK, until Michael shouted into my ear, "Watch what you're doing, you stupid fucking bitch."

I'd felt the surge of blood in my veins. My heart beating too fast. My brain fizzing with the onslaught of the adrenaline coursing through me. It was a risk, but I didn't stop to think. I turned hard, gripping tight, as the back of the bike lifted off the ground and swung out fast. Michael wasn't expecting it; he'd just got over the previous skid. The bike flipped, with me still attached and Michael not. I landed hard, the engine still running, the wheels whining, and I felt the shift in weight as he lost his grip and flew into the air, landing

220

with a hard crack on the rocks that lined the side of the road. I let go of the handlebars and the bike pinwheeled away from me. People came running, shouting, from all directions. But I'd heard Michael's skull crack open like an egg. Remember — it's the driver who wears the helmet.

A terrible accident.

I was treated in the hospital for shock, but by the time his parents came to collect the body, I was long gone. Luckily, for me, they didn't even know he had a girlfriend. Luckily for me, I was able to blend in, slip away, and before long, I'd met someone else.

The phone on the centre console rings again, and I snap back to the present. The car is weaving in and out of traffic, and he ignores it. I still can't remember his name, but I see his ID badge, partially obscured by the ringing phone. He works at a bank. I turn away, facing out of the window, remembering now — the pub, the rough men . . . my saviour. I'd joked that I needed a loan. He'd joked that he would look after me.

Finally, I start to recognise the streets.

"You can just drop me here. I can walk the rest of the way."

He doesn't argue. Just slams the car to a halt, a metre from the side of the road. I climb out, and I'm closing the door when he leans over and says, "Be careful." His voice is kind, and I think he means it. Then he yanks the door shut and drives off at speed, cars tooting horns behind him as he swerves into their path.

I walk to the far side of the pavement, away from the road, and I sit down for a minute on a low wall. My head is a mess, but I need to get myself together. I picture Carrie, and wish she was still with me. Too much has happened now for me to sort things out on my own — but she's gone, and it's all my fault.

I walk back to the hotel, keeping my head down, avoiding the gaze of people on their way to work, school — doing normal things. I feel like a mess, so I must surely look like one. As I pass the receptionist, she makes an uncharacteristic move.

"Hey, lady," she says, "you still need to pay."

I can't deal with this right now.

"I know. I know. I'll sort it later, I promise."

"You pay by six, or manager will come," she says. Then she disappears back behind the counter, and the volume of the TV goes up again. Somewhere nearby, there's the sound of furniture being dragged across the floor. A vacuum cleaner starts up.

I hurry up to the room, and see that the "do not disturb" sign is still hanging on the door. Good. I hurry inside, locking the door behind me. The room still smells strongly of bleach, and I yank open the balcony doors to try and air it. As I do, the room seems to tilt around me, and the scenes from the night before flash in front of my eyes.

The blood. The balcony. Carrie screaming at me to stop.

I slide down onto the floor, hugging my knees to my chest. Staring across at the one remaining rucksack. You wouldn't even know Carrie had been here at all. I stare

222

at the rucksack with the contents spilling out of the top. The side pockets bulging with God knows what. And then I see it. A glimpse of silver poking out from the flat bottom pocket. Something that shouldn't be there. Something that's been left behind in a rush of panic.

Something that gives me a brilliant idea.

To: lauralee@gmail.com
From: carrie82@hotmail.com
Subject: Changing the subject

Hi Laura,

Thought I'd start a new thread as my emails were getting a bit over the top. Hope I didn't worry you too much. All is well, and I am heading off on my own soon for some calm times, maybe a retreat for a while. Not sure how much I'll be online. Hope your arm is healing well!

Love and hugs,

Carrie xoxo

★ ★ ★

To: carrie82@hotmail.com
From: lauralee@gmail.com
Subject: RE: Changing the subject

Er . . . WTF?

Who are you and what have you done with Carrie?

Haha. Seriously, you sound like a different person. Have the drugs permanently mangled your brain?

And my LEG is doing well, thank you.

Seriously . . . I can't imagine you at any sort of retreat, but it sounds like you might need one.

Lx

CHAPTER
TWENTY-EIGHT

Irkutsk–Moscow

I barely sleep, tossing and turning most of the night. I can't stop thinking about Carrie. About everything that happened that night. That pig, Sergei. Hurting her. Well he can't hurt her anymore, that's for sure. And thanks to good old Ivan "not so terrible" he is long gone. Carrie is, too, and I need to get her out of my head.

My phone is charging beside the bed, and I pick it up and go straight to Facebook. I was shocked when I realised that Carrie hadn't been updating her page throughout the trip, but then when I thought about it, she hadn't really been taking any photos either. It was as if she didn't want people to know what she was up to. In fact, she barely seems to use Facebook at all. Most of her posts are "friends only" so it's just as well that she accepted my request that first night in Beijing. Thinking about it, she did say that she didn't really use it much. I suppose it's not that unusual; it's just that I always enjoy keeping up with people on there. Not that I comment, or even like things. I suppose I could be called a lurker . . . but I'd say it's more that I prefer to live vicariously. Or perhaps I am just a bit of a voyeur.

Carrie's last post is from more than a month ago, a photo she's been tagged in. A bunch of people in a pub, holding glasses aloft. Carrie is almost out of shot, not looking at the camera. She's not someone who likes to be photographed, I think. Definitely not a selfie-taker. It's a shame, as I'd love to look at more photos of her, but either I don't have the level of access I need to see them, or there just aren't any there. I don't know why I expected any updates — I've seen this photo before, and I know that she hasn't added anything since, but I'm still disappointed.

I type in Sam's name and go to look at his page instead. As usual, there are several new posts since I last looked. I'm getting a little bored with all the party pics, and the mad-for-it status updates — not to mention the myriad of hangers-on, and the Botoxed females. Sometimes I look at these pictures and think how lucky I was to get a piece of him at all, even for a short while. I am definitely not like any of his other lovers.

I suppose that's why it was never going to last.

Enough now.

I give myself a mental shake and climb out of bed. I know I should have a shower while I have the chance — I don't even know where I'm going to be sleeping after I leave here — but I can't be arsed. Most of my things are already packed, so I quickly throw on yesterday's clothes and toss everything else into the rucksack. I do a final sweep of the room, making sure nothing's been left behind, under the beds or in a drawer or some other stupid place that will end up incriminating me, then I grab one of the towels from the bathroom and begin the process of wiping everything down.

The blood might be gone, and I have Ivan to thank for a good job there — but I can't actually remember him doing it. I assume I had passed out by then. I can't trust him to have wiped down everything else that I might've touched, and besides, I've been in there another night. I bundle up the sheets and pull off the pillowcases and roll them all into a big ball, then I hitch my rucksack onto my back, and have one final glance around. I catch sight of myself in the mirror, and I'm not surprised to see that I look like complete shit. My eyes are bloodshot, red-rimmed and decorated with dark circles beneath. My hair is greasy and matted — I don't even know when I last washed it. My skin is a disturbing shade of grey.

I look away from the mirror, not wanting to dwell on it anymore. I shove a hand into my shorts, making sure I still have the cash, and then I pick up the bundle of sheets and towels and slip out of the room. The maid's trolley is at the end of the corridor, but she is nowhere to be seen. I toss my laundry into the cart, then jumble it around a bit with the other stuff in there. No one will know which room it came from — it will all get thrown into the washer together, and if there does come a time when the events that occurred in my room are investigated for some reason, I'll be long gone.

I take the stairs instead of the lift, knowing that there's no way the receptionist or the manager will be walking up them to try and corner me before I do a runner. I have the cash to pay now, but that makes it even more invigorating as I open the fire escape and head outside. I let Ivan in this way the other night, so I already knew that the door isn't alarmed. I hurry down the alleyway, not looking back. I pause for a moment as I pass the dark stain on the ground, closing my eyes briefly — remembering what happened to Sergei. Then I blink it away, and carry on. I need to get away from here. The good thing is, there is no record of me being here at all. Another one of the benefits of sharing Carrie's accommodation.

No one is looking for me, because they don't even know that I exist.

It's strange being on the train without Carrie. Even stranger not having a cabin, or a ticket, but as long as I keep moving I'm pretty sure I can get away with it. I just need to be careful at the station stops, make sure I avoid the guards. I walk up and down through the carriages until I find a luggage rack with some space at the end of the standard-class dining car. Perfect. I push my rucksack as far back as it will go, then cover it with a bright-red wheelie suitcase. It reminds me of some of the luggage on the first train, where Carrie was chatting to the tour group. That couple she befriended . . . Steve something. Street? Yes, Steve and Marion Street. The couple she planned for us to meet up with in Moscow. Well, that's not going to be happening now. It was all so effortless for Carrie — the way she slid into the seat beside them, started charming them, making them laugh. I wasn't interested then, but I might have to dig

229

deep if I want to make it to Moscow without attracting any attention from the guards.

I'm sliding the red suitcase back into position when I realise that neither the main compartment, nor any of the pockets on the front or back, are locked. I smile to myself. Rookie mistake. Everyone knows you're supposed to lock up all your zips when you leave your luggage on an unattended rack on a train. Especially in a strange country. Didn't these people read the guidebook? I think about the long cable padlock that Carrie had, and I wish I'd bought one for myself I didn't before, but I have something in my bag that's worth stealing now.

Glancing up and down the carriage to make sure that no one is going to come over and disturb me, I carefully unzip the pockets of the red suitcase one by one. Nothing much of interest in the front. But in the back one, I strike gold. A cardboard wallet, the kind you get in the travel agent's when they hand over the currency you ordered. I open it, fully expecting it to be empty, or maybe with just a receipt inside, but no. There are several fresh, crisp notes.

Someone has been very irresponsible leaving them in this case like this — but I'm not going to hang around and wait for them to realise their mistake. I slide the notes out of the wallet, then put the wallet back inside. Then I pull my rucksack towards me again and open the top. I fiddle around inside until I find the zip for the secret pocket, and then I slide the notes in, zip it up and close the flap again. I push my rucksack back to the corner of the rack, leaving the red suitcase back in its original position. If they do come back, wondering where their money is — they'd never think to look in the bag next to it. I imagine a husband and wife arguing about which one of them was stupid enough to leave the wallet in the bag, and which one of them didn't bother to put on the padlocks. Neither of them will ever know that their money is less than thirty centimetres away, but lost to them forever.

I'm humming a little tune to myself as I saunter off down the carriage and into the dining car. I realise now that Carrie was holding me back My feelings for her clouded my judgement, dulled my senses. She made me weak, helpless — humbled by her sexy charms.

Well, not anymore. Because the real Violet is back.

The dining car is already nearly full, people chattering over maps and guidebooks, teas and beers. I stop at a table where two women in their sixties are pouring small bottles of tonic into tall glasses filled with ice and lemon. They look up when they see me standing there, and I give them my best, most vulnerable smile.

"Do you mind if I join you, ladies? I don't want to impose . . . it's just, well . . . I'm traveling alone, and I was mugged last night." I pause to push out a tear, and I rub at my face, pressing my fists into my eyes, then I look back down at them, and they are looking up at me sympathetically, thinking, "This could be my daughter . . . this is someone's daughter . . ."

"Oh you poor thing," the one on the left says, eventually. "Please, sit down with us. What happened? Do you have any money at all?" She slides her drink towards me. "Here, have this. I think you could use it more than me. I'll get another." She turns, gesturing to the barman, and the other one lays a hand on top of mine, and I close my eyes, remembering. Soft hands, soft lips.

"What's your name, dear?" the other one says.

I sniff, stifle a sob. "Thank you both, you're so kind. I'm . . . I'm Carrie. My name is Carrie."

CHAPTER
TWENTY-NINE

Moscow

The journey wasn't so bad in the end. The three-and-a-half days flew by. After the charming hospitality of the gin-and-tonic ladies of the standard-class carriage, and their insistence on pushing 100 dollars each on me "to get me through", I'd almost felt a little guilty when I saw them lifting that red wheelie case off the train, waving at me as I calmly walked away from them along the platform. They had no idea what they'd given me, and neither did I, until I opened it, sitting on a bench outside the railway station. Fifty thousand rubles. That will certainly "get me through" — thank you very much, ladies. It's their own fault for being so stupid.

I'd spent that first night in the dining car, playing cards and drinking with the other night owls, then moved elsewhere in the morning. It was just as easy to find new companions for the other two days. Befriending the French students and finding out about the spare room in their four-berth had been another stroke of luck. I got off the train with a spring in my step, the events of Irkutsk and all that went before erased from my mind — for a while, at least.

I asked the taxi driver — another ubiquitous track-suited, chainsmoking oaf — to take me to the best hotel he knew. Quite the opposite to the arrival in Irkutsk, when Carrie had insisted on being taken to the dump that she'd pre-booked — which was a blessing, in the end. It's much easier to get away with things in places like that, where the staff don't really give two fucks about what their clients are up to.

That's not what I'm after now, though. What I'd like now, is a little luxury for a while. A decent base for a few days, while I work out what to do next. I barely notice the car speeding down the wide boulevards, swinging hard around the corners. I'm already thinking about a long soak in a scalding, scented bath — taking some time to cleanse my soul. I think it's about time. I laugh a little, remembering something that Carrie said — her fearful flashback to the nomadic festival, and what the shaman said about me. I'd brushed it off as nonsense, but what he'd said was true. I am not a nice person. There is something fundamentally wrong with me.

My parents tried to fix me when I was young — they could tell early on that I wasn't following a normal developmental path. But when the counsellors failed, my mother gave up on me. I tried to change then, realising my mistake — realising I was invisible to her, and that I'd taken things too far — but I found out it's not that easy to change, and maybe it's right to say I was born, not made.

We pull up outside a glittering facade, but when I climb out of the car, I see that the gold is flaking in

234

parts and the stairs are scuffed — and the doorman, when he arrives, is wearing a suit that is shiny at the knees and elbows, frayed at the cuffs. Perhaps this is not the right place after all.

"Two thousand rubles," says the bored-looking driver. I hand over the money, even though I know it's too much, and head up the steps. Inside, the lobby is as I expected — it was once opulent, but now it is faded and tired, but at least the receptionist is a little livelier than the one in the last place.

"*Privet*," I greet him, my accent as perfect as I can make it. "Do you have a room, please?"

He smiles at my Anglo-Russian attempts and taps on his keyboard. "We have only the Lenin Suite available, I am afraid. It is very expensive." He cocks his head to the side in a slightly pitying, slightly patronising manner. I get it now. I'd forgotten about the state that I'm in. My filthy hair and clothes, and the battered rucksack.

Then I remember an article I read, about Anna Delvey the fake, possibly Eastern European socialite, who managed to trick the best hotels in New York into letting her stay for as long as she wanted, charging everything to her room, telling them she was waiting for a business deal to go through. "Fake it until you make it", that's what they say, isn't it?

I pull the wad of rubles out of my pocket and lay them flat on the counter, locking his gaze as I say, *'ideal'no.'* Perfect. "That would be just fine." I pause, then I cock my head, coo, mirroring him, and say in a low voice, in English this time, "This will more than cover my stay ... and don't try and rip me off, you little weasel. My father is a British diplomat and he will have you out of this job and in the gutter faster than you can say *trakhni svoyu babushku*." I take a step closer, pushing the money forwards as I do, and his hand appears from behind the counter to grab the notes, like one of those grabber machines with the crappy toys at the fair. He's not too concerned with the threat against his grandmother I've made.

He blinks, once, and the smile slips, just for a moment, and then he says, "We're delighted to have you here with us, Miss —"

"Osborne," I say. "Carrie Osborne. I'm afraid I'm waiting for new documents to arrive, but I have this." I slide Carrie's driving licence across the counter. Another useful nugget that was left behind amid her rapid departure.

He pushes it back, and gives me a small nod. Then he hands over a brass key on a huge metal fob. "Your suite is on the twelfth floor, Miss Osborne. Please let us know if we can do anything else to assist."

CHAPTER
THIRTY

Although the hotel isn't quite as flash as I'd hoped, it is a good room. Far too big for just me, but it's nice to be somewhere like this for a change. The bed is huge, wider than a king, and with crisp white linens that contradict the bling of the rest of the place. I like it. The bathroom doesn't disappoint either.

I fill the huge, deep bath almost to the brim, adding all the fancy-looking toiletries that they've placed beside the green marble sink. I hesitate for a moment, wondering if I can call housekeeping and get them to bring me some hair dye, but I decide to hold off and get it done properly somewhere. My hair feels like matted rope, but when I slide down into the floral-scented waters, it soon fans around me and begins to soften. I lather on shampoo, and then the whole little bottle of conditioner, and leave it to soak in while I shave my legs and armpits, and give myself a proper scrub with the helpfully supplied loofah. You don't get real loofahs at home anymore. Something to do with the environment I expect. Not that I give two shits about that. Finally, I run my fingers through my hair, detangling it, then rinsing it in the dirty bath water, which has formed a distinct brown scum around the edges. The water is murky and opaque, as if all the grime and gunk that I have been carrying around with me, unnoticed, has finally leached from my skin.

Wrapping myself in a fluffy white towel, I inspect my face in the mirror and conclude that I look a lot better than I did yesterday. I have colour in my cheeks now, and instead of dark rings and blood, my eyes look as bright and shiny as a pair of new buttons. I think I have the ladies on the train to thank for helping to sort out my demeanour. Perhaps taking Carrie's identity is what's perked me up. At the back of my skull, a small bead of worry is undulating under the skin, but it soon works its way back inside. The old Carrie is gone. The new one is right here.

I choose the cleanest, neatest clothes from my mediocre selection, but they are worn and crumpled, and even Carrie's strappy vest top doesn't make the grade, but it'll do for now until I get something new. I pick up my small bag, and make sure I have all my cash, then I head out for some entertainment.

No one pays me much attention as I hurry along the wide boulevards, not having any real sense of where I am going. I have in mind to find a department store, grab a few things from there, but I'm conscious that my cash isn't going to last forever, and I'm concerned now that none of the cards I have will work. Most of them I picked up in Thailand, from drunken Brits, who'd been waving them at the distractingly pretty staff. I got three in one night, all from the same crowd of idiotic rugby lads who really should've known better. I had developed a foolproof scam of standing close to them

238

while they tapped their pin in to the card reader, then pretended I'd been jostled into them, grabbing their waist to stop myself falling over, sliding a hand into their pocket to remove the freshly used card. In most cases, they'd wait until the next day before cancelling, so I was able to withdraw the maximum, twice. I kept the cards as souvenirs, and I marked them with a code on my little piece of paper — the code being a quick drawing of the place I'd taken it, or the person that I'd taken it from.

I stopped doing it for a while, when I met Sam. I'd assumed I wouldn't need to — that he would be happy to pay for things for me — but that was just something else I got wrong about him.

I have no idea where I am, but I don't feel like I am in the main hub of the city yet. So far, Moscow is not nearly as pretty as I'd imagined. The streets are grey, the buildings nondescript. I'm not sure what I expected, but I know that when I get to the river and Red Square and St Peter's Basilica, it will look like all the photographs I have seen online over the years. So far it's not unlike Irkutsk: harsh apartment blocks, small, soulless squares, bored-looking people sitting on benches, unapologetically drinking from cans of beer or bottles of vodka. The people I pass are hurried, drab and uninterested. Where are the glamorous hooker-types like the girls at the party?

I turn the corner and there is a row of sad-looking shops, the signs old and faded. Even the mannequins in the windows look bored. But the clothes look half decent, and I imagine them to be cheaper here than in the centre, so I go into the one with the least depressing display.

The assistant doesn't look up from the counter, but I'm getting used to this now. I walk around the edge of the shop, trailing a hand across the hanging garments, stopping occasionally to push the hangers back and pull something out for a better look. I choose a simple cotton dress, navy blue with an anchor pattern, which at home I would laugh at, but somehow seems fitting here. I wander into the centre of the store, where a variety of shoes are on display — none of them particularly nice, but neither are they particularly awful. I lift up a tan ankle boot, checking for the price on the sole. It just happens to be my size, and the other one is there, too — not a common occurrence in any decent shop, in case you pilfer them.

I genuinely hadn't come in here to steal anything, but the assistant hasn't even looked up yet, never mind greeted me, and a small ball of annoyance bounces up my gullet, a burning lump in my throat. I'm sick of being ignored. Of being sneered at. I could just pay for the dress and the boots and be on my way, but what's the point? I'd be far better keeping my dwindling cash reserves for other things.

I take a breath, then ask, loudly, "Do you have this dress in a medium?"

She looks up, then looks me up and down. She mutters something in Russian, then disappears through the back. I don't think about it any longer. Don't consider that she might have a big, burly boyfriend waiting through there, ready to pounce. I quickly roll the boots inside the dress and stuff it under my arm like a rugby ball, then I hastily leave the shop. My heart starts pounding as I skip down the few steps, and then I start to run.

Still no idea where I am, I run across the street and around the corner, and then I just keep running, faster than I've run for a very long time. I didn't even glance back before the shop was out of sight. I have no idea if she is currently calling the police, or if she has even returned from the back of the shop, but I don't care. My lungs burn, my thighs burn, and I just pump my legs harder, but only one arm — so I don't drop my illicit wares. Eventually, when I can't run any further, I stop, letting the clothes fall to the ground. I lean forwards, panting hard, trying to catch a breath — and then I start laughing. I stand, glancing behind me, but no one is there. No one has followed. I laugh until my chest feels like it might burst, until tears are running down my face.

When I've managed to compose myself, I walk across the road to one of the small drinks kiosks, and I realise then that I am on the banks of the river. The Moskva is vast and grey, and I gaze down at it for a moment, the river that gave the city its name.

Then I point to a small bottle of vodka. The kiosk worker hands it to me in a brown bag, and says something I don't understand. I hand him the cash, and then I head over to a bench facing the river, and I sit down, and finally, I relax.

CHAPTER
THIRTY-ONE

Glancing up and down the murky river, I spot the big wheel of a fairground on the other side and realise that it must belong to the famous Gorky Park, and the Scorpions' song "Winds of Change" immediately starts playing inside my head, lifting my mood. I'm not a fan of fairgrounds in general, but I've had just enough vodka to think that it might be fun. I'm bored on my own, after the initial buzz of the shoplifting and the running, and I definitely don't want to go back to my hotel alone right now. I have a quick look around me, hoping that there might be somewhere I can change into my new clothes — a public toilet with wash facilities would be preferable, but in the absence of that, anywhere nearby. I settle for the shade of a tree. I'm not exactly concealed, but I don't really care.

I pull off my sweaty, grubby clothes and ball them up, then I step into the dress, sliding it up over my hips, twisting my arm behind my back to do up the zip. I smooth the material over my thighs, swish the material back and forth. It's a perfect fit. I take off my filthy sandals and pull on the ankle boots, without socks. I need a mirror to sort out my hair and face, but I look better than I did before. I head off along the riverbank, tossing the old clothes into the water without looking back.

Carrie is hardly going to miss that top now.

I cross the river at Krymsky Bridge and enter the gates of the fairground. It's one of those places where you don't pay to get in, and just buy tokens for the rides. I listen to the rattle of the ancient rollercoaster and the shrieks from the people riding it, and decide to give it a miss. There is something very out of control about rollercoasters, and I'll never understand why people go on them. I'd rather be in charge of my own adrenaline surges, with much more thrilling activities. What happened in Irkutsk has awakened something in me that I'd thought was safely buried away. I'm like a vampire — lain dormant for years until the smell of blood has me wanting more. Of course I like to try and convince myself that all the things that have happened to me over the years have been accidents, but in an occasional moment of honesty, I recognise what they really are. What I really am. I take a swig of the vodka and realise that I've nearly finished the whole bottle, and I can't help but laugh. What must I look like, to others? Bedraggled hair from the run, out-of-place clothing, swaying slightly from the alcohol — laughing to myself in a park.

Mothers with children swerve to avoid me, throwing me filthy looks. A couple of men leer at me in that way I've noticed here many times now — they don't care if I'm drunk, if I stink of booze and sweat. If I'm vulnerable. They'll fuck me if I ask them to. What they don't realise is that I don't actually care about fucking them, or talking to them, or anything else. What they don't realise is that I am looking for something that none of them can give me.

A traitorous tear slides down my cheek, and I wipe it angrily away, then I toss the vodka bottle into a bin and ignore the staring children and the snotty mums, and head over to a row of colourful stalls on the other side of the park.

By the time I get there, I've pushed the tears and the regrets back into their box, and I'm feeling a bit brighter. I stop to look at the items that have been arranged neatly in rows, according to height. Babushka dolls — some out on display as the full set of seven, the rest of them with their interlocking babies safely stored inside. They are painted in every colour under the sun, with different faces, different styles of dress. There are even "novelty" ones, with faces of celebrities and politicians.

When they see me looking, the stallholders start to demonstrate with their dolls, twisting them apart, taking out each nested doll from within, setting them out in a row like ducklings following their mother. It's mesmerising, and joyful, and I feel another wave of deeply hidden emotions threatening to push themselves up and out of me. A wave of panic and dizziness hits me, and for a moment, all of the dolls seem to be un-nesting themselves, coming towards me, circling me, and I take a step back and try to breathe, but it's too hard to catch my breath — my throat starts to close up and the light around me begins to shrink until there's nothing but a pinprick.

244

There is chattering in Russian, and shrieks of children and the clatter of the old rollercoaster as it whizzes around above my head, and I feel myself falling, blackness taking over and I want it to end . . . and then . . . arms, grabbing my arms, someone talking in my ear. I feel weightless, and then I feel nothing.

I come to on a bench, my head between my legs, staring down at cracked concrete. Someone is rubbing my back.

"Hey, you're back. You kinda scared me a bit then."

I don't know who this is. I turn my head slowly in the direction of the voice — American, I think, or it could be Canadian. I can't really tell the difference.

"Hey yourself," I manage. My mouth feels like sandpaper. Tastes like shit.

I sit up slowly, and wriggle away slightly, so he stops rubbing my back.

"Do you need to be sick? Here, I got you some water."

He hands me a plastic bottle, the cap already off, and in other times I would query this as being very unsafe, but right now I need water, and if he's decided to drug me then good on him, because I'm not too scared of oblivion. I've often thought that date-rape drugs are the best way to go, because if you can't remember what happened, then did it really happen at all? More rational people would question this logic, but I am long past any form of rationale. I gulp the water down and sit up.

"Who're you, then? My guardian angel?"

He laughs. "I'm Brad. I saw you pass out and I thought you might need a friend."

He's being nice and I should thank him, but part of me remains deeply cynical about people who like to "help". What's in it for him? I give him a proper once-over, and decide that a lot could be in it for him, as it happens, and maybe for me. He's late thirties, fresh faced, well dressed — in that preppy kind of way that I wouldn't normally go for, but that screams *money*, and that is really the prevailing thought in my head right now.

"Look," he continues, "this might sound really creepy, so feel free to tell me where to go, but my hotel is just there . . ." He pauses and points through the trees at a towering concrete block next to the river. "And maybe you could do with some place to get cleaned up? Have a lie down?"

Cleaned up? I'd like to be offended, but I can actually smell myself through the clean clothes, and it's not particularly fragrant. I should tell him where to go, just for his assumptions. I was clean before I came out, wasn't I? This is obviously a combination of the sprinting, the adrenaline come-down and the vodka leaching out of my pores. I should tell him where to go, and I should head back to my own hotel and sleep, but instead I say, "That's very kind of you. I'm staying in a crappy hostel and it would be nice to go somewhere nicer for a while."

He squeezes my shoulder. "See? That's exactly what I was thinking. I was thinking: *This girl is backpacking —*

this girl would just love to come and see the massive tub in my en suite . . . Am I right?"

He grins, displaying his perfect white veneers, and I think: I *know your type, Brad But I can handle it.*

Then he stands up and holds out a hand for me to take, and I take it, like some grateful little college girl so pleased to be with this handsome man, and I think how much I am going to enjoy the rest of the afternoon — and not for any reason he thinks.

CHAPTER
THIRTY-TWO

It turns out that Brad is staying in the Royal Bolshoi Plaza, which is considerably plusher than my hotel, so in some ways I'm not even lying about how nice it would be to have some proper luxury. The staff here are well groomed and slick, and none of them bats an eyelid as we walk past the desk. I'm sure in my hotel there would have been a hint of a sneer at least, after thelr snotty non-welcome when I checked in.

Brad calls the lift using his key card, then extends a hand as the doors slide open.

"After you, honey," he says, with a wink.

I get a strange little chill, then. Not sure why. But something makes me think that "Brad" — if that's even his name — has done this before. The way he'd "rescued" me and brought me back here seemed a little too easy. Or maybe that's just because of my own messed-up head. If I hadn't passed out like that, I fully intended to swipe at least one of those babushka dolls. Not because I even want one, but because I'd enjoyed the thrill of the earlier shoplifting and fancied another buzz.

The effects of the vodka have worn off now, and it doesn't appear that Brad has tried to drug me . . . yet.

I'm in dire need of another lift. I'm running on fumes now. I don't even know when I last ate.

I purposely turn my back to the mirror in the lift because I don't really want to see myself right now, and I'm amused but not surprised that Brad uses the thirty seconds or so until we reach his floor to check himself out.

What exactly does he want from me?

Someone like him — good-looking, money, flash hotel — if he wants a bit of rough he could pay for one better than me. I could be anyone. He clearly has no qualms at all about inviting strange women into his room.

He grins at me, as if reading my mind. "You're probably thinking I do this sort of thing all the time, but I don't, honestly" The doors slide open and he gestures for me to step out, then he follows and the doors slide shut again. "In fact," he continues, taking his key card back out of his pocket again, "I'm happy to leave you in the room to have a bath or whatever. I can go down to the bar. Come and join me whenever you like."

He turns left along the corridor, and I follow. The walls are papered with a shimmering gold. The burgundy carpet, adorned with a gold crested pattern, is soft and spongy beneath the thin soles of my boots. It's been a while since I've worn anything other than hiking boots or thick, rubber-soled sandals. I'm not used to feeling the surfaces that I'm walking on.

When we reach his room, he swipes the card and the sensor glows green. The door opens with a little click, and I follow him inside. The far side of the room is floor-to-ceiling windows with an incredible view of the river, and the park beyond.

Half of me wonders if he was watching me from here, then hurried down when he saw I was in distress. Is this the kind of thing that Brad would do? Given that I don't know him at all, I have no idea. All I do know — as is now confirmed — is that he is clearly very rich.

"Make yourself at home," he says, grinning. "I'll go downstairs . . ."

I decide to call his bluff. "Thanks so much. I really appreciate this." I glance around the room, taking it all in. He has a fancy, slim laptop on the desk. Expensive jackets hang in the wardrobe, the door left open for me to see. "I promise I won't steal anything."

His grin drops, just for a moment, then it's back. He laughs, but it sounds hollow. "Good one. Actually . . ." He sits down on the plush, gold velvet armchair that faces the window. "Maybe I'll stay, if that's OK with you? I have some work to catch up on. Don't worry. The bathroom door has a lock."

Oh, for fuck's sake. Maybe he hasn't done this before. Maybe he is just ridiculously nice and stupidly naïve. I guess I'll go back to plan A. Not that I had any other.

"I don't think that'll be necessary, will it?" I give him my best come-on smile. "Let me go and freshen up. Maybe you can order us something to eat? I'm absolutely starving."

250

"Sure," he says, happy again. "I'll get us some champagne too. They have an excellent vintage Krug that goes perfectly with their lobster and caviar platter."

Of course they do.

"Whatever you think," I say, pulling the bathroom door closed. "Oh," I call from the other side, "and when I come out, you can tell me all about yourself."

I hear him laugh. "You, too, sweetheart. You know I don't even know your name?"

After a very brief pause, I reply. "It's Carrie."

I decide on a shower rather than a bath, and I think about calling on him, asking him to join me, but decide against it. It's Carrie I think of as I soap my body with the expensive shower gel. It's Sam's face that I see when I close my eyes, letting the strong shower jets course over my skin. I work myself into a frenzy, but then I stop, holding back. I need to leave a little bit for Brad.

I rough-dry my hair and comb my fingers through it, then I use some of Brad's toothpaste to finger-brush my teeth, gargling with a cold glass of water to freshen my mouth. I slip on one of the fluffy white robes and give myself a quick glance in the mirror. My skin is pink from the heat; my hair looks better now that it's damp.

The doorbell goes as I am about to walk out of the bathroom, and I hold back, to let Brad deal with it. I hear the sound of a trolley being wheeled inside, low voices. The door closing again. Then the sound of a bottle chinking in ice, and I open the door.

Brad is in his underpants, running a finger under the foil on the champagne bottle. His eyes flick up to my face, then down the robe, and he tilts his head to one side — then holds up a hand and opens two fingers, grins.

I run a hand down the front of the robe and prise it open, just a little. Not enough for him to see anything. Not yet. He's going to have to do better than that. But it was enough to confirm my earlier suspicions. He has definitely done this before. He is confident bordering on arrogant, and he is trying to hide it under a "knight in shining armour" facade. Suddenly, I have a flashback to the room in Irkutsk — Sergei's grunting face as he pounded himself into Carrie; Carrie too weak from that stupid drug she'd smoked to fight him off. A wave of revulsion skitters over my skin, leaving goose bumps. The robe falls open to the waist.

Brad grins, holding up the bottle, and the cork pops.

What a fucking cliché.

I don't want to be here. I shouldn't be here. I was supposed to be careful, after what happened in Irkutsk. I was supposed to keep a low profile. Keep myself to myself. I shouldn't be getting involved with anyone else.

I should not be in this room.

Brad pours the champagne into two flutes and takes a step towards me. He hands out one of the flutes to me, and holds the other aloft. "Cheers," he says. "To you, *Carrie*." It's the way he says it. The way he doesn't believe that it's my name. "Isn't this just perfect?"

Then he makes a fatal mistake.

He turns away to look out of the window. Still trying to impress me, with this view that he has bought, before he plies me with champagne and caviar, and makes me suck his filthy cock. *You're just the same as the others, aren't you, Brad?*

I swing the champagne bottle like a baseball bat, at the perfect spot on the back of his head. He literally doesn't know what's hit him. He falls to his knees, still gripping the flute, and then he tips forwards, his hands thrust in front of him, and there is a strange gurgling sound as his face hits the floor. He starts, as if he's been electrocuted, or is having some sort of a fit, and an arc of blood jets out from under him.

It takes me a moment to realise that he has landed on the flute and that it has smashed under him, impaling him like a chunk of chicken on a skewer.

CHAPTER
THIRTY-THREE

Moscow–Berlin (flight)

Thankfully I still have my own ID to get on the plane. I'd felt a moment of panic at the immigration desk, wondered if my passport might have a flag on it, but after a moment of jobsworthy pageflicking, the po-faced guard stamped it and pushed it back under the glass.

Ivan had been seriously unimpressed with my latest request for him. I'd called him from my mobile while still in Brad's room. He'd been enjoying a rare day off, after working twenty-four hours straight on a job that he'd flown here to do after he'd dealt with my little problem in Irkutsk, while I'd been idling away my time on the train for three days. I didn't ask him about the job. I know from my own experience that he is far more than just a taxi driver.

It had taken him less than two minutes to break into the bedroom safe, finding Brad's passport and visa documents, his credit cards and wads of cash.

"Another wolf?" Ivan had said, impassively flicking through the pile of US dollars.

I nodded. "I told you before. Lots of them about."

He sighed. "You need to get out of my country, *leetle peeg*. You are very dangerous person. This is going to be a very — how you say? — *treecky* job for me to do, you understand? Very difficult. Very expensive."

I wanted to protest. It was an accident, that's all. OK, so I had hit him with the bottle, but that's because I'd realised what he was. I'd seen beneath his skin. The wolf in handsome-man clothing. All I'd wanted to do was knock him out for long enough for me to get into the safe and then get out of there. I'd planned to take the laptop, too — I reckoned it was worth at least a grand and would be easy to flog.

Ivan had tossed the bedspread over the top of Brad so that we didn't need to see him, and while he continued to count the cash, I let the robe fall off me and climbed into the bed, under the sheet. I smiled as Ivan looked up, pausing his counting.

He muttered something in Russian that I assume was a swear word. Then he sighed. "Very nice, *leetle peeg*, but no time for this. Not even for you."

I stuck out my bottom lip, mock-offended. "Then how am I going to pay you?"

He held up the cash, and the laptop. "I give you enough to get plane ticket, and you get the fuck out of here, now." His voice was harsh, and for the first time, I felt a little afraid of him. I'd thought I had him wrapped around my finger, but he was always the one in charge, I realise that now. It would have been easy for him to kill me. To get rid of me, and all of the mess I'd caused — but for some reason, he let me go free.

Perhaps he felt sorry for me.

I almost got myself lost on the way back to my hotel to grab my stuff. Nearly freaked out on the confusing

Moscow Metro, with its circular map crossed with far too many snaking lines, the signs all in Cyrillic and not having a clue which direction I was going in; but a kindly couple had taken pity on me and I'd had a flash of a memory to Steve and Marion Street — Carrie's friends from the train; we were supposed to meet them in Red Square, and I wondered if they turned up — if they expected us to be there too.

The tears are flowing now, as I strap on my seatbelt, preparing for take-off. I'm trying not to think about everything that's happened, but it's impossible. I close my eyes, wishing I could transport myself back to the start, before all of this began. The tannoy announcement starts, and I open my eyes.

I don't even know what the start is.

The plane picks up speed on the runway, and I grip onto the armrests, barely aware that I am doing it.

The smartly dressed woman next to me leans over, bringing a cloud of cloying perfume and a soft Welsh accent. "I used to be such an *awful* flyer," she says, rolling her eyes and handing me a wrapped caramel sweet. "But since I started with this meditation app, it's really helped." She shows me her phone, the app open — a lilac pulsing light taking up the screen. She hands me an earbud, and it feels churlish to refuse. I push it into my ear and the soothing sounds of waterfalls come through the tiny speaker. She pats my hand, and I give her a small smile.

Let her think I'm a bad flyer. If only that was the truth. If only that was the only thing that was wrong with me.

256

Don't be nice to me, I think. Nothing good will ever come of it.

CHAPTER
THIRTY-FOUR

Berlin

The first thing I realise when I land at Berlin Schonefeld Airport is that I have no euros to get myself into the city. I can probably jump on the S-Bahn without paying, but I'm not sure what I'm going to do when I get there. I have no contacts here, nowhere to stay.

For the first time in a very long time, I feel a little afraid.

What happened in Irkutsk, and then in Moscow . . . I hadn't expected things to take such a dark turn. I'm grateful to Ivan for sorting everything for me and leaving me enough cash to buy a plane ticket out of there, but even he had looked at me with disgust in the end.

He doesn't understand. No one does.

Things have happened to me over the years. Ever since I was a little girl, it seems that I was in the wrong place at the wrong time. That misunderstandings and accidents have happened around me, and somehow I've been to blame. I know that this is why my mother was so horrible to me. Tried to push me away.

But Daddy never did.

After that horrible incident with Ophelia Morgan in sixth form, I was as traumatised as everyone else — but for some reason I was eyed with suspicion, just because I happened to be there when she'd decided to jump off the clock tower. I'd been trying to coax her down, not wind her up. But then it all happened so fast. Daddy paid the Morgans off so that they wouldn't investigate further, and I had to leave school just before my final exams, but I didn't care about that. What I cared about was how everyone was so quick to judge. Ophelia had been my friend. OK, so it had to be in secret because the rest of her stupid little clique hadn't approved, but that doesn't make it any less real. It was real to Ophelia and it was real to me.

I'm not sure I've ever really gotten over that.

Daddy was the only one who gave me support, stepping in when Mummy stepped back. He was the practical one. He'd accepted my grief without question. He'd sorted everything out. When I left home, I tried hard not to call on him for anything more, knowing how much it upset my mother, but I'd had to call him after Michael, and I realise that I'm going to have to call him now.

Thankfully, my mobile still has charge.

I drop my rucksack onto the floor, and sit down on top of it. It's midday, so that means it's 11:00am back home — too early for golf, but he might be in a meeting. The phone rings a few times and I'm about to give up, when he answers.

His breathing is fast, rasping, as if he has had to move quickly to grab the phone before it rang off. I try to picture him in his office, or maybe he was in the kitchen making tea. Mother would be out at one of her classes, I imagine. Not that she would answer the phone anyway, if she saw my name flash up on the display.

His breathing slows at last, and then there is a small sigh, before he says, "Veronica? Is that you?"

I open my mouth to speak, but suddenly my throat is constricted, and tears start to fall. Hearing his voice like this, I have so many memories. I have a dull ache in my stomach, a sudden, intense longing to be at home. Back in the mansion in the countryside, surrounded by fields and flowers and fresh air. Away from this place, this too-bright, echoing space filled with adrenaline and anxiety and too many chattering voices.

"It's me, Daddy. How are you?"

He lets out a longer sigh now, slow, steady. I imagine him slumping down onto the sofa in his office, sinking into the squashy, cracked leather. That sofa is older than me, and I had always loved sitting there — curled up, watching him work at his wide desk, framed by a picture window looking out onto the manicured lawn and the open fields behind.

"Where are you, Veronica? We've been very worried —"

"No need to worry," I say, cutting him off. I hold the phone away from me for a moment while I sniff, and wipe my face quickly with the back of my hand. I don't want him to think I'm upset. I can't be upset. He's always said that I am so strong. "I'm in Berlin," I tell him. I considered lying, but he does need to know where I am if he's going to be able to help me. "Not sure how long I'll be here. Thing is —"

"How much do you need?"

It's my turn to sigh. Is this all we are now? Two people who only speak when one of them needs money. One of them being me.

"Thing is," I start again, "I've actually lost my bank cards." This isn't a lie. Ivan made me get rid of every single one. Cut them up and burned them and threw the ashes in the Moskva. It's like he knew that what happened in Irkutsk wasn't the first time. I mean, of course he'd know. Any normal person would've called the police.

I hear the sound of a keyboard tapping down the phone. "I can arrange a new card and account at Targobank — the branch on Friedrichstraße. Can you get yourself there?"

"Yes, I —"

"Good. Good." His voice is clipped, the warmth of his initial greeting gone. "I need to get on, Veronica. I've got important meetings today. Your mother will be home soon."

Subtext: your mother will be home soon and I need this transaction dealt with before she comes back and finds out what I am doing. I get it.

"Thank you, Daddy. I'll pay you back soon, I promise. I'm thinking of coming home . . ."

The keyboard tapping stops, and I hear the sound of a door slamming shut.

"Don't come home, Veronica. Goodbye."

He cuts the connection before I can reply.

Shit. *Shit!*

I just hope he puts enough money in the account so that I don't have to call him again. I'm annoyed with my brief moment of vulnerability, but the sound of the door slamming pushed it away. He won't tell my mother that he spoke to me. As far as she's concerned, I no longer exist.

I slide my phone back into the front pocket of my bag, then lift it back up and hoist it onto my back. I'm sick of this travelling now. I want a bit of luxury for a change. I watch people push expensive wheeled cases over the concourse. Glamorous women in high heels tap-tapping on the marble floor. Over at the cash machines, people are fumbling with small travel bags, stuff wads of notes into hidden pockets, and I think for a moment about strolling over and robbing someone while they faff around with their wallets, but I decide against it. It feels riskier here, somehow. Despite everything that's happened to me in one of the most dangerous countries in the world, I actually feel more intimidated here in this airport. It would be much easier for me to be extradited from here, and I'd rather not take the risk.

I follow the signs for the trains and hope that they haven't changed their security systems since I was here last — when there were no barriers and rarely any guards doing spot-checks. There are electronic adverts on various screens as I walk towards the train platform, advertising the Westin Grand, and I decide that it must be fate. I wait for the correct train, and jump on. It's a much easier system to navigate than in Moscow, and with a quick change, I am there.

The Französische Straße U-bahn stop is right next to the hotel, and I'm pleased with myself for getting here without any bother. There were no guards, as I suspected, and no one really paid me any attention. I'd like to go straight into the hotel — the glass frontage and the properly attired doorman are much better than that Soviet fleapit I had to blag my way into in Moscow. That was a blip, and I'm over it now. Back in charge of things. Or at least I will be, when I get my money. I quickly Google the bank where Daddy has arranged my new card, and I'm pleased to see it's only a couple of streets away. It's almost like he knew I would come to stay here. It's the last place we visited as a family, and despite it being many years ago, I do remember it fondly. I imagine my mother would have a different view. If I remember rightly, there's a Ritter Sport chocolate shop not far from here. It's been too long since I had any decent chocolate. I'm walking up the street when I have a flashback to the very first night on the train — when we left Beijing for UB and everything was still fun. I'd been dozing on the bunk, enjoying the rhythm of the train sending me to sleep, but then I'd realised that Carrie was meant to be coming back with cups of tea for us.

I found her in the dining car, squeezed into a booth seat with a bunch of people wearing beige and brown tour company T-shirts, all with little shot glasses of vodka in front of them. Carrie was in her element, hands waving in front of her as she regaled them with something hilarious that made them all laugh. One of them sensed me staring, and there was silence for a moment, and Carrie turned and saw me, her smile lighting up her face.

"Violet! There you are. Come and join us . . . We're discussing the best chocolate in the world. This is Steve, and his wife Marion . . . and this is George, and his friend Sandra, and her sister Maude . . ." She's babbling away, and the others are muttering hellos, and giving me little waves — and I remember feeling that stab of annoyance, right there and then.

No, I'd thought. Carrie is *my* friend. This is *our* trip.

They're all talking over each other, saying Cadbury's, or Swiss or Belgian, and it's unanimous that they all think that American chocolate tastes like sick — except for Peanut Butter Cups.

"Stop!" I shout, and they all do. Mouths hanging open. I hadn't meant to shout, but the noise was too much, frittering around my brain, and I was sick of their inane chatter. I wanted a proper conversation with Carrie, in our cabin, about life and love and things that matter. But I could see the look on her face — that wary look that I've seen people get before, and I realised my mistake. So while they're all still staring at me, mouths agape, I gestured to the barmaid to bring more drinks, and I said in a stage whisper, "I'm sorry, but you're all completely mad. Everyone knows that the Germans make the best chocolate. Have you never had Ritter?"

And then the babbling starts again, and the drinks arrive, and Carrie grins up at me and I know I've got away with it, for now.

"Hey, watch it." A short guy in a tight suit bumps me out of the way, and I realise I've daydreamed my way all along the street. Somehow, on some in-built autopilot, I've made it to the bank. It's useful when your father is a real VIP, with fingers in many businesses and banks around the world. I catch sight of myself in the shiny metal entrance next to the glass doors. I look bedraggled, and in need of some proper attention. All I need to do now is pick up my card, draw some cash, and then I can sort everything out. Hair, clothes, proper hotel. Everything is going to be just fine.

It always is.

THIRTY-FIVE

It feels good to be wearing new clothes. I chose the orange-and-yellow halterneck dress, with a pair of black strappy sandals. I caught a glimpse of myself in the mirror in the hotel lobby and at first I thought I was looking through a window at someone else. The blonde highlights shimmer as I move slowly from side to side, catching myself under the myriad of lights. I'm usually wary of using stylists in foreign countries, but it's like she looked into me, and saw who I really am, and gave me the look to reflect it. I remember the little card she handed me at the till, scribbling her name on it for me so I'd know who to use again. She gave me a look too. Appraising. Intrigued. Perhaps I'll contact her. See if she fancies having cocktails with me. She looked like a cocktail sort. From what I've seen of the city so far, the styles fall into two distinct camps — if you exclude the tourists, of course: that kind of industrial, grunge freaknik vibe, with the crazy colours and the piercings and the tattoos; and then the other vibe, the more Parisian-type style. I wonder if the Berliners would be offended by the comparison. Designer dresses and expensive highlights. Perfect nails and Instagrammable entertainment habits. I could've chosen either way, but

I am sick of feeling grubby and cheap. I don't want to pour my own stein and wolf down bratwurst. I have gone for elegance, but just like Julia Roberts in *Pretty Woman*, when she's finally managed to get herself a fancy dress and a classy chignon, I am not what I look like in the mirror.

The hairdresser has chosen to see a certain version of me, a version that I have chosen to reveal to her. The real me is much more difficult to define. I tilt my head, give myself a small, coy smile. The version of me smiles back. I am ready.

I check Sam's FB one more time while I wait for the doorman to hail me a cab. His last check-in was the Roofer Club in Mitte, several hours ago, and since then there have been several photographs posted — fancy, multi-coloured drinks in expensive glassware, adorned with exotic fruits. Delicious, bite-sized canapes on giltedged trays. A plethora of greenery and luscious-looking plants with an array of pretty blooms. And then there's Sam, looking tanned and oh-so handsome, lounging on leather sofas with a selection of beautiful people. His friends? Or just others sitting nearby? The women are gorgeous, with just the right level of potential sluttiness, and I wonder if one of them is his girlfriend. Not that it matters, because when he sees me he will surely disregard these vacant imposters. It has been a few weeks since he last saw me, and I've lost some weight, making my collar and cheekbones more prominent. My hair, my clothes, my make-up — all expertly styled. Quite different from the sweaty, slovenly beach look that he last saw me in. I scroll through the photos; some are not his, he is tagged by someone — Bethany — and I wonder if she is the one who has stolen him from me.

Not for long, *Bethany*. Your fun is over now.

I don't want to make a scene. I want to glide in there and watch his jaw drop. I want him to see me. I want him to want me.

The doorman opens the door of the yellow cab and I climb in, depositing a euro into his palm and smiling at him. A few people outside the hotel peer over at me, wondering if I am someone special. My attire and my elegance giving the impression that I'd hoped.

I am no one, of course. But as long as I act like I am a princess, then they will believe it. Like Cinderella, I might only be a princess for one night, but I shall go to the ball.

The driver asks me where I want to go, and I tell him the address in perfect German. He glances in his rear-view mirror, smiles.

"Where are you from?" he asks, in German.

I pretend not to understand, give him a small shrug, then I stare out of the window. He gets the message, and doesn't try to engage with me again.

Thankfully the traffic isn't too bad, and I continue to stare out of the window, taking in the sights. The river Spree is murky and grey, and not at all appealing, but from what I have read about the area, there are some "beaches" where the water looks cleaner, more alluring. I watch a tourist boat trundling along, leaving trails of white foam in its wake. We stop at traffic lights — the cutesy Ampelmannchen sign switching from green to

268

red as pedestrians start to cross. A girl in shorts carrying a backpack skirts past the car, and for a brief moment my heart stops. I watch her retreating form, see the tattoo of a snake sliding down from her shorts, and I know it's not her. Carrie didn't have any tattoos. And she would never get one so vulgar. Besides, she can't be here. Not here. She only exists now inside my mind. A beautiful memory, that one day will start to fade.

The car carries on, for another block, and then it pulls in to the side.

"Twenty euro," the driver says.

I take the money from my purse. We're here.

I am going to see Sam. My heart starts fluttering in my chest as I step out of the car. Of course he was going to end up here in Berlin, with his new German mates. But it's lucky I checked his Facebook in the cab to the airport in Moscow, or I'd have ended up flying somewhere completely pointless and random. As it is, it feels like fate. I can't wait to see him again.

I take in the grand entrance, the potted palms, the sharply dressed doormen. The entrance is in stark contrast to the grungier buildings that sit alongside, and I wonder if they are trying to be ironic — having this blingy venue in the punky east — or perhaps everything is starting to become one amorphous lump, losing its identity. That's something I can relate to, as it happens.

"Where is the party?" I say, again in my perfect German.

"Rooftop," says doorman one, giving me a lascivious sneer as he opens the huge glass doors.

I smile and glide in, looking like any other girl that is meant to be there.

Looking like I belong.

CHAPTER
THIRTY-SIX

The doors of the glass elevator slide open and I take a lurid peach martini from a tuxedoed waiter holding a tray. I think I get this place now. The ride up had revealed that most of the floors were bare — random pieces of old furniture, scuffed floors and walls covered in mouldy, peeling paint. Someone has had the idea of turning the top floor into a luxurious hedonist's dream — the transparent walls of the lift exist solely to show the guests what was there before, to make them feel elite. It's an artwork, of sorts, and I try to be impressed, but as I glance around the space, taking in the types of people that are in here, drinking, laughing, sizing each other up, I have a feeling that most of them probably don't really get it.

I take a sip of my drink, then walk across to a high, glass bar. The whole frontage is completely see-through, highlighting the bare legs of the staff serving on the other side. Above the bar level, they are in crisp white shirts and black bow ties; underneath, their toned, hairfree legs are on full display beneath their skimpy white underpants. I feel a wave of disgust at this, and try hard not to look beneath the counter, but at their faces and their torsos, at their expert hands

271

holding diamante-encrusted cocktail shakers, high-pouring into rows of different-shaped glasses.

A man in an open-necked cream linen shirt, artfully half tucked into dark, perfectly fitted jeans, walks towards me, a look of interest and intrigue on his face as he runs a hand through his floppy blond hair.

Here we go, I think, and drain the rest of my drink. There are pros and cons of dressing to fit your environment and, sadly, this is one of the cons. On another night I might've been interested in him, but tonight there's only one man for me. I turn away from the approaching man and scan the room for Sam, but I can't see him. I'm not worried. Not yet. I don't think he will have left while the party is in full swing, and judging by the layout, I expect there are some hidden nooks and crannies for me to explore.

"Well, good evening," the blond man drawls. He is not German, but I can't place his accent yet.

"Hello," I say, making sure to look him in the eye. "Nice party."

He smirks. "Glad you approve." He holds out a hand, which is strangely formal in this setting, but I take it anyway and try to hide my confusion. "Sorry," he says, stepping back again, that smirk still firmly fixed on his face, "I'm not sure we've met?"

"Oh." I give him a brief, girlish giggle, sure that this is what he wants. "A friend invited me . . . I think he's already here."

He laughs. "Did he now? Funny, it was specific on the invites that this was *not* a plus-one situation, but as

272

you're here . . ." He pauses, looks me up and down. "I'm not going to turn away a pretty girl."

I don't like the way he's looking at me now, and in my peripheral vision I spot a couple of extremely glammed-up girls in the shortest, tightest dresses I've ever seen — perfect cleavage spilling over the top, and endless legs on expensive heels below. One of them widens her eyes, and the other gives the tiniest of headshakes, and I realise that I may have made a huge mistake.

"Perhaps I should go?" I lay my empty glass on the bar and turn away, but he grabs my upper arm, a little tighter than I'd like, and spins me back to face him.

He leans in close, pulling me in as if in an embrace, and whispers forcefully into my ear. "This is my party, little girl, and you'll stay now that you're here." Then he lets go of me and does an air kiss on each side, saying, "So amazing to see you again, Alyssa." And then he turns away and heads off towards a cluster of people who are grouped around the far end of the bar, whooping and chattering at the bar staff as if they are performing monkeys.

Shaken, I wait for a moment more, then head towards the lift, but, as I do, I spot him — at the far end of the room, heading through a door that I'm sure I hadn't noticed before. Time seems to stand still for a moment, as I watch him disappear through the gap, the door swinging back into place — fake bookshelf and all. If I wasn't rattled by my encounter with the horrible blond, I would be rolling my eyes at the cheesiness of this hidden door set-up, but right now, all I want to do is stay invisible for long enough to find the right time to go through it and confront the man who has been haunting my dreams since we parted ways almost three weeks ago.

I take another of the peach drinks from a tray and walk slowly around the edge of the room, taking it all in. The women are very beautiful, but most of them are incredibly drunk — draped in pairs over far less attractive men. Then I spot the two girls from earlier, as they glide in unison towards a table in the corner, where one man sits, a bucket in front of him with a bottle of champagne, three glasses on the table next to it. They sit down on either side of him, and then they lean in and kiss his cheeks, as coordinated as synchronised swimmers — and that's when I realise that the women aren't "guests", they are employees. "Alyssa" is who the arrogant host has decided I will be for the night.

No.

I turn away from the coordinated whores on my left and make my way across the room towards the secret door. No one has followed Sam up there, and I'm wondering if it's out of bounds, or maybe there will be some sort of keypad, and I will end up getting caught and thrown out before I can get the one thing that I came here for. I glance around, trying to look casual, but also to make sure that no one is watching me. I recognise someone else. One of the German guys from the hotel in Bangkok. Of course — Sam wouldn't even be here if it wasn't for them. I wonder if they've offered him a job, or something. Or maybe this awful host has.

Maybe that's why he's here. I don't like to think of Sam mixed up in a place like this.

I worry for a moment that I won't be able to locate the sensor to open the bookcase, but I needn't have panicked. As I walk slowly past a line of five red books clumped together, purely for the colour of their spines, rather than their content, a small, green light blinks at the back of the shelf and I reach in, as if to take a book, and there is a small click, and then the door swings open. This time I don't bother to glance behind me; I just hurry through and hope that no one has noticed me going inside.

As I walk slowly up the dark glass staircase, I take a deep breath, trying to calm the nerves that have had the cheek to make themselves known. I don't know why I am nervous — it must be because I am so excited to be seeing Sam again; and partly because I'm scared that he won't want to see me . . . and partly because I know I could be putting myself in danger. I have no idea what lies at the top of this staircase. This could be where people go for the "real" show. One of those sex parties that you hear about and can scarcely believe actually happen.

But it's too late now.

As I reach the top of the stairs, it becomes clear that I'm not entering another room. I'm going outside, onto a rooftop garden.

It's dimly lit, with only fairy-light bulbs pinned around the sides of the walls, and a dark glass floor, like the stairs. The space seems to be empty, and at first I think that there is no one up here at all, and that Sam must've gone back down another way, but then I near noises. Soft snuffles and grunts, whispers and moans, and the rhythmic squeak of something moving against leather.

I blink, trying to get my eyes to adjust to the light, and then I see that there are some small glass cabins in the middle of the roof space. The doors are closed, but the glass walls are clearly not soundproof. Maybe that's meant to add to the experience, knowing that whatever it is you are doing in your cabin, others are doing the same right beside you. Perhaps they can all see out of the glass, but I can't see in. Part of me wants to run back down the stairs and out of this place — the feeling of it is all wrong, just like that party in Irkutsk. But something is drawing me to investigate further before I go. I have to assume that Sam is inside one of these cabins, and I don't want to imagine what he is doing, or what is being done to him, but on the other hand, I feel a stirring deep inside, and I realise that the whole thing is turning me on.

I walk slowly past the cabins, trying not to make any sound, not letting my heels clip on the floor. There are more cabins at the back, but there are no doors on this side, so I can only assume that they are all linked, and I try to blink away further visions about what might be going on in there.

Then I see him.

He is standing on the far side of the roof space, leaning back against the wall. I see the silhouette of smoke curling above him against the inky sky. He sees me, and I see the flash of white teeth as he grins. He turns away, and then hoists himself up onto the wall. Sits.

"Hello," he says. He tips his head towards the cabins. "Don't bother to try and coerce me, darling. It's not really my scene."

I swallow. He doesn't recognise me from here. I can make him out because I knew he was up here, and because I would recognise him with my eyes closed. But he can't see me yet. Besides, I don't really look much like I did the last time he saw me. And I'm out of context, he won't be expecting to find me here at all. I smile to myself, pleased at the surprise.

"I'm not here to coerce you," I say. "Not really my scene either. Thought you'd know that." I take a few steps closer, teasing it out.

He sounds amused. "Do I know you? I don't think I saw you downstairs. Are you one of Hagan's new girls?"

I shake my head. "I guess Hagan is the arrogant prick with the blond flick? I don't think he likes me very much. I kind of blagged my way in."

He laughs, then flicks his cigarette over the wall, turning to watch it fall. "I've never heard of anyone crashing one of Hagan's gatherings before. Most girls run a mile once they realise what goes on here."

"And what about you?" I say, taking a few more steps closer. I can see his face now, and I long to put my hands on his cheeks and pull him towards me, to feel his soft lips on mine. "Do you like what goes on here?"

His face darkens. "Not really," he says, under his breath, "but I'm pretty close to getting a job with the

277

firm, and from what I can gather, this stuff is compulsory. This is my third time, and I've always just snuck up here and hidden in the corner for a while. I don't think anyone has realised that I don't partake." He pauses, peers at me. "Are you sure I don't know you? There's something a bit familiar about you."

I smile and walk further over, until I am only a short distance away from him. He can't fail to recognise me now.

"It's me," I say, tipping my head to the side and giving him a coquettish smirk. "Violet."

He looks confused for a moment. "I don't know anyone called Violet . . ."

I take a step closer. "Ohhh, sorry," I say. "You didn't know me as Violet, did you?" I slap my forehead with the heel of my hand. "So silly. I got the new ID on the Khao San Road. I'd forgotten that was *after* you left me."

"Ronnie? That's it, isn't it?" he says, shaking his head. "Jesus, is that you? You fucking mad bitch. Stefan and Pauli told me I should've called the police on you, but I was worried you'd end up in one of those crazy Thai prisons — and no one deserves that, not even you . . ."

It's my turn to look confused. "You left me, Sam. We were happy . . . we were —"

"We were nothing. You stalked me and tricked me into a one-night stand and then you fucking robbed me . . ."

"You said we were going to travel together."

278

He snorts. "Did I fuck! Bloody hell, wait until the guys hear that you've turned up. How did you even find me?"

The rage starts to bubble. "You're such a fucking narcissist, Sam, checking in every place you go on Facebook. It's not hard to keep track."

"And you're a fucking fantasist! Jesus. Have you been keeping track on me since Bangkok?"

I take a step closer, giving him my best smile. I flick my hair back, then I smooth down my dress. I raise an eyebrow, saying, "Look at what you're missing."

He shakes his head. "What have you done to yourself? I barely recognise you. You know, I don't think Hagan is going to like it much that you've crashed in here. He'll try to put you to work. You should go."

He shuffles back a bit on the wall, and I see from the look on his face that he's not comfortable with me showing up like this. Fair enough; maybe I should've messaged him first to let him know — but then what would be the fun in that?

His look changes again, and I realise it's not discomfort. It's fear.

Good. I gave him a chance to be nice to me. I gave him a chance to want me.

"Look . . . what do you want, Ronn —"

"Violet. It's Violet. You know what I want. I want to take everything." I pause, then lower my voice. ". . . Don't I, Courtney?"

He shifts on the wall once more. "Who the fuck is Courtney?"

I smile at him. Courtney Love's voice fills my head. The song — my namesake — keeps playing in my head, and I forget that only I can hear it.

He's still looking at me with that mixture of fear, confusion and revulsion as I take a final step forwards and push him hard in the chest. It's so quick, I don't think he even remembers to scream. I lean over the wall and peer down, but it's too far away for me to see what's down there. Too far, even, for me to notice anything other than the heavy liquid slap as his body lands on the concrete.

It's his own fault. If he'd even been *slightly* pleased to see me, he might've lived.

I was ready to front it out, walk back to the glass stairs and through the sleazy party, but I notice that further along there are a couple of steps up and over the wall, leading to the fire escape.

This has all been less satisfying than I'd hoped.

Ignoring the sounds of grunts and moans behind me, it's clear that no one has noticed what just happened, so I take the opportunity and climb over the wall and onto the iron fire escape beneath. It's a lot of floors, but I figure that no one's going to be looking for me just yet.

I take my phone out of my bag and open up Facebook, clicking "unfollow" on Sam's profile, then I start to make my way down the stairs, barely noticing the descent because my body is so pumped full of adrenaline that I am both shaking and numb.

280

To: carrie82@hotmail.com
From: rosieposie1985@gmail.com
Subject: Hi

Mum says you're on some retreat thing and you might not get this. Don't know if you're planning on coming home this year, but just in case you are, I'm getting married. Fancy being a bridesmaid? *GRIN*

Rx

P.S. Don't take the piss. Be happy for me!

CHAPTER THIRTY-SEVEN

I sleep like I am dead. And when I wake, it takes me a moment to work out where I am. My head is fuzzy, but not from alcohol. I felt like this in Russia, too, after it happened. After all of those things happened. My first instinct is to aim for oblivion again, but it's starting to wear thin, even for me. It's temporary, at best, and when it goes, I'm back to where I started. There's another option, of course — a more permanent one. But I'm not sure if I am ready for that.

People say that suicide is selfish, but that's only if you have anyone to leave behind. Who's going to care about me when I'm gone? I'd thought that I still had Daddy, but even he now seems to be tiring of me — pandering to the whims of my mother, listening to her lies about me. I was never who she accused me of being. It's almost as if she wanted me to be bad, so that she could justify to herself why she was a useless excuse for a mother. I feel nothing for her now, and my feelings for him are waning.

And there is no one else.

I never expected to be alone in this world. As a child, I'd imagined a big family full of fun and laughter, bickering over Christmas dinner, falling out with my siblings and then making up, knowing that they would always be there for me, no matter what.

But I never had any siblings. My mother made sure of that. I suppose I've been subconsciously seeking out that love ever since, confusing friendship and family, becoming obsessed, I suppose, although I am loath to admit it. The truth is I have been let down. By everyone I've come into contact with. That's hardly my fault, now — is it?

I drag myself out of bed and into the shower, dressing quickly in one of the more muted outfits I bought when I arrived — dark jeans, red Converse, a striped vest and a neat, grey cotton jacket on top. I tie my hair back and stuff it into a baseball cap, and don a pair of sunglasses that block out most of my face.

I'm invisible now, as I head through the foyer and into the street. I am not the glamour girl from before. There is no reason for anyone to notice me.

Back in the same hair salon — I can't help myself — my friendly stylist from before is not on duty. I feel a prickle of disappointment, but I blink it away. It's for the best. I shouldn't even have come back here. The allocated stylist is punky and bored-looking. He ignores my attempts at conversation. He doesn't care who I am. I point at an image in a magazine — chosen entirely at random from the first page I'd opened it at — and he raises his expertly pencilled brows, just for a moment, and then he shrugs and gives me something close to a smile. I've piqued his interest now, and he tries to engage me, but I stick my nose back in the magazine and ignore him.

I get through the process — cut, colour, rinse. A young girl in a candy-pink dress with goldilocks-style plaits sweeps away my blonde hair, and I don't look in the mirror again until it's done.

"You like it?" the stylist says, holding up a mirror so I can see the back. He's grinning now, pleased with his work. "I *really* like it."

I stare at myself in the mirror. At the black, sweeping fringe, edged with a neon pink tint. I turn my head side to side, taking in the swept-back sides that blend into the shaved back. I blink, not quite able to believe it. I've had many transformations, but none quite so bold. I want to laugh at how ridiculously un-me it is; but on the other hand, it's absolutely perfect. No one is going to link me to that blonde from the rooftop sex party. No way.

"*Danke,*" I say, "it's *perfect.*"

It's only when I pull out my purse to pay that I realise I've lost my new bank card. *Shit.* Shit!

Luckily I took the extra precaution of withdrawing a load of cash, so I pay, leaving him a generous tip, and head out of the shop, trying to keep the panic that is beating a loud, rhythmic drum in my chest.

I think about heading back to the bank for a replacement card — but worry that this would be too conspicuous, after only getting it yesterday . . . and I worry about where I might have dropped it. I know I had it when I went out last night, because I used it to pay the cab there — but I walked back, winding through the streets, trying not to draw attention to myself. I didn't want a cabbie to remember picking me up from near that place. If I dropped the card in the rooftop bar, then there's a good chance that it's been found — and if it's been found, there's a good chance that someone might already be looking for me.

285

To: carrie82@hotmail.com
From: lauralee@gmail.com
Subject: WHERE ARE YOU??

CARRIE!! Please call me. I'm so scared for you! I know you're not with her now, but she's all over the news! You were right to be suspicious . . . Her name's not Violet.

HER REAL NAME IS VERONICA DELAUNEY, AND SHE IS EXTREMELY DANGEROUS!!!

They've been looking for her for almost two years. She's killed people, Carrie . . . She's been on the run, but they'll find her. They found her ID and bank card and they know she's in Berlin.

PLEASE reply as soon as you get this.

I'm scared that she's going to come looking for you!!!

Please call me. Please come home.

Lxx

CHAPTER
THIRTY-EIGHT

I don't want to go back to the hotel yet, so I walk back from the salon a different way and end up on the edge of the famous Tiergarten — the huge park in the west of the city centre, famous for nude sunbathers, secluded gardens and a pretty boating lake. I remember coming here with my parents, on that trip so long ago, and it feels like fate that I should end up here. I was too young to care much about the bar when I was younger — but I remember it vividly.

I check the signs to make sure I am going the right way, and then I hurry into the park, the trees screening the sounds of traffic nearby, and by the time I have been walking for a few minutes, it feels like I am a million miles away.

Maybe my bank card is back in the hotel, and I'm overreacting. I have enough cash to keep me going for now, so I decide not to worry about it for a while.

The sunlight tries to push through the thick canopy of trees, but the light fades as I go further into the woods. Shadows dance on hidden sculptures, and the place seems to fall silent for a moment, and I stop to take a breath. I look up at the sky through the clearing and have a sudden feeling of claustrophobia, as if the branches reaching up are beginning to change direction, swirling and winding, seeking me out, ready to grab me and smother me in their wooden embrace . . . and then the sounds return. Birds chirruping in the trees, the scurrying of small animals in the undergrowth, and a flurry of voices carrying on the wind.

I blink, rub my face with my hands. *Get a grip.* Then I start walking again, quickly, over a small bridge and towards the sound of the voices. When I come out of the trees, the world returns: a road, nearby, and on the other side, the bar that I remember — long wooden tables, fairy lights strung across trees. The tables are filled with the after-work crowd, mingling with tourists, drinking steins of cold, pale beer and eating pizza.

I take a breath and feel calmer at last. I follow a couple into the self-service area and get myself a beer and a pretzel, then head out to find a good place to sit and reflect. I have to work out what to do next. Staying in Berlin isn't really an option now, after what happened at the rooftop bar, but for once I am at a loss as to where to go. I wish I could go home. Move back in with my parents. Shut myself away for a while. But from my conversation with Daddy, I don't think I am welcome. I suppose it's no real surprise that he's given up on me, just like everyone else.

I take a bite of the pretzel, enjoying the soft, salty warmth. Then I wash it down with a glug of ice-cold beer, and take Carrie's laptop out of my bag. The photo on the wallpaper is of the two of us on the train — taken on our first night, and the only photo of us that I think there is. I run a hand across Carrie's face and

288

wish that things had turned out differently. I'd thought we were so alike, that first night in Beijing — but it turns out we weren't alike at all. She just wanted fun, no matter the risk, no matter who got trampled along the way. I'd wanted a friend . . . more than that. I'd wanted someone to love me.

I click open the photos folder and delete the picture, then empty the trash. Then I gaze across the lake, at the couples laughing, rowing their boats, having fun together. Carrie would like it here, I think. I take another sip of my beer, and I try to block out the chatter around me, zoning out as I remember the last time I saw her.

She'd grabbed me from behind, trying to pin my arms to my sides. Trying to stop me from smashing Sergei in the face with the lamp. He'd staggered back, and I'd pushed, and she'd pulled . . . and it was an accident. But it was her fault. I close my eyes.

"Violet, stop!" Carrie screams in my ear. She's yanking at my T-shirt, and I shrug her off, but she won't stop.

Sergei is stumbling, trying to right himself. There is a lot of blood, from where I've hit him on the back of the head, and he reaches a hand up, touches it. Looks confused. He is muttering something in Russian, but even in another language it sounds garbled and nonsensical.

He is almost at the balcony.

Carrie is on my back, gripping me like a monkey. "Violet, you need to stop." Her weight causes me to lurch forwards, and I almost lose my footing, but I throw out my arms to break my fall, and I connect with Sergei's chest, and he flies back, colliding with the low wall of the balcony. The wall is too low. I said this to Carrie when we arrived. It's dangerous, this low wall. It's a health and safety concern. Just one of many in that horrible place.

The shock of the impact causes Sergei to awaken from his stupor, momentarily at least, and he rises up to his full height, his face contorted in anger.

"You fucking *beetch*," he shouts, and I lunge forwards, lifting a shoulder hard at the same time, and I feel a huge weight lift off me as Carrie loses her grip and crashes to the floor. I barrel into him like a charging bull, and I hit him just in the right place.

His arms windmill as he falls back, realising that there is nothing behind him, and he bends in half and topples over the balcony. After a moment, there is a wet, crunching sound as gravity deals with this rotten apple of a man. Not a man . . . an animal.

A wolf.

I'm relieved that the hotel is practically deserted.

I peer over the edge, and see the lump of flesh and bone on the concrete below. There's no way he can have survived that fall. I take a step back and let out a long, slow breath.

"It's OK," I say, quietly. "He's gone, Carrie. He can't hurt you anymore."

No answer.

I turn, expecting to see her crying on the floor, but that's not what I see.

290

She is on the floor, but she is not crying. She's not moving. Her face is turned away from me, a small pool of blood forming on the floor where she has hit her head on the edge of the bedside cabinet.

Oh God . . . oh God . . . oh God.

Carrie is dead.

A creak brings me back to the present, movement on the bench as someone sits down at the other end, a little distance away from me. I open my eyes and wipe away my tears. I never meant for that to happen. Of all the things, I never meant for that. I can see the new arrival out of the corner of my eye — a young woman in a long floral dress, floppy sunhat and huge shades. She seems to be alone.

Can I risk another friendship? Perhaps, but I have to sort out some admin first.

I open the email app on the laptop and scroll back up to the top of the list — to the most recent email from Laura to Carrie. It must've come in while I was in the hair salon.

HER REAL NAME IS VERONICA DELAUNEY, AND SHE IS EXTREMELY DANGEROUS!!!

I laugh out loud. I can't help it. The stupid cow still thinks she's talking to Carrie.

I type a reply to the message:

What's with the dramatic caps, Loz? It's fine. I am safe.

Then I delete it, and type instead:

My name is VIOLET, my dear Laura . . . and they will never find me.

I delete this too, then snap the lid of the laptop shut. I'll deal with it later.

"Too nice an evening to be working, right?"

I turn towards the voice. The girl in the sundress. She's taken off her sunglasses and placed them on the table.

"You're right, there," I say. "I love your dress, by the way."

"Oh, thank you!" She grins and her whole face lights up. She's younger than I first thought. Her English is perfect, but with the hint of an accent. Not German; Swedish maybe. I see a lock of white-blonde hair poking out from under her hat and think that I'm probably right. I keep looking at her dress.

"I'm Daisy," I say, reaching out a hand, "like your dress."

"That is so cool! I love floral names. I'm Annie."

"Like the orphan."

She laughs.

"My mother wanted to call me Violet," I say. "But my father thought it was too dark."

She laughs again. "They are a bit sinister, aren't they? Daisies are beautiful though. Sunny and bright and perfect." She grins, and then she turns away at the sound of her name being called from another table.

"Nice to meet you," she says, gathering up her sunglasses and her bag. "My colleagues are over there. I didn't even see them."

292

I swallow back my disappointment.

"Have a lovely evening," I say. I hear her laughing when she reaches her friends, and I want to run over there and grab her and shake her and scream.

But I don't.

I glance around, at the groups of people, at the couples, looking for someone else who might be more promising. Someone else alone. I see a woman with long dark hair poking out from a cowboy hat. Sitting with her denim-jacketed back to me a few tables away. I pause, glancing around, but she's the best candidate. The only candidate.

Then I pick up my things.

I'm going to go to the toilet, and then I'll get myself another drink . . . and if she's still alone when I return, I will go over and join her.

To: lauralee@gmail.com
From: carrie82@hotmail.com
Subject: Chill

Laura! Don't panic! Really . . . I told you, I'm not with her
— it doesn't matter who she is or what she's done. Well, it
does, matter — but really, I am fine! I promise! I'm trying
to decide where to go next. I know you want me to come
home, but I'm not ready. Honestly . . . I am having a ball.
I've made loads of new friends. I wish you could meet
them! Maybe when you're all healed you can come out and
meet me for a holiday?

To be honest, I don't think I'm coming back . . .

Love you, Loz.

Carrie xx

★   ★   ★

To: laura.mclean@exhon-services.com
From: carrie.osborne@btinternet.com
Subject: The Eagle Has Landed

She's here. She hasn't spotted me yet, but it's only a matter of time. I've got everything set up. Talk to you later, when it's done. C.

CHAPTER
THIRTY-NINE

The girl in the denim jacket is still alone when I return with another beer. I hesitate, just for a moment. Do I really need to talk to another girl right now? Maybe I should look for a man instead. I'd thought a friendship was what I needed more than a lover, and I'd even thought that Carrie might become both, but things aren't going to plan and maybe it's time for a break.

I can't see her face. It's obscured by her long hair, her head tipped forwards as she types fast on her phone. A frantic conversation, by the looks of it, or a rant. I walk closer, and see that in front of her on the table is an ice bucket with a bottle of something fizzy, beads of condensation running down the sides. Two flutes and one pretzel, sitting expectantly on a plate.

She's waiting for someone.

I almost walk away. I do a quick scan, looking for another likely candidate, but everyone else is in couples or groups, and I never join a group if I can help it. Far too risky.

She drops the phone on the table and sighs dramatically. Perhaps she's been stood up? I take it as my cue.

"Mind if I sit here?"

She doesn't look up. "Sure, go ahead." She has an Irish accent — Northern, I think. Something about it is familiar, but I blink it away. She uses a nail to slice the foil on the bottle, twists it off and rolls it into a ball, then sets about untwisting the wire mesh.

I sit down opposite her, put my beer on the table, and try not to stare. She's wearing a straw cowboy hat with a black rim. Huge, amber-tinted sunglasses. Her hair is dark and sleek. From the angle, I can't see her face at all. I'm not going to be pushy. I open my bag and take out Carrie's laptop, and place it down in front of me, but I don't open it yet. I take a sip of beer, try to be casual. I'll wait until she talks to me, because if she does, then I'll know I was right to come over.

Her hands are working on the cork, and she mutters something under her breath, and I have this sudden flashback to the night I met Carrie, and her accents, and . . .

She lifts her head, just as the cork releases with a loud pop, and I see her face for the first time. Even with the sunglasses and the hair and the hat, I'm not going to fail to recognise those lips. Her perfect rosebud mouth.

My own mouth falls open in shock. The pop of the cork has given me another flashback — this time to Brad and his fancy hotel. Blood pooling under his face on the posh carpet. I blink.

She takes off her sunglasses and hangs them on the front of her loose T-shirt, exposing smooth, milky skin. I stare, open-mouthed, as she plonks the hat on the table, slides the dark wig off her head and shakes her own shorter blonde hair loose. "Surprise," Carrie says, grinning. "Nice laptop. I used to have one like that, but some fucker stole it." Her Scottish accent is back, and it's dripping with venom.

"You're . . . you're supposed to be dead. I —"

"That's right, Violet. Don't make a scene, now. Christ, you took your time. I thought for a minute you weren't going to come over." She leans across the table, whispers, "You *thought* I was dead. You didn't check though, did you? I woke up in the stinking boot of that Lada, face pressed into your man Sergei. I'd thought he was decent at the party, but he was a right shady fucker, as it happens. You did me a favour sorting him out, so I thank you for that, although you did take your time, to be fair. You let him get his filthy cock inside me before you caved in his skull. He wasn't so good-looking after being launched off that balcony, I can tell you that."

I lean back from her, shocked. Unable to take it in. "I didn't push him. He . . . he fell."

"Course he did. Just like I did when I tried to stop you from pushing him or battering him to a pulp with that lamp. Hit my head on the bedside cabinet. Even I thought I was a goner. You know you're meant to check breathing as well as pulse?"

"I . . . uh . . ." I can't get the words out. "He carried you downstairs. Out the fire escape. I took your bag . . . well, it was my bag, as it turned out — Ivan was grabbing things and tossing them in. I got confused with all the commotion. Didn't realise until I woke up later. Anyway, I took it and walked past reception with

298

it. Shorts on, sweatshirt hood up. Not hard to pass myself off as you. I knew the receptionist wouldn't be paying attention . . ."

She rolls her eyes, mocking me, and it lights the touch paper.

My shock soon morphs into embarrassment and anger. I ball my hands into tight little fists. I don't like to be made a fool of. My voice is cold, flat. I need to deal with this now. "I assumed Ivan would've made sure."

"You picked a dud there, love. Turns out he actually *was* Ivan the Terrible after all. Terrible at doing your dirty work. Should've seen his face when he opened the boot and I leapt out. We came to a wee arrangement, though — I'd say nothing about the body with a head like a burst watermelon in his boot; he'd let me go, as long as I paid him fifty thousand roubles and disappeared. You were never to find out, of course. Until I saw what you were up to. That first email you sent to Laura almost gave you away."

I nod. Calm again now. I know I've messed up. It was a risk, and it could've paid off, but it didn't. "I realised that. I was terrified that I'd given myself away straight off . . . then she replied, and I thought it was OK."

"She was suspicious, but I got to her fast. I spoke to her. I told her we'd just have to come up with a wee plan of our own. If you were pretending to be me, then I would pretend to be her. She gave me her email login, and the two of us kept in touch via different email addresses and on the phone. I'm not sure what you were hoping to achieve, pretending to be me — maybe

299

just to give you enough time to detach yourself from me, so that when people at home sussed out that it wasn't me writing those emails, you'd be long gone? Tell me, Violet. Tell me, because I am genuinely interested in how your psychopathic brain actually works . . ."

Something occurs to me, and I realise what an idiot I've been. How my plan was flawed from the start. "How did you know I was here?"

Carrie barks out a laugh. She nods towards the laptop. Her laptop. "You kept *that* — but you forgot to disconnect it from the cloud. Ivan gave me my phone, and I was still connected to it via the cloud. I kept expecting you to notice, to realise what was going on. If I hadn't had my phone, I don't think I could've done it — not without another device back-up. I told you Ivan was an idiot. *Find my device* is much more accurate than tracking people via their Facebook check-ins."

I smirk. I still have an ace up my sleeve. "I read your drafts, Carrie. I know what you did . . ."

Her face clouds for a moment, and then she looks down, won't meet my eye. "What *I* did was an accident . . ."

"I doubt Greg sees it like that."

She lifts her head and sighs. "You're right, V. It's something I need to take care of. I know that. Things got out of hand. But you don't know Greg . . . you don't —"

"You hit him." My voice is incredulous.

She sighs again. "I know exactly what I did, and I'm not proud of that. I've spent this whole trip feeling

300

guilty. Trying to block it all out. And it's something I'll have to face when I get back. But it's something I *will* face. I'm not running away from it. I know I did something wrong. But you . . . *you* don't seem to know the difference between right and wrong. You pushed a man off a balcony. You thought you'd killed me too. I'm pretty sure you don't have the moral high ground here. I was angry and upset. Betrayed. I lashed out. But you —"

"I don't have to listen to this." I stand up, but she leans across the table, reflex quick, and grabs my wrist.

"Sit down."

I'm too shocked to respond, and I fall back heavily onto the bench. The man sitting at the far end says something in German, and he and his companion laugh, but I ignore them.

"You know you dropped your ID near where they found Sam? Jesus, what did that bloke even do? Did you actually know him, V, or was he just one of your mad obsessions?"

"I told you. I don't want to talk about Sam."

She slams a fist on the table. "Sam is dead. They're looking for you, V. They'll find you."

"They'll never find me."

She smirks. "You know," she says, pouring champagne into the two flutes, "it's funny that I always called you 'V' — like I actually knew that your name wasn't Violet."

I pick up the bottle, and take a long swig. "So what happens now?"

"Well, you killed me . . . remember? Then you pretended to be me. But you're not as bright as you think you are, *Violet*. Or should I say Veronica. Veronica Delauney from Windlesby Manor in Surrey. I knew you were home-counties spoiled rich trash, but I didn't expect this. Your poor parents. Daddy's a diplomat, isn't he? Not sure he's going to manage to get you out of this one. I imagine the paparazzi are already at the gates."

I make a face. "As if they care . . ."

"Oh, have they disowned you? That wouldn't surprise me at all. I wonder if they even know what you're really like?" She picks up her glass and downs the contents. Refills it, and does the same. "Cheers."

She's smirking at me, and I don't like it. How dare she call me stupid?

"You've got no idea what I've done. What people have done to me . . . I've defended myself, that's all. I've done it many times, and I'll do it again if I have to. People like you, you'll never understand what it's like . . ." I pick up the champagne bottle, but I don't take a drink.

A dark cloud crosses my vision and I zone out. A selection of interconnected scenes slot into my head, as clear as a cinema reel — me swinging the bottle, the bottle connecting with Carrie's face . . . screams, blood, my arms being pinned behind me. Sirens, police with guns. Court. My mother's blank expression as she watches me from the dock. Prison . . .

Perhaps prison wouldn't be so bad. Plenty of opportunities in there, for someone resourceful like me.

The sound of sirens jolts me back to life.

I've taken too long.

I turn around, scanning the exits, the bar, the other tables — but she's gone. I put the bottle back into the ice bucket. I can hear the sounds of car doors slamming, shouts. Running feet. Through the trees, I see the sun glinting on the boating lake, and I wonder if I have time.

I can't swim, remember? This could be the perfect, sweet, release. I stand up, smiling now. It's all going to be over soon enough. It takes me a moment to realise that people are being ushered away from their tables. Their drinks and food abandoned. There's a cacophony of chatter and fear. I catch a glimpse of a red rowing boat, an oar dipping into the cool water. Too late now.

"Veronica Delauney?"

Two armed police stand in front of me, their expressions stern. I should get them to call Daddy. I wonder if I'll get diplomatic immunity.

"Veronica Delauney, you must come with us now."

Give me a minute.

Surely another few moments won't make a difference now. I'm not going anywhere. I close my eyes, drifting off again, and I remember those big skies in the desert, Carrie's arms around me. Her lips on mine.

"*Violet . . .*" she'd whispered. "I think I love you."

The policemen are talking on their radios. They flank me on both sides, and one lays a surprisingly gentle hand on my arm. I turn to him, and smile. *She'd thought it, even just for a moment. I'll take that.*

"It's Violet," I whisper, as I let them lead me away. "My name is *Violet*."

Epilogue

The daylight has faded to a smoky grey, the low-hanging clouds threatening rain. The harsh interior lighting of the concourse makes her wince as the automatic doors slide open. She glides her new wheeled suitcase towards the check-in desks, feeling light, at last, after finally ditching the rucksack. It had been a cheap buy from Mountain Warehouse, she and Laura buying the same ones in matching colours. Giggling as they'd picked up and put down the weird little camping and hiking trinkets on display near the tills. Laura's rucksack will still be pristine — probably still in the cellophane. She hopes they'll get a chance to use it together some day, although she's not sure that another backpacking adventure is going to be on the cards for a long while yet.

God, she misses Laura. Can't wait to take the piss out of her pale, scrawny leg, free of the plaster-cast at last — just in time for her getting back home. There's so much she needs to share with Laura, about everything. But there are some things that will have to stay locked away for good.

Violet thought she knew the full story, reading those emails about Greg that she was never going to send. Yes, she did hit him. No, she's not proud of it. But after what happened, it was him or Laura who was going to have to face her rage — and she cared more about Laura. She didn't want to destroy their whole friendship over a man. Certainly not a man like Greg.

That's why her fall had to look like an accident.

"Where are you flying to?" the neatly made-up woman at the check-in desk asks.

"Edinburgh," she says. "Oh no, sorry. It's via London."

The check-in woman smiles. "That's fine. I can see it's with one of our partners. I can check you straight through." She taps away on the keyboard, and Carrie examines the little sign with all the prohibited items on it. The gas canister reminds her of the day that she and Laura bought the rucksacks.

Carrie had gone home to dump her shopping and get changed for their usual Friday night out — it was only a week until they were due to fly out on their trip of a lifetime. The message had pinged in while she was finishing her make-up, the phone sitting on her dressing table. She didn't recognise the name of the sender, and there was no profile photo. Normally she would just delete messages like this, but something made her open it. A moment after that, the photo appeared.

The thing was, she had never contemplated for a moment that something like this would happen. Laura wasn't even particularly keen on Greg — although it would appear from the photo that she'd changed her mind about that. The image was slightly blurred, taken at night under streetlights, with that sort of grainy discolouration that sometimes happens. Maybe zoomed-in too, unless the sender was standing right next to them.

Laura against a wall, Greg pushed up against her.

You could interpret the image in many ways, if you were so inclined, but the fact that his jeans are around his ankles and Laura's legs are wrapped around his back is a bit of a giveaway.

She waits for him to come home from work. The time stamp on the photograph is from two weeks earlier, and she's no way of knowing if this was a one-off thing or not, but what hurts the most is that she remembers that night — she and Laura had been meant to go to the cinema, and Laura had texted last minute to say she was ill and couldn't make it. Carrie had decided not to go either, and with Greg apparently at a work's night out, she'd had an early night and thought no more about it.

By the time he arrives home, she's drunk three-quarters of a bottle of Bacardi that was in the back of a kitchen cupboard, and Greg's six-pack of Stella from the fridge. She can barely remember hitting him, and if it hadn't been for the bruise on his cheek the next day, she would've convinced herself it didn't happen. He'd left, then, and, thankfully, he'd decided not to tell anyone what happened.

Laura was a different kettle of fish.

She was jumpy and paranoid every time they met, and Carrie had tried to bring it up several times, trying to keep the anger at bay — knowing that it didn't matter anymore, now that she'd split with Greg — but really, everything was ruined.

They'd had a lot to drink that night, on their own wee leaving-do. The others had left early, leaving Carrie and Laura to stagger down the High Street on their own. They'd been laughing and joking, and Carrie had almost forgotten what a cheating bitch her best friend was, but then she'd recognised the wall — something about the angle, the way the light hit it and left it in shadow. Here. Right here! Her best friend and her boyfriend. The bastards. Pushing Laura down the steps had been a spur-of-the-moment decision. That split second when life can go one way or another. She'd thought she could forget the betrayal, but the fact that Laura still hadn't confessed was what pissed Carrie off in the end.

Anyway. A broken leg can heal, just like a broken heart . . . and if it hadn't been for that moment, she'd never have ended up on this trip alone.

She'd never have met Violet.

Carrie smiles at the woman at the gate as she scans her boarding card. She's looking forward to going home. The trip has been fun, but completely removed from reality, and it's time she got back to it.

She clicks on BBC News while walking along the gangway, and the headline jumps out at the top of the page:

UK WOMAN ARRESTED IN BERLIN:
SUSPECTED OF MULTIPLE MURDERS

Poor Violet . . . or Veronica. Or whoever she really is. It's not often you get to hang out with a real-life psychopath and escape unscathed.

Who knows who anyone really is, anyway?

Sure, Carrie did a bad thing. A stupid thing. But she's been paying for it since. The unbearable guilt eating away at her, trying to swallow her whole. The only way to block it out was with drink, and drugs . . . and toying with Violet. She'd had no idea what she was dealing with there. She shudders. She's had a lucky escape.

She slides into her seat — window, near the back — and quickly checks her emails. There's one from Laura, from her alternative email address — they'd had to use covert ops while Violet had control of her real email:

Well done, love!! They got her! I was so worried!! Please tell me you're on your way home?! Can't wait to see you! X

Carrie smiles and types a quick reply:

On plane. Can't wait to see you too! X

It's almost the truth.

She *is* looking forward to seeing Laura again. She has been Carrie's best friend since they were five years old. They need each other.

No one has to find out what really happened that night when Laura fell down the steps. If there's one thing Carrie has learned from Violet, it's that you can't always trust people, no matter how much you love them. Carrie herself turned Violet into the police without a second thought. You can't have people like that roaming the streets, can you? Seeing Violet that last time, drinking the champagne, Carrie had felt a weight lift off her — the fear and guilt she'd felt since she'd left home for the trip of a lifetime was grabbed by the bubbles and popped away.

Hopefully Laura's learned her lesson. She might even think she deserved to have that accident. Karma. The Universe. But there's been no sign of an apology. No explanation. She said in one of her emails that she thought Greg was seeing someone else . . . Was that her way of trying to tell Carrie something? Was she waiting until Carrie got back home to confess all? Or was she going to stay silent, hoping that Carrie would never find out? Was it a one-off, or was it more? How long had it been going on? Carrie doesn't even know who sent the image, or why. Was someone else out to hurt her?

Carrie's chest flutters, and she feels a sudden urge to cry. It was easier to keep her emotions in check when she was filled to the brim with drink and drugs. Now, in this sober return to reality, the betrayal hits hard. A lump sticks in her throat, and she has to cough to release it.

To breathe.

The voice on the tannoy tells everyone to turn off their electronic equipment for take-off. She clicks her phone on to flight mode and leans back in her seat. Outside, the dark clouds have gathered, the day appearing like night, but for a slice of sunlight snaking through.

It's going to be a bumpy ride, she thinks.

Oh Laura . . . what am I going to do with you?

Acknowledgements

In 2006, I took a round-the-world trip with my (not yet) husband, Jamie (aka JLOH) — including several (smelly) days on the Trans-Siberian Express. While on it, I read Stephen King's brilliant *On Writing* and decided that I would start writing my own book. This is not the book that I started then, and there have been five others in between, but it was inevitable that the trip would feature in one of my stories one day . . . and that day has finally come.

He normally gets the final line in my acknowledgments, but in this case, he's going at the top. Thank you, JLOH — for spending six months with me and two rucksacks, having fun and adventures across several continents (visiting many Irish bars along the way). Apart from anything else, we now have a shared, life-long love of Chinese dumplings, and memories that will last forever — some of which have been) fictionalised* and included in this book. (*Ewe's milk tea, however, is very much real. Eeuw.)

Thank you, as always, to my brilliant agent, Phil Patterson, for always believing in what I do — and to all at Marjacq Scripts for their unwavering support. I couldn't do it without you.

Huge thanks to Karen Sullivan and all of #TeamOrenda for continuing to publish the most beautiful, diverse and special books with a level of passion and enthusiasm that cannot be matched.

Thank you to my most active cheerleaders: Steph, Ed and Vicki — whose regular messages of encouragement throughout the writing of this book were the only things that kept me sane. Thank you too, to all of my friends in the crime-writing world, who make the whole thing a joy (even when it isn't). A special thanks to Paddy, too, for being in the right place at the right time.

Thanks to all of my faithful readers, bloggers and reviewers, who say lovely things and who make the whole, long process from idea to draft to final version worthwhile.

Massive thanks to Steve Street for his generous CLIC Sargent bid to have his name in this book. Very much appreciated, and I hope you and Marion enjoyed the ride.

Thanks, as always, to my friends and family — who are constantly supportive, encouraging and proud (even when I don't see or speak to them for weeks on end while I am locked away in my fictional world). It's always a bit terrifying when family read my books, a bit like those online reviewers who like to say exactly what they think . . . So an extra special thanks to my sister, Abby, who read the proof and loved it!

You can find out more about me and my books on my website, *www.sjiholliday.com.* where you can also sign up to my mailing list for excusive news and updates, and find links to my social media accounts. If you enjoyed Violet, I would love to hear from you!

Other titles published by Ulverscroft:

LIGHT TOUCH

Stephen Leather

Working undercover is all about trust — getting the target to trust you and then betraying them in order to bring them to justice. But what do you do when you believe an undercover cop has crossed the line and aligned herself with the international drugs smuggler she was supposed to be targeting? When Lisa Wilson stops passing on intelligence about her target, MI5 sends in Dan "Spider" Shepherd to check that she's on the straight and narrow. Now two lives are on the line — and Shepherd discovers that the real danger is closer to home than he realised. As Spider finds his loyalties being tested to the limit, an SAS killer is on a revenge mission in London, and only Spider can stop him . . .

JOE COUNTRY

Mick Herron

"*We're spies, Standish. All kinds of outlandish shit goes on.*" Like the ringing of a dead man's phone or an unwelcome guest at a funeral . . . In Slough House memories are stirring, all of them bad. Catherine Standish is buying booze again, Louisa Guy is raking over the ashes of lost love, and new recruit Lech Wicinski, whose sins make him an outcast even among the slow horses, is determined to discover who destroyed his career. And with winter taking its grip, Jackson Lamb would sooner be left brooding in peace, but even he can't ignore the dried blood on his carpets. So when the man responsible breaks cover at last, Lamb sends the slow horses out to even the score. This time they're heading into joe country. And they're not all coming home.